Praise for *What About the Scientists?*

What About The Scientists? is a stunner: absorbing, compelling, thought-provoking: a mosaic of stories and storytelling built around a compelling central mystery. Travel, as reader, to the remote scientific research establishment and uncover the nature of the experiment performed upon its test subjects. You'll emerge a different person to the one who went in.

Adam Roberts,
Professor of Nineteenth-century Literature,
Royal Halloway University of London

What About the Scientists?

ERIC PERCAK

A Blackwater Press book

First published in the United States of America by
Blackwater Press, LLC

Library of Congress Control Number: 2026941739

ISBN: 978-1-963614-16-9

Cover design by Camilla Malachin

Blackwater Press
120 Capitol Street
Charleston, WV 25301
United States

blackwaterpress.com

Foreword

Eric Percak's extraordinary novel *What About the Scientists?* is a compelling work of speculative fiction. The premise is classic: a mountaineer in the wilderness unwittingly discovers a bundle of papers, a wrapped-up manuscript concealed in an isolated landscape. Leaving it behind, he returns early the next morning, finding it impossible to believe it is worthless and merely abandoned: it must have been left there to be found. The mountaineer, the narrator, becomes "The Editor", and we find out what the manuscript reveals.

A group of people have been gathered in a state-of-the-art "facility" and invited to spend a year there. Officially, they are attending a writers' retreat—whether they write words or music. In fact, they have agreed to take part in a long-term scientific experiment on human health, led by the mysterious and menacingly reassuring Dr. Samesong. At the center of the study is a remarkable new pill, the "medicament", whose essence seems to have been extracted from fruit—or perhaps something animal.

Throughout the manuscript narrative, the writer, Lily, whether recounting her experiences in the facility on her own in isolation or interacting with others in the assembled company (Hector, Peggy, or Quinn and Anna, who have their own relationships, tensions, and predilections) or writing home to her mother, gradually introduces us to her new world and her own background and history. The manuscript narrative is intercut with the Editor's interventions, so there are multiple strands of suspenseful bagatelle. Where is this taking us? Where are we going with this? The questions are intrinsic to the story as it unfolds, but they gather power as they continue incrementally without a final answer.

By now the Editor has traced the manuscript itself to the geographical site of the long-abandoned "facility" and starts to explore it, finding the rooms, domestic, communal, and the laboratory, which the manuscript has referred to, so we start to piece together the two major narratives which sustain the novel, and "What happens next?" becomes an increasingly urgent question.

The Editor begins to uncover what we have suspected: "For those that had come before, it didn't end well." The foregoing delineates the main strands of the story. The last third of the novel brings it to a resolution, with more characters coming to various points of mortal crisis and Dr. Samesong revealing his own story as more about "the facility" is disclosed to the reader: "In order for the scheme to work, the recruits needed to buy in with limited knowledge. Only bits of information could be revealed before inking the deal to ensure their society remained a secret. The recruits were asked to feel the truth and accept it without further evidence. Only then could they take a leap of faith and sign the contract."

What's going on is described in a chillingly naturalistic way, but clearly the metaphoric impact of the whole work is primary. This is going to be a recurring story, a tale of frighteningly eternal return, dependent upon faith and ignorance: "Within a year, the team had met quota. Ten new recruits."

The Editor leaves the last word to the survivors—including Lily—or, perhaps, the presumed survivors, whose discovery of the purpose of their lives within the facility, the experiment itself, has come to its irresolvable conclusion.

Their proposed activity—creativity—the scientific priority within their practice and their human lives, individual, communal, mortal—are all brought to bear upon each other. "I need to make my own mistakes." We cannot live with "too much certainty" or too much security, too much safety, too much enclosure. This is what the novel has been leading to, and it is a well-earned and firmly delivered, cautionary note on which to close.

As a work of speculative fiction, Eric Percak's novel sustains a cool seriousness while the emotions and enquiries extend, entrap, boil and recoil within the characters. And the questions at the novel's heart are perennially pressing, pertinent in our own time as much as any other, past or future.

Professor Alan Riach, University of Glasgow

Arrival

January 3, 1991

Snow is pelting my face, but I don't feel cold. The anesthesia hasn't completely worn off, and I'm still groggy. The tarmac I walk on is covered with blue rock salt. Ice and slush have been plowed to the edges.

I've regained lucidity while walking, but I'm still too disoriented to think anything's strange. Skipping over hours of time shouldn't feel comfortable, but it does. I'm leaning into someone for support as I walk, but I don't know who they are. I don't bother to glance up at this person since they walk with an authority I find trustworthy. I'm nestled into their shoulder and the creases of their waterproof outerwear scrape against my face.

The landscape is beautiful. It's the half-light of dusk (or maybe dawn, depending), and we're amid a valley surrounded by mountains and forest and snow, but I don't pause to marvel. Though my senses are numbed, instinct and my escort guide me to the shelter ahead. We've probably walked a hundred steps or fewer, but it feels like miles. The shelter is impossibly far.

It looks like something out of the future, or what they imagined the future to look like years ago. Geometric shapes of glass and polished steel arranged like a space station docked into the earth. A large white globe looms atop the structure. I try to say it looks like Epcot, but my mind and tongue aren't in sync yet, so nonsense spills out of my mouth. My guide responds with a reassuring, "Almost there, Lily."

We enter a tunnel to shield us from exposure, but there's still some distance to a door ahead. The tunnel's corrugated iron reverberates a low moan, and with the natural light outside fading to the dim glow of industrial lanterns overhead, I feel as though I'm walking into a machine. Still, I step with more confidence now, free from the assault of wind. For the first time I look behind me.

I am the first in the line of people marching towards the facility. Three of them and their escorts struggle forward as the green and red runway lights flicker beside them in the hazy light. Beyond them, a small airplane sits on the runway, looking as if it'll be swallowed by the elements, too, if it doesn't find shelter.

With my body still numb, I can hardly feel anything as they continue to move me toward the entrance. They need me to go inside. They need me to be warm. They need me to rest.

Note From the Editor

When I stumbled upon the cache, I nearly did nothing with it. I shouldn't claim discovery; actually, it was my dog, Germany, who found it. Protruding from the ground, the case's rubber corners made an appealing chew toy.

Inside, the documents looked like junk or, at best, a lost manuscript. The paper was worn and water-damaged along the edge, and the pages stuck together a bit, though I could see they were still legible. The stack was about an inch thick, and since it was tidy and unshuffled, I doubt anyone had touched it in years. I didn't want to add the weight to my pack, so I left it behind.

I continued my hike and gave it little thought.

It wasn't until I set up camp that the obvious dawned on me. They weren't dropped from a loose bag. Nor did they arrive by the happenstance of erosion. They were there because someone put them there. Whoever it was hoped someone would find them.

It was a time capsule.

* * *

The adventure piqued my curiosity, and my imagination ran wild with ideas of an intercontinental treasure hunt. I almost ventured back during the night to reclaim the cache before realizing that if it had been there this long, it was not in jeopardy of discovery.

Still, when the Alaskan summer's sunrise greeted us at three a.m., we wasted no more time returning to the site. Germany seemed to remember the path as we neared and did a playful bounce and dig when he sniffed his way to the cache.

Reading through the first few pages, I noted the sentences:

They want me to go inside. They want me to be warm. They want me to rest.

Who were *they*? The word instilled a curious mix of obedience, admiration, and fear.

I'm not a journalist, a historian, or a scientist. I'm a storyteller. Lily was one of the characters, but *they* had hidden a story. I spent the next five years piecing it together.

—Eric Percak, Editor

Day One

I wake in the most comfortable bed. It's so cozy, I could easily fall back asleep, but the drug haze has dissipated, and I desperately need the bathroom. It's been, well, I guess I don't even know. Long enough. I check my wrist, but I'm not wearing my watch, and I don't see a clock anywhere.

I muster the power to fling off the blankets and throw my legs to the side of the bed. Dim lights illuminate the room automatically as my feet touch the floor. Cool. The room is bigger than my last apartment and reminds me of a hotel suite from movies. I don't pause on the details because the bathroom is my priority.

I'm still half-asleep as I relieve myself. It takes a moment to realize the floor tiles are heated. Actually, the bathroom is incredible. There's an extensive vanity, a rainfall shower with frosted-glass walls, and a separate bathtub—a Victorian claw-foot with a copper finish.

The room is so clean it makes me conscious of my stench. I'm wearing the same clothes I had on when I left, but I'm happy no one has changed me out of them. Clean clothes hang on the backside of the bathroom door.

I peel off my clothes, toss them into a basket labeled "Laundry," and take a shower. The water pressure is perfect.

Since it feels like a five-star hotel, the bathrobe is the right choice. I explore the rest of the room. It takes me forever to find the light switch. It's unlike any I've seen: a digital panel which modulates the light as I track my finger up and down. There's a large mahogany desk with a lamp and leather desk set. The rug beneath me looks handcrafted, and I'm beginning to realize the amount of money they've invested in this place. They want us to be comfortable or, at least, impressed.

The closet isn't anything special. Inside are nothing but plain T-shirts, sweatshirts, and cotton pants. All baby blue. I check the drawers, and both the socks and underwear are baby blue, too. Everything is my size.

There's a bookshelf next to the bed with a random assortment. It's as though someone tried not to select more than one book from a single genre. There's a pulpy whodunit called *A Moment to Live* sandwiched between a copy of *Jane Eyre* and *Catch-22*. A shelf below, there's a photographic *Reptile Encyclopedia*, a tattered World War II history, and a biography of an English race car driver. Another shelf holds faux books made of cardboard boxes with spines labeled to look like a few classics.

I realize the room feels less like a hotel than it does a staged room someone could hypothetically live in. I'll need to add some of my own touches to give it character at some point. There are a few framed prints on the wall I would never choose for myself—a couple of minimalist drawings and a placard stating, "*Make Every Day Count,*" in elongated cursive.

I move to the window and draw the curtains. The windows stretch from the floor to ceiling, another fancy and expensive detail. It's nighttime; the view of the sky is obscured by the reflection of the room, but I can still see thousands of stars. It's a clear night and the air breathing off the window draws me back to the memory of the bitter cold outside.

The quiet strikes me for the first time. No traffic. No neighbors. No TV. There's not even a buzz from the lamps or a hiss from the vents. The sound hasn't been turned down; it's been muted.

I move to the desk and rummage through the drawers. Notebooks and loose-leaf paper and Post-its and notecards and pencils and ballpoint pens and even inkblot pens. Sitting in the desk chair, a high-backed leather swivel, I lean forward to mimic a few writing poses, test it out, and see if it feels right.

I'll have to rearrange the desk to face the window. It's far too heavy to move on my own. I make a quick sketch and figure there's enough space to swap the bed and the desk. It'd be too drafty to sleep under the window anyhow.

There's a knock at the door. I walk over, and without opening it, I ask, "Yes?" My tongue still feels fat in my mouth, and my voice is unnatural. The drugs haven't completely worn off after all. They said I'd feel the effects for up to sixteen hours, so I'm trying to do the math of how long it may have been since I was sitting in doctor's chair while they injected me and asked me to count backward from twenty.

"We saw that you're awake. Is there anything we can get you? Something to eat, perhaps?" says a muffled woman's voice on the other side of the door. She sounds pleasant, or at least accommodating.

I'm not hungry, but I don't want to seem ungrateful. "That sounds good. Let me get dressed," my fat tongue slurs every few words and causes me to pause. "I'll be right out." I'm basically shouting. I could hardly hear her through the door, so I tried to project my clumsy voice.

"Take your time. No rush. You'll find the dining room at the end of the hall on your left," she shouts back. With the soundproofing, I can't hear footsteps to tell if she's gone or not. Either way, I don't want to keep her waiting, so I get dressed in the baby blue outfit, which, even though it looks new, has a worn-in softness. I'm comfortable and impressed.

I give myself a quick check in the bathroom mirror. My hair is still wet, my eyes look sleepy, but I don't want to take any more time to freshen up. There don't seem to be toiletries in the room beyond shampoo and soap, anyhow.

I have no trouble finding the dining room since it's the first door with a window. Through it, I see a man and woman talking to each other at one of the tables. I hesitate, not wanting to interrupt, but the man spots me. He smiles and waves me in.

As I enter, the two of them rise to greet me. He emphatically extends a hand as he approaches, saying, "There she is."

"Here I am," I shrug as I shake his hand.

"I'm Doctor Samesong. Peter Samesong," he says, making intense but agreeable eye contact. His eyes grab me with their blueness. "And this is—"

"Margaret. Or Peggy. Whichever you prefer, really," she takes a small step forward to shake my hand before taking a step back again to cede the floor to her colleague. They're much more put together than I am. She's wearing light makeup, and her hair is tied back, but it doesn't look messy. It's a composed look of confidence and sportiness that makes me think there must be a gym at the facility.

"It's nice to meet you both," I slur with my unnatural voice. "I'm sorry. It seems—"

"No need to apologize," Samesong interrupts. "A residual effect. It happens to everyone. Peggy was lisping for at least two days after she arrived." I make a mental note that he called her Peggy, not Margaret. "But you know the best remedy?"—he doesn't give me time to respond—"Waffles!"

I look around the large dining room, which could seat at least fifty, and spot a full waffle bar to my left. It's elegantly arranged to impress: waffle irons, batter in a large carafe, glass-jarred (thus authentic) maple syrup, bananas and strawberries, and chocolate chips. It seems dubious that it'll help my tongue, and I envision drooling syrup down my face, but I smile anyhow because that's obviously the reaction he wants.

Sensing my reluctance, Peggy chimes in, "Of course, if you're not hungry, don't worry. There's also some coffee or tea, if you'd like." They're both looking at me, so I take a banana and fix a cup of chamomile tea.

"Did you sleep well?" Dr. Samesong asks, shifting away from the unappreciated waffles.

"I did, thanks. That bed is amazing."

"I know, right?" agrees Peggy. "The doctor sure has spoiled us, hasn't he?" She glances at Dr. Samesong.

"Here, please sit," he says, pulling out a chair.

We all sit, Peggy to my left and Dr. Samesong across with his elbows on the table as he leans in. I realize the lighting is softer than I'd expect for a dining room. No fluorescent lights; instead, sconces adorn the walls, and mini stained-glass chandeliers dangle over each table like in a fine dining restaurant. "Before you came in, Peggy and I were talking about what a fine group we have with us. You'll meet everyone soon, but I assure you they're all good people. Interesting people, too. Which is good because, well—"

"You'll be spending a lot of time together," interrupts Peggy with a chuckle to follow.

"Yeah, that's right. But my guess is the time will fly by."

I steep my tea bag up and down and watch the steam rise. I must look anxious because Peggy cuts the silence, "Please relax. And enjoy yourself."

"Thanks." I sip the tea and it's far too hot, but the warmth feels good in my hands. "Would I be able to wander around a bit, get my bearings?"

They exchange glances before Dr. Samesong says, "We'll

save the tour for tomorrow. There's a lot to see, and I'm sure you're exhausted."

We make small talk, mostly about the cold weather. It seems perverse to be discussing something mundane given the atmosphere, but no one really knows what else to talk about. They haven't mentioned the experimental drug, so I'm not going to bring it up. Everything is pleasant enough, but undoubtedly peculiar.

Dr. Samesong is handsome in a traditional way—sharp jawline, high cheekbones, and mystifying eyes. He must've had a haircut recently, and he looks like the sort who never misses a day shaving. I'm surprised by how young he looks, probably under forty. He's confident, too, though I'm not yet sure if that's attractive or unattractive.

Peggy is probably a few years older than him, and she also has a certain attractiveness to her, though hers is less noticeable at first. It might be the dreadful yellow she's been saddled with. I'm sure if she tried to doll up, she'd turn a few heads on the street, but instead I'm fixated on the clash between her blond hair and Tweety Bird yellow clothes. It makes me thankful for the baby blue I've been issued. Dr. Samesong is in white, of course. I decide they're both good-looking enough to be on TV. Maybe not as actors, but as news anchors. Though this could be because they enunciate with noticeable precision—each syllable detached, and with an attack on the consonants. It makes me conscious of my mumbling and fat tongue.

They run me through the nearby topography, Dr. Samesong telling me about a river and a glacier before he moves to the window to point out the surrounding peaks, which are barely visible in starlight. He's telling me about the one he assures me is just beneath the moon, which is the tallest peak on the entire range at nearly 10,000 feet, when I see he's distracted. I follow his eyes to a series of four light bulbs above the door. One is illuminated and another is blinking.

"Quinn is starting to stir," he says before checking his watch and returning to his seat to write a quick note. I piece together that I'm the illuminated bulb, thinking I might've triggered it with the floor sensors in my room. "Let's give him a few minutes before we check in." Peggy checks her watch as well. There aren't any wall clocks.

"Hey, what time is it, anyhow?"

They pause for a second before Dr. Samesong answers, "Oh, um, it's just after four."

"A.m., right?"

"Ha. Yes, a.m." He makes a few more notes and Peggy moves over his shoulder to point at something on his paper. She whispers something I can't hear.

I take the opportunity to announce my exit, "Wow, this chamomile has done its job. I think I might need to lie down again."

"Of course, of course. Get some rest. Please."

I stand to leave. "It's been really nice meeting you," Peggy says. "I look forward to working together. We'll be seeing you soon enough."

"Nice to meet you both, too," I say as I smile, before remembering, "Oh, I don't have a key."

"Use your thumbprint," says Dr. Samesong.

As I leave, they're fixating on something in the notes. They whisper to each other and don't look toward me again.

Before I return to my room, I stroll past my door to the end of the hallway. There's a nameplate on my door and three others, which are labeled "Anna," "Quinn," and "Hector." The next door is labeled "Utility" across the hall from "Storage Annex." The hallway dead-ends at what looks like a vault. It's steel with a round wheel in the middle and a large, hydraulic locking mechanism. There's a small window through which I can see the corrugated tunnel extending back to the airstrip. I notice a glass plate and a digital screen, and try my thumbprint before it blinks, "Unauthorized. Clearance Needed." I try again with the same result and then notice the security camera mounted in the corner overhead. I give it a shrugging wave before returning to my room, where a thumb pad now grants me access.

It's quiet in my room. I write a note to ask for a record or cassette player. They probably won't have much of a collection of albums, but anything is better than silence. I tuck the note into the jamb of the door to remind me, and I brainstorm if anything else is urgent. I'm trying to clear my head before I shift to the desk and settle in to write.

* * *

1/3/1991

Mom,

You won't believe where I am. A writer's retreat. Well, not really, but that's what I'm calling it.

I actually don't even know where I am. And I don't mean that figuratively.

But don't worry, I'm okay. I'm part of an academic study and they're paying me to stay put for a year. It may sound a little strange, but I could use a change.

They say I'll have plenty of free time, since they won't need me for more than an hour or two each day. I'll have to write lots if I don't want to die from boredom.

You're right. I always made excuses. Worse, I believed the excuses. I couldn't write when I was overworked, or when money was tight, or when I had to take care of our family, or after everything else that happened to us. It's funny. I used to envy those types of lives, the ones that were rough, because they forced you to *feel*—to give you something to write about. Because that's what I've always wanted—to create something.

My God, it was so easy to make excuses. I was lazy, but mostly I was scared. As long as my writing didn't exist, it couldn't be bad. It was a whole lot easier to live with the fantasy of the great American novel in my head than a not-so-great one on the page.

But look! I've written a page already. I kid, but I'm going to keep it up, I swear, it's coming this time. I apologize in advance if I write anything that's not accurate. I'll do my best to tell the story as I know it.

It's cold here, but I keep hearing you say, "It's not cold. It's cozy." I think the snow is whiter than we used to get, but maybe I'm just imagining it. I hope Russell is still coming by to shovel. I paid him in advance, and he was always a good kid, but, like you said, you never know, right?

They say I won't be able to mail anything, but I'll keep writing to you anyhow.

Love,
Lily

The Guests

I'm trying to look nonchalant, but I'm sure it's obvious I'm trying and instead I look terribly "chalant." I doubt that's a word, and I shouldn't be thinking about whether or not it's a word, but that's all I'm thinking about while Hector introduces himself. My head is nodding along, but I'm retaining nothing, which I know is rude, so I command myself to focus. But I fail and don't focus on him. I feel my eyebrow dancing without settling on one expression, so now I'm thinking about eyebrow positions. They've gone from quizzical to concerned to amused in two-and-a-half seconds, and he's picked up on this. His eyes have shifted to my forehead like he's afraid of what the brows will do next.

"Don't worry," he smiles. "I'm nervous, too."

I exhale with ridiculous emphasis and bulge my eyes out in agreement. "I know, right?" It's the first human moment since I've arrived. He smiles, and so do I.

"Let's try this again," he says, extending a hand, which I shake with ironic formality. "My name is Hector."

"Lily. Pleasure to meet you." I let his hand drop, and we do a little nod to each other. We breathe. "So, um, where are you from?" I'm remembering how to do this.

He lights a cigarette, and I notice the ashtrays around the dining room. I'm not sure where he got his cigarettes, and I don't want to ask for one in case he has a limited supply. "Colorado, originally, outside of Denver, though I haven't lived there in some time. I've been living in California for the past thirty years."

He moves to the counter to pour himself a cup of coffee. When he came in, I had been adding milk to my coffee, intending to sneak back to my room to drink it. The jet lag has my body wanting to start the day even though it's not even dawn, yet. It feels like we're breaking the rules by chatting before we're scheduled to formally meet.

For some reason, I didn't picture anyone older coming. Not that he's ancient—probably in his sixties—but I expected everyone to be roughly my age. The blue in his eyes is brought out by the outfits we're both wearing. I'm slightly envious. His hairline has receded, but he's constantly combing his remaining hair to the back of his scalp with his hand. It's a tic that gives me the sense he's always deep in thought.

He's sort of a park ranger, he says. Not a nature guide and such, but the maintenance side of things. He makes sure cacti aren't growing too close to trails and garbage cans are cleared out. If there's a problem with plumbing or electricity, he'll take a crack at it, but he admits he isn't an expert.

"It's how I make a living," he says, "but it's not my passion." He lowers his voice, "I make homemade liquor."

"Really?"

"Well, liqueur, actually," he takes a sip of coffee and it's clearly still too hot. "From prickly pears. The cactus fruit."

I don't know what to do with my hands. I've finished my coffee, but I keep attempting to sip from the cup.

"And where are you from, Lily?"

"You know those towns you're desperate to get out of as a teenager. One of those."

"Ha."

"But really, I doubt you've heard of it. Chippewa Creek,

Wisconsin. Kind of the middle of the state. It's not all that small, there's even a college, but I don't think many people end up there by choice. There's a historic downtown that's kind of cute if you need to kill an hour, but the rest of the town is basically strip malls."

He nods to acknowledge my rehearsed spiel. "Need a refill?" he asks.

"I shouldn't. Makes me bouncy if I have too much."

"Bouncy?"

"Yeah, like I bounce from one thing to the next." I gesture with my hands and let my eyes dart back and forth. "I can't stay focused."

"This is coffee we're talking about, right?" I smile and shift my weight. There is nothing in the kitchenette besides coffee and each other, but he picks up on my cues. "I'm going to talk to someone and see if we can get an early tour," he extends his hand. "It's been a pleasure to meet you, Lily."

"You too…"

"Hector," he rescues me from lapsing on his name. He smiles before wandering off.

There's no one left in the room, but I don't want to leave right after him. I resist glancing up at the security camera blinking above me. Try to ignore them, they said.

***

It's orientation and we're seated around a conference table in a classroom. I'm trying not to be quick to judge, but I'm pretty sure Anna and I are not going to get along. I get it, she's interested, and she has a lot of questions, but she will not stop babbling. She uses twice as many words in a sentence as necessary and doesn't seem to realize it's bothering everyone else. Or she doesn't care. Either way, fine, I'll admit it—I don't like her. We're probably about the same age, and we're wearing the same clothes, but she looks much better in them than I do, more confident, at least. I would bet money she was popular in high school.

Peggy is keeping it together so far, but Dr. Samesong has a look on his face of "what did I get myself into?" His fist rests over his mouth, and his eyes blink emphatically as Peggy answers yet another of Anna's questions about the schedule.

She's seated near the head of the table, and her body language only acknowledges Peggy and Dr. Samesong. We stir while Anna plays the role of a parent hijacking the Parent/Teacher Conference to talk about their kid. The other blue shirts have formed a silent alliance against her already. Hector might be asleep with his eyes open, and Quinn has started doodling. They didn't give us much of a chance to chat before they started orientation, but I can tell Quinn is the youngest. Maybe a year or so out of college. He's got thick, black-rimmed glasses, a stubbly beard and messy hair which probably looks unkempt the day after a haircut. He bummed a cigarette from Hector but has only been fidgeting with it unlit while bits of tobacco leak onto the table. He seems a little shy, but, then again, I'm sure I do, too. Since Anna isn't going to be my friend, Quinn needs to be one. Cliques will form quickly.

I flip through the packet to dispel some of my aggravation. There are stock photos of doctors chatting with patients and pills spilling out of a prescription bottle and a man trying to walk with the support of those parallel bars they use for physical therapy.

"Okay, let's move on," Dr. Samesong jumps in during a momentary lull in Anna's barrage of questions. "Now I will take us through the nitty-gritty details of what to expect from the study."

The lights dim before a slideshow presentation begins on a slide projector. It's painfully boring. It seems as though he's used the same presentation before, but it must have been tailored to a group of doctors, and he hasn't bothered to tone down the medical jargon. I pick up on a bit about jellyfish chemistry and extracting a protein from the skin of red grapes, but then he's deep into biochemistry: "Glucuronidation may occur in the intestine as well as in the liver, but we know for certain sulfonation not only happens in the liver but in the intestine and through microbial gut activity." Then he's on to diagrams of atoms and neutrinos: "Here are the two geometric isomers, with the *trans* isomer shown in the top image." Then he walks us through the data from clinical animal trials and physiological effects not replicated in double-blind studies that were "obviously problematic, but we found the source of the discrepancy, don't worry," he laughs to himself. This must have been a joke. This is what makes Dr. Samesong laugh.

The presentation's only mercy comes from Anna's lack of interruption. At the start she'd been taking diligent notes, but now her eyes are as glazed over as mine. I glance around the room to find Hector is fully asleep and Quinn has lit his cigarette but has let the ash build for several minutes since last inhaling. There's no clock in here either, and the bulbs over the doorway are all illuminated. I look for a security camera but don't find any.

Dr. Samesong says "medicament" for the hundredth time. That's what they're calling it. Rhymes with predicament. Each time he says it with a distinct cadence, adding a lilt to the second syllable to give it a lyrical quality. It bounces out and becomes a refrain to his speech in an almost exciting way.

I'm relieved when he places the projector's controller onto the table to indicate we're done with the slideshow. The projector holds the final slide, *Your Health,* which relates unspecific bullet points about quality care and comfort next to a photo of a smiling woman sniffing a flower in a meadow. We're willing him to wrap up with our faded expressions. "And that about covers it. Of course, you'll have your weekly checkups with me, but you won't see me much of the time. I'll be in the lab tracking your progress—"

Anna's hand shoots up. "Is it safe?" she asks.

The rest of the group snaps out of their stupor. Dr. Samesong fields the question, "I'm glad you asked, Anna." He meanders through the room as he delivers his monologue. "There's always risk when we move to clinical trials, but, given the evidence from our lab work and animal testing, we're confident there won't be side effects. Headaches, maybe," he pauses like it might be a joke, but no one cracks a smile. While he paces, he alternates between clasping his hands together and gesturing back towards the final slide. "Of course, your health and safety are our top priority, and, though we don't have reason to suspect there will be even the slightest negative effect, we will be vigilant in monitoring any changes during the routine exams."

He's looped the room and leans forward to rest his hands on the back of his chair. "And you'll be updated on your test results constantly. Remember, it's always your choice to continue and we will support any decision you make regarding your own well-being." The room looks unmoved by his canned delivery, so he adds, "The Medicament is not much different than the vitamins you get over the counter. Part of a daily routine that makes you feel better." He smiles. "We're still working on slogans." Anna seems satisfied so he claps his hands together. "Now, let's watch the video before we take a much-needed break."

Transcript of Orientation Video

[recovered by editor during research]
(full color film)

Video begins with computer-animated polygons coming in and out of focus while in motion, accompanied by an upbeat, synthesized composition. A laser beam appears, carving the initials SL on a granite tablet, which centers on the screen above the words 'An SL Corporate Production.' Scene fades.

Frame changes to a man sitting in a maroon leather chair in a private library. He is dressed in a white button-down shirt and dark pleated pants. He is Caucasian, middle-aged with dark brown hair, a full mustache, and wide-framed glasses. He smiles, then speaks in a low-pitched voice with an indistinct accent.

"Hello, I'm Arthur Romaine, owner and president of the SL Corporation. We've primarily been involved in the excavation and refinement of precious metals in Eurasia; but we also have personal and business interests in other sectors, including real estate, banking, and transportation. Recently, we have spread our investments into medical research, hoping to use our success to help others in need."

He stands, moves to a small table to pour a glass of water.

"That's enough about myself, though. Let's talk about you and why you're here. I'm certain you're a bit apprehensive and anxious at this point, and I do apologize for all the clandestine behavior you've encountered thus far. However, I assure you these were necessary measures to ensure the safety of everyone involved, and we promise to be much more accommodating in the future. Unfortunately, these security measures have become necessary. It is our fear the findings of this study will be targeted by those looking to secure the information for their own benefit."

He leans against a large desk in the library's center. Camera zooms in and refocuses on his face.

"That being said, I would like to formally and graciously welcome you here. By accepting our invitation, you have become an integral part of our revolutionary research. Some of you may have enrolled in our program only to receive the compensatory package we offered, and despite that seeming to be a large enough enticement in itself, I assure you that your time here will exceed even your highest expectations. Our qualified staff and state-of-the-art facilities are here to ensure your comfort. Most of the time, I believe you will view your stay here as a vacation, a time to relax and reflect with minimal obligations to cause you worry. The freedom will seem almost endless and will allow you to pursue any personal interests and goals."

Camera switches to wide shot. A globe rests in a wooden stand beside the desk. An abstract marble sculpture adorns a gap in the bookshelf behind him. He leans back and drinks.

"All that we ask for in return is your cooperation. That is not to say we discourage any sort of debate or discussion, but rather that you do not refuse or disregard the small things that we ask of you. It is inevitable that some frustration and disagreements will develop in the lengthy time spent here, but you should remember everybody, including you, is working together for success. Right now, you may be a bit ambivalent towards our project."

He crosses the room, places a hand on the back of the leather chair.

"Please understand that although the research will be performed with the utmost care, it is still a relatively new field of study. Previous testing has revealed a remarkable level of safety, and we believe this stage will be no different; but it is impossible for us to absolutely guarantee your health and safety. I understand this may concern you, and justifiably so, but we would not be proceeding to this stage of research had we not exhausted tests at all other levels with entirely positive results. If you feel conflicted though, and do not wish to participate in our program, it is at this time that you must make your final decision. For security reasons, we are unable to divulge any further information on our project for fear word will leak to the press or competitors. I recognize that we are asking you to make a difficult decision and are not providing answers to many questions you surely have, but our offer and promises are guaranteed."

Camera zooms in. He removes his glasses.

"Please consider your decision carefully. Think of the fantastic possibility we are offering and compare it with the life you have left behind. Do you want to have a future of familiarity, or does the idea of great innovation entice you? Will you return to your former life and constantly wonder what could have been?"

Camera zooms out. He retakes his seat in the leather chair and picks up a newspaper from the side table before crossing his legs.

"We will give you time to consider your decision. If you choose to stay and sign the preliminary agreement, you will then receive further orientation. Once again, I would like to welcome you to our facility, and on behalf of everyone at SL, thank you."

Scene fades. Block letter message appears on a blue screen.

'MONITOR: Please distribute the agreement form.'

Introductions

"Question 1: If you could be any animal, what would you be?" Peggy prompts. After orientation they gave us a long break, which I spent failing to fight jet lag and napping two hours straight. They've set up a make-your-own-taco station in what they're calling the lounge. There's a couch, a loveseat, and two recliners arranged around a coffee table and framed to face a projector screen on one side of the room. The other side has a card table, dart board, pinball machine, and bumper pool table beside a stereo system and a collection of records. On the walls are some abstract art prints and a framed Rolling Stones 1972 Tour poster. The lights have been dimmed to create a more relaxed atmosphere and they've popped champagne to inaugurate the project.

I'd be a migratory bird. Preferably waterfowl because who wouldn't enjoy flying and swimming and seasonal travel?

I'm pleased with my answer. It came naturally even if it sounded rehearsed. Hector says he wouldn't mind being a house cat, and Anna and Quinn both say they needed to think about it, so come back to them.

"Question 2: Why did you decide to come here?"

There was an accident about a year ago and, since I didn't have insurance, I was basically ruined by the hospital bills. Creditors were aggressive, and I wasn't making enough to pay even a fraction of what I owed, so when I saw the opportunity to make all this money, I took it.

This wasn't untrue, though it wasn't everything, either. It doesn't seem like I'm the only one to omit parts of their story. Hector and Quinn both said it was primarily for the money, and Anna said she liked the idea of being part of something so exciting. This may have been somewhat true. She does seem excited; or, at least, she has a lot more energy and enthusiasm than the rest of us. Yes, there was money; yes, there was intrigue to the project, but the four of us chose to be here for reasons we weren't going to share on question two of icebreakers.

"Question 3: What are you hoping to gain from your time here?"

Our answers are interrupted when Dr. Samesong notices a blinking bulb over the doorway and excuses himself. Peggy tells us to continue to mingle and lets us know, "There's plenty of champagne, but you might not want to go crazy, you all have a big day tomorrow," before she follows Dr. Samesong. The interruption is merciful. I don't want to come out as a writer just yet. People act differently around writers. They think you're taking notes.

Hector doesn't hesitate when the staff leaves. He opens another bottle of champagne and tops up each of us without asking. My jetlagged body isn't sure it wants the alcohol, but I find myself sipping quickly.

We give up on formal icebreakers and, well, we gossip. Apparently, I'm not the only one to wonder if Peggy and Dr. Samesong are an item. There is evidence in the looks they give each other, and their rapport. They literally finish each other's sentences. We laugh about how proud they look when the other is speaking. Anna is especially enthralled by the gossip. Okay, she could be part of our alliance. It makes more sense if it's us versus the staff, anyhow.

I'd normally be afraid of Anna's intense eye contact, but I don't find it unpleasant. Again, that's probably the wine. It doesn't hurt to have one of us taking this seriously, too. Our point person. If we're confused, she'll help us out. She'll be the kid in class who does her homework and lets us all copy. She is a dork, though. She laughs at her own jokes—well, snorts at them, actually.

"I was so nervous, I couldn't stop asking questions. I don't know how everyone else was so calm. Ha." My eye contact falters and I look to see we're on to our fourth bottle between the four of us. Still four, I should say, since no one hesitated to sign the contract at the last chance to opt out. Peggy and Dr. Samesong insisted we have fun getting to know each other on our own.

I'm going to give Anna a second chance. She's a good listener, as in, actually absorbs details as you talk. And yes, she's pretty, too. She makes me conscious of the fact I'm talking to a pretty person. Definitely popular in high school, probably even won a superlative in her yearbook. I was reciting the usual bits I talk about when I talk about my life—growing up in a medium-sized town that felt smaller and smaller as I got older, traveling when I could afford to and even when I couldn't, my family, my mom, sort of—and she interrupts to ask if the accident was hard on my family.

"Oh, well, the accident was only recently." I guess I shouldn't be surprised she took note of the accident. It was one of the only memorable parts of icebreakers.

"And don't forget the altitude," Quinn says to Hector as my conversation with Anna fades and we turn to join them. "Thin air gets you drunk quicker. I mean, who knows how high up we are exactly, but I'm guessing it's not sea level.

"Well, we're in the northern hemisphere still. Daylight hours tell us that much."

It never occurred to me that we might not be.

"You know, I heard a story about a guy, Scottish, I think, or maybe I'm just thinking that because he..." Quinn mumbles. I smile to myself, glad not to be the drunkest. "Well, he climbs Everest and does a shot of Scotch at the top to celebrate, and cuz of the altitude, right, he's hammered from one shot. And he basically falls back down the mountain."

The group seems likable enough; at least, I'm not worried about spending the year with them. We learn none of us has a brother or sister. "What are the odds?" I ask.

"Hmm. Let me see," Anna begins. "I think I heard about 20 percent of households have only one child so with four of us that would be... math wasn't my strongest."

"Ha. I wasn't being literal," I laugh.

"Actually, I had a brother," Hector adds. "Sorry for bringing the mood down."

"Well, I need another glass," I say to lighten us up again.

Quinn is indeed the youngest, and when I ask him where he's from, he tells me, "All over" before clarifying he's a military child and spent years living near bases across the country. He did one semester of college before realizing it wasn't for him and has worked in restaurants the past few years, admittedly partying too hard while doing so.

Anna is from Long Island and divorced her husband about a year ago. She was young and dumb, she says, which means married at twenty-four, apparently. I do the math to determine an eight-year marriage ending last year would make her thirty-three or thirty-four, about three years older than me. Divorce was the right move, she tells me, but she didn't expect to feel so isolated afterward. "We had all the same friends, you know? And the ones I did keep up with started having babies, which… I've never been a baby person."

"Cheers to that," I say, clinking her glass. There's a lull in conversation, and with my inhibitions down, I blurt out, "So this is weird, right? Being here?"

"Ha. I was wondering when someone would say that," says Hector.

"I know," Anna says. "Like, I kept waiting for it to be a scam. Even though my lawyer looked through it and said it was legit, and I made all the preparation and put everything into storage, it wasn't until they stuck that needle into my arm that I started to realize, wow, this is really happening."

"Yeah, I mean, I still didn't believe it even after I saw the first deposit in my bank account," I add and realize we've started whispering. "Even then I was skeptical. But, like you said, at some point—"

Peggy returns and we all go quiet. She's come back to apologize for their hasty exit. We'll finish orientation in the morning, she assures us, apologizing a few more times for good measure. I invite her to stay and have a drink with us. She tells us to have fun. The light bulb has stopped blinking.

* * *

My head aches. It's made all the worse knowing I won't be able to fall back asleep again when I'm hurting so bad. The bed is still immaculately cozy, but it's become a sweat cocoon as the alcohol escapes my pores. I force myself up and retrieve a glass of water. Somehow, in the mirror, I look even worse than I feel. Eyes bloodshot and dead. Skin draping off my bones like it wants nothing to do with what's happening inside my body. It was fun last night, I'm glad I'm getting along with the others, blah blah, but why did I do this to myself? I drink a glass of water, refill it and have another before returning to bed. Even if I can't fall asleep again, I can lie still and feel sorry for myself for a few hours.

I'm back among the living by breakfast, but I'm still pretty rough. Anna and Quinn look in poor shape, too. They're sitting quietly at separate tables, eyes lost in empty space in front of them. A bowl of oatmeal sits untouched in front of Quinn as if its presence might help him work up the courage to move, maybe eat. Anna cradles a coffee mug without drinking.

Hector is unfazed by last night's debauchery. He's kind of singing to himself, almost dancing as he ladles more syrup onto his pancakes. Sure, he was my first friend here, but, in this moment, I wish him ill.

Transcript of Orientation Video; Part Two

[recovered by editor during research]
(full color film)

Text appears on blank blue screen, 'MONITOR: Confirm all subjects have signed the preliminary agreement form before proceeding.'

Text fades. Scene begins with computer-animated polygons coming in and out of focus while in motion, accompanied by an upbeat, synthesized composition. A laser beam carves the initials 'SL' on a granite tablet, which centers on the screen above the words 'an SL Corporate Production.' Scene fades.

A computer-animated interlude begins with a blue sunburst effect. The word 'Orientation' slides across the screen from right to left as a brief synthesized drumbeat and keyboard play.

The frame changes to a mid-range shot of

Romaine standing outside a modern white building with mountains visible beyond.

"Hello again. I am pleased you have decided to join us in our project. Without you, our research would not be possible. It is my sincere belief that over the course of the next year you will be regularly comforted in knowing you made the right decision."

He walks to his left. Camera zooms out.

"It would be hard to regret your choice when you wake up to this view every morning."

He gestures with arms widespread. Camera pans right and zooms out. Frame depicts mountainous scenery. Birds and a stream are audible. Camera tracks back to Romaine.

"You will be given a tour of your accommodation shortly, but without further delay let me take you into the heart of the research facility."

Scene fades out. Text appears on a black screen: 'The Medicament.' Frame changes to a mid-range shot of Romaine standing in front of a steel door marked 'Laboratory. Authorized Personnel Only.' He is wearing a white lab coat. He unlocks the door with a keycard and enters the lab. He stands in the middle of the large room. Lab equipment can be seen in cabinets on all sides. A man in a lab coat is working at a station to his right.

"This state-of-the-art laboratory provides our scientists with the resources they need to ensure success. Though I don't want to disturb him too much while he works, here is our chief researcher, Dr. Peter Samesong."

He gestures to the man working at the station. He pauses from his work to wave at the camera. Text appears on the bottom of the screen identifying the individual. Romaine walks backward further into the lab. A couple of other unidentified researchers take turns looking into the eyepiece of a microscope. Another is taking notes while observing a centrifuge.

"Now I would like to introduce you to another essential member of our team."

He stops next to a large glass cabinet, opens the door, removes a jar and pours the contents into his hand. Camera zooms in on several small green capsules.

"Trans-trihydroxystilbene. Or as we've been calling it, The Medicament."

Camera zooms out.

"At the heart of this incredible pill is the skin of grapes. After promising studies revealed increased longevity in those who drank a glass of wine daily, we took it a step further, isolating the source and magnifying its effects. In our animal testing phases, we found not only an increase in lifespan, but also remarkable recovery from a wide variety of pre-existing conditions, with virtually no side effects. Essentially, we created a miracle drug."

He places the capsules back into the jar, which he returns to the cabinet. He slowly walks backward while facing the camera.

"To put you at ease, it is important you know our animal testing phase had a nearly one hundred percent success rate. In fact, you can meet some of the early experimental candidates right now."

He opens a door marked 'Exam Room' and enters. Several cages filled with mice, rats, and rabbits are visible. He opens one of the cages and removes a light brown rabbit, cradling it in his arm.

"When we first began our testing on Henry here, he was hardly the adorable pet you see now."

A photograph appears on the lower right corner of the screen with the date 2/15/89. The rabbit is covered with patches of blistered flesh between its sparse fur.

"He was suffering from a bacterial infection his immune system was unable to fight on its own. However, after only a few days' treatment with The Medicament, he showed signs of recovery and has been healthy ever since."

He places the rabbit back in the cage, exits the room and returns to the laboratory.

"Now, despite our exceptional results in animal testing, our scientists have worked arduously for the past several years to ensure The Medicament is ready for human use. It is our shared belief that The Medicament will yield nothing but positive effects in our next phase as well. We are giving you the opportunity to become the first people to experience the benefits of our miracle drug. On behalf of our entire team, I would once again like to thank you for your cooperation and commitment to this endeavor."

Scene fades out.

Text appears on a blue screen: Please pause the tape at this time and distribute the orientation information packet.

A computer-animated interlude begins with a blue sunburst effect. The words 'Daily Routine' slide across the screen from right to left as a brief synthesized drumbeat and keyboard play.

Tour

Day two of orientation is a slog, physically and mentally. We finally take a full tour, which I've been eager for, but I've entered the hangover stage of not quite wanting to die, yet not being too happy about being alive, either.

This is where we have our checkups: a small room with an exam table, a physician's scale, some medical equipment, a sink and cupboards.

This is where we can exercise if we're so inclined: a motel-size gym with a mirrored wall and angled colored stripes along others. There are free weights, a multi-function weight machine, a treadmill, and an exercise bike.

This is where we can cook if we feel like cooking: a large and spotless kitchen attached to the dining room where every surface appears to be stainless steel. We need to put in a request in advance so the gas stoves and ovens may be turned on. Safety first. There's also an array of microwavable meals if we prefer not to cook.

In case we forgot, this is where we can watch movies and play board games and bumper pool and get shitfaced on champagne.

The hallways are quiet. We've been walking a lot, and I haven't seen anyone else. It feels like being in a school after all the kids have gone home, except there's not even a custodian moving from room to room consolidating trash bins.

Peggy and Dr. Samesong show us the pantry, which is the size of a small bedroom and is lined with well-organized boxes and cans of food. We have access any time. There's a ridiculous amount of alcohol along one wall, wine in racks along the base and liquor bottles arranged from light to dark on shelves above, both brand names and generic labels. Cases of a beer I don't recognize are stacked in the corner. Nothing is dusty.

"We want it to be as normal an experience as possible. People drink," Dr. Samesong tells us. But no booze tonight, they say, since we're doing our physicals tomorrow. That's perfectly fine. I swear I won't drink again. Today, at least. Before we move on, Hector inquires about cigarettes and before he's done asking, they've retrieved a carton for him. Near the entrance they gesture to a hallway of doors they call the storage annex. They don't anticipate needing everything, but they have plenty of backup supplies.

We go outside briefly. They tell us our thumbprints have been authorized for access now that we've signed the forms. It's clear but bitter cold. We stand on the edge of the runway, which has been dusted with a fresh coat of snow. An airplane hangar sits on one side, its corrugated iron doors shut to protect the only means of transportation in or out.

The air rushes over the mountaintops, making a howling sound and bringing flakes of snow downward. The nearest peak is craggy and would require gear and expertise to summit. Other peaks have a more gradual ascent, but still look formidable while covered in snow. A glacier sits between two peaks opposite the facility and opens into a gully and stream parallel to the runway. Along our valley is a scattering of evergreen trees which looks to become dense forest as it follows the river. The only sign of wildlife are white speckled birds which flit from one tree to another.

Beyond a ridge in our foreground, they tell us, there's a pond we can ice skate on, if we want, but we might want to wait until it's at least tolerably cold, say, twenty degrees. We reenter the facility, and they reveal the storage room by the entrance to be filled with ice skates, snowshoes, and hiking boots. I notice a frisbee and a croquet set, as well as some folded-up lawn chairs. It must warm up eventually. Northern hemisphere and below the Arctic Circle. And mountains. My Siberian geography is shaky; there may be mountains there. I can't rule it out.

The library perks me up, I'll admit. I'd been expecting a droll set of cubbies like the forgotten corner in a thrift store. Romance paperbacks and essays from obscure politicians and Time-Life books that refer to Asia as "The Orient." A place where books go to die.

Instead, the library is my favorite. It's not only my favorite room on the tour, but possibly the nicest room I've ever been in. Shelves of enough books for several lifetimes of reading. At a glance I note the range of genre and era. Enough to satisfy any mood. More impressive than the collection is the space itself. The ceiling is much higher than the other rooms, and an upper register of stacks is accessible by ladders wheeled on a track. Elegant sconces jut from the walls between oaken shelves, and despite everything looking crisp and new, it maintains a rugged coziness in contrast to the futuristic feel of the rest of the facility. There are a few reading tables outfitted with green desk lamps and high-backed leather chairs which, to sit in properly, you would need a Sherlock Holmes pipe.

And, magically, at the library's center a spiral staircase leads to a glass-domed conservatory with stunning panoramic views. I'm now able to take in the scenery without shivering. We are shaded from sunlight by the nearest towering peak, but the bright reflection of snow makes me squint. The glacier is even more expansive from this angle, with forest and wilderness extending indefinitely beyond. There's no cloud cover, but I can see a generator puffing plumes of steam past the edge of our building. Apart from the runway and our facility, nothing else manmade is in sight.

It makes sense to end the tour here. Peggy fails to conceal her pride. She smiles watching me bounce back down the stairs.

The rest of the day is ours, they say. I linger in the library, placing my claim on it early as my space. I'm not going to be possessive about it or anything. If other people want to use it, they're more than welcome. If anyone ever needs to find me, though, this is where I'll be.

CHAPTER 1

I got my first job when I was eleven. Our neighbor was an older woman, who probably wasn't all that old, but to an eleven-year-old she seemed ancient. She might have been eighty-five, but she might have just as easily been sixty. I didn't know my grandparents, so I had no frame of reference for estimating the age of anyone older than my mom.

She lived by herself and didn't leave the house apart from excursions to her mailbox at the end of the driveway. Since this was her only trip into public view, she made a show of it, dressing in lavish clothing and not once repeating the same outfit as far as I could tell. Her colorful dresses fit perfectly and were complemented by a pair of open-toed shoes, but even more impressive were her hats. These wide-brimmed hats affixed to her head so naturally, I couldn't picture her without one. As the seasons changed, her footwear would switch to leather or fuzzy boots, but the hats continued, becoming more rugged, but still wide-brimmed.

The routine was orchestrated like a whimsical opening to a musical. The mail truck slowed to a stop with screeching brakes, her door creaked open, the truck puttered along to the next house, she made her entrance—a runway walk down the gravel driveway, always the same number of steps.

It was a dazzling display, more so since she delivered this daily performance for no one. The neighborhood was quiet.

Our house sat opposite and was the only one with a view of her driveway, which nestled into a little gully surrounded by overgrown brush on one side and a drainage ditch on the other. She couldn't possibly have been doing this for us. She never made the slightest gesture in our direction. Still, it was her way of making sure the world knew she was there.

Her groceries were delivered once per week and left on the doorstep. In strange contrast, when she retrieved these items, it was without pageantry, often dressed in a bathrobe and huddled over like the task took every ounce of her strength.

During the summers, I spent a lot of time on our front porch. The marginal relief from the stale indoor heat was worth sacrificing TV. On the porch, the only entertainment was my books and the daily appearance of the neighbor. Our swing was too creaky, so I'd pull off its cushion, place it on the porch and lay prone at the top of the stairs facing the street. The mail came just after noon, so I'd wait for her, then go inside to make myself lunch. When I heard the mail truck, I'd look up from my book and watch the scene, wondering what color she'd be wearing that day, trying to puzzle out her philosophy for the ensembles. Were plaid dresses reserved for Saturday? What weather necessitated a scarf? Did she work backwards and choose her shoes first before she assembled the rest of the outfit?

One day, before the rumble of the truck, with my nose deep in a collection of *Grimms' Fairy Tales* I'd reread dozens of times, I was startled by a voice, "You read." She was gesturing to my book; it was more a statement than question.

"Yes, I—"

"You write, too?" This time it was a question, not wanting to assume one truth necessitated the other. She stood at the base of the stairs, her straw sunhat flopping over in a way that made only one of her eyes visible to me.

"What do you mean? Like stories?"

"No. You can scribe. Handwriting."

"Yes, I can scribe." Not sure I was using the word correctly.

"Can I see?"

I brought out a pen and paper and lay on the porch to demonstrate. "You want me to write my name or something?"

"That's fine."

I wrote giant letters with as much precision as possible before holding it up for her approval.

"How about cursive?"

"No."

"We can work on that." The mail truck made its appearance at the end of the street and, summoned, she turned her head, putting a hand on her hat to secure it in the breeze. "Are your parents home?"

"My mom is running errands."

"If it's okay with her, would you like a job?"

"Doing what?"

"Writing letters."

"For you?"

"For me. I'll dictate them. I just can't scribe."

"Dict—?"

"I'll tell you what words to use," she shifted backward toward her mailbox which was now filled. "It's not hard. Talk to your mom."

"I'll do it," I shouted after her. I didn't think to negotiate pay. Her shoes told me she could afford something reasonable.

* * *

Since she refused to come inside, and there would have been no way to bring a table or desk outside without a daily ordeal of removing door hinges and bending furniture at impossible angles, we conducted our writing sessions on the front porch. I lay prostrate, supported by an elbow while she dictated (a polite word for bossed) from the swing, which squeaked with her movement. I'd left her the cushion on the swing and lay on an old blanket to protect myself from the flaking paint of the floorboards. The cursive lessons were little more than repetition from a page she'd ripped out of an old textbook. I'd copy and recopy sentences that need not exist were it not for their usage of every letter of the alphabet—*The quick brown fox jumped over the lazy dog* and *Bright vixens jump; dozy fowl quack.*

While she rocked in the swing, she crossed her arms. When she walked over, she kept her hands behind her back, and on her way home she held them clenched in front as though praying. She didn't use her fingers to point out my script errors; she robotically recited the number of the line where I'd made the error. The lessons ended promptly with the arrival of the mail truck.

On Sunday, the day without mail, her outing was to deposit an envelope in my mailbox stuffed with fifty dollars in random denominations. I didn't tell my mom about the lessons. If she didn't know about it, she couldn't object. It was more money than an eleven-year-old knew what to do with, but I still didn't want to risk losing it. I'd been receiving pay for three weeks before we began scribing the letters.

The first draft was rough, and I'd have to rewrite it.

Dear ~~Matthew Son Matt~~ Matthew,

Thank you for writing. I look forward to every one of your letters. Everything here is the same as it's always been, ~~though, nothing is quite the same without you here.~~ I'm thinking about taking a vacation soon, but I can't decide where to go. ~~I'll probably stay put, though.~~

Love,

"How should I sign it?"

"Mom."

"Would you like to write that part?"

"No."

"It feels weird for me to write it."

I practiced writing "Mom" after our lessons ended. I figured it was important to have those letters look right.

* * *

Enough time had passed that I couldn't ask her name. If she had told me, I didn't remember. I knew enough about manners to know it would be rude to ask after so long, but continuing to not know it was even more rude. Since she took her mail the second it arrived, I couldn't check there. I didn't want to ask my mom, because I didn't want her to have follow-up questions for me, and I doubt she knew anyhow.

It became awkward during our lessons. If I wanted to get her attention, I'd have to cough or raise my hand or do an extended *ummm* and wait for her reply. It didn't help that she used my name constantly. She'd end sentences with it in a display of etiquette, "Good morning, Lily," or "Nice work, Lily," or "I'll see you tomorrow, Lily," and I'd disguise my ignorance in response—" I'll see you… too."

I hadn't ever snuck out of the house before. Finding out the name of my employer was as good a reason as any for my first escape. Mom's snoring made it easy to tell she was asleep. The TV she left on in her bedroom added cover for my footsteps.

The neighborhood was different at night. With the house lights off and not a car to be heard, I became a trespasser, not just of the neighborhood, but of the world. It was like one of those science fiction stories where someone finds a magic watch and everyone else freezes in time—stopping mid-sentence, or mid-drink, or mid-fistfight or whatever—and there's one person who can roam amongst the frozen bodies unnoticed, gathering secrets. Crickets and cicadas tuned their songs as if trying to find the proper pitch while never quite arriving, a circuitous intonation that would continue through the night until they took a break and vowed to resume tomorrow. Each step I took was a violation of the nighttime order. My eyes swallowed every hint of light as they adjusted to the dark and I crossed to Mrs. Whoever's house.

I'd assumed her last name would be written on her door knocker, as it was with ours, but when that proved false, I needed another plan. Her garbage must have had some junk mail, so I went around back. She had loud metal garbage lids I was sure would give me away. Using the skill of a spy, I managed to remove each lid with the muted timbre of a kid who thinks they aren't making any noise. To my dismay, the cans only possessed stinky scraps rotting in the summer heat, not a trace of discarded mail.

My last chance for mission success was to peer in the windows. Perhaps she had a plaque or knick-knack along the lines of *God Bless the Smith Home*. Each window was guarded by a fully drawn drape. The only chance was the small window of the backdoor. On my tiptoes I could barely see into the house of my employer. Everything was dark, frozen, asleep.

Despite my obscured vantage, I could make out the newspapers: stacks and stacks piled up to the ceiling. They towered over the room like cathedral walls, yellowed-gray in the diffused light. My curiosity piqued, I made a stepping stool of the garbage can, and I stood on it to see fully inside.

The newspapers were only the beginning. Walls of newspaper turned to piles of clothes to stacks of dishes to mountains of unidentifiable junk that filled every recess of the house. The only empty space was the trail that had been carved through the canyon. It sprouted tributaries leading to further tunnels through bric-a-brac until there was no outlet. Floor to ceiling stuffed with clutter, an impossible collection of nothing.

She would stay nameless.

* * *

Writing sessions continued and I gave no hint to what I had seen. I wanted to ask questions, but a combination of guilt and pity kept me quiet. The letters spurted from my pen without the words registering. If I didn't know how to spell a word, I pretended like I did for fear that a pause in scribing might cause me to blurt out something I couldn't take back. So, I wrote silently and mechanically and made the corrections she requested without curiosity. And I never asked why, if her son were a soldier, the letters were addressed to Canada and not Vietnam.

It was August when she stopped showing up. The weather had turned wet, and, for a while, I figured that's what kept her away—her dresses too susceptible to the mud.

When her mailbox overflowed and the grocery deliveries attracted the attention of stray cats, I needed to investigate. The doorbell made an odd sound, probably muffled by heaps of junk, and she didn't answer when I started to knock. I went around to the backdoor to see inside. Nothing unusual, not counting the hoard of whatevers. The doorknob turned, and

I nudged my way inside, shifting the balance of a stack of *Gourmet* magazines that wobbled for a moment before settling again. The top cover featured an illustration of a table set for a holiday meal, labeled December 1955 and retailing for fifty cents. I called out, but there was no answer.

Following the well-trodden trails, I searched the house. I was too overwhelmed by the stench of musty newspaper and mildew to detail the contents of each room, but suffice it to say, every space had been consumed by a pile or a stack or a cluster, often smothering furniture beneath. Walls showed the remnants of decor, but frames and hangings had been smooshed by the stacks and hung askew.

As I continued my search upstairs, the bathroom door wouldn't open. I could see light over the transom, but the door stuck after an inch, so I put my shoulder into it. A few hard nudges were enough to create a gap I could squeeze through. It was her body that turned out to be the reason for the jam. She lay wedged between the door and bathtub. Her back was against the door, intentionally obstructing the entrance. My heaves must have made her give up. She was so still, I thought I might have killed her.

Unlike the rest of the house, the room was spacious and orderly. Resting on the floor was a twin mattress fitted with a clean set of sheets and pillows. In the windowsill nested a hot plate and kettle filled with the remnants of a stew. Books sat on a shelf above the mirror. A small jar of potpourri and a candle lay atop the toilet. Toiletries in a basket hung from the showerhead.

She had been crying, that much was obvious. Unshielded by a hat, her eyes were puffy and red, and she wiped away a tear. I was too uneasy to say anything, but she proffered the answer by handing me an envelope. Her hand, mangled and unsightly, could hardly grip the simple weight. At her wrist, the joint bent at an unnatural angle, and her fingers looked lifeless, the tips a haunted purple with cracked yellow nails. I took the envelope and read.

> Mom,
>
> Please stop writing. Every time I read your words, it is a reminder of what I did. You may say you have forgiven me, but I still haven't forgiven myself.
>
> Love,
> Matthew

"I wasn't always like this, Lily," she held her wrist, her weakened hand relying on the other. "We had been planning to go to the draft office together the next morning, but I woke up with my hands tied to the bed. He was kind enough to leave slack so I could reach the phone, but I couldn't bear calling anyone. So, I had to free myself. And snap! I know I should have gone to a doctor." She paused as if remembering I was the one listening, "I'll pay you for this week's lessons. Don't worry."

It wasn't long before a caretaker began coming to the house. Loads of junk were hauled outside by men who wore bandannas over their faces to protect from dust. Trip after trip, the contents of her house became junk in a dumpster.

She still made her daily appearance for the mail, but the outfits repeated themselves. I counted out all my cash and saved it in an envelope in the back of my closet. Two hundred and forty-five dollars. I wished there were more.

The Medicament

It's green and it looks like a jellybean. Unlike most pills, it's not firm but instead coated with a squishy substance. It feels like you could compress it and make its liquid core explode. I haven't tried. We take it orally, once per day, every day.

At noon Dr. Samesong comes over the intercom and tells us our medication is ready. Exactly at noon. Down to the second, which means he's sitting idly for a minute or so, waiting for the clock to change. It's an odd choice since we don't actually ingest the pill at that precise moment. Still, at twelve p.m. sharp we're summoned, and each of us retreats from the library or the lounge or the kitchen or our bedroom to march to the lab. He punches in a key code and unlocks a cabinet filled with hundreds of bottles of pills. We're given the green pill in a small paper cup. We wash it down with a drink of water and then open our mouths and stick out our tongues to show we've swallowed it.

"Science," he says each time like a joke to break any possible tension.

When we are weighed each week. "Science."

When he asks about our bowel movements. "Science."

When he asks me about my cycle. "Science." Actually, he doesn't say it then, but I still imagine him saying it in my head.

The exams don't take long. We run through the questionnaire in about five minutes, and the physical takes another ten. So, we maybe spend an hour with him each week. It's so infrequent, I almost forget it's why we're here.

I don't feel different. Not really. I don't have more energy or feel clear-headed or anything like that. I certainly don't feel stronger or smarter. They said we might. Not that I've been going to the gym. I'm no quicker solving a moderate crossword puzzle.

Well, there's one noticeable effect. Hangovers. Gone. And we had a serious bender one night, too. We were playing cards and drinking whisky for a few hours, one of those nights where a few drinks became a few more and the drinking became something unconscious we were doing with our hands without pausing to consider if we were overdoing it. At one point Anna tried to excuse herself with a line about a busy day tomorrow, but the group knew we all had nowhere to be, so peer pressure won out, and Hector topped off her glass. I fell asleep with shoes on.

But I woke up the next morning feeling top notch. I know they have grandiose ambitions with The Medicament, but they could probably make pretty good money selling it as a hangover cure. I'd endorse it.

Though without the hangover as deterrent, I have been drinking more. I find myself saying, why not?

There's only so much time I can spend writing in a day anyhow.

We aren't getting sloshed routinely, but I'll work up a healthy buzz most nights, well, every night. It's fun—it makes me social, makes us all social, which we need. For our mental health. For science.

Quinn's Music

I'm trying not to seethe when Quinn tells me he came here to write—write music, but still write. Writing was supposed to be my thing. Well, we have different mediums, I tell myself. There's enough room.

"You'll have to play for us sometime," I say with my best poker face, hoping he'll play for us and prove to be terrible so I can claim the title of the creative one.

"I don't know."

"Oh, come on."

"We'll see."

He's not doing that thing I've known musicians to do. The thing where they want you to beg them to play and they're all faux embarrassed, but then they play and slobber up all the praise. But his body language suggests he doesn't want me to egg him on; his upper body has clenched, and his eyes have fixated on a loose thread on the arm of the couch. He doesn't want to play, which means he's either no good (win), or he's shy like me (I don't like it).

Anna walks in on our conversation. Everyone keeps to themselves in the morning, but at some point in the afternoon a few of us will congregate, this time in the dining room where we're refilling our coffee. She forces him to play. Won't take no for an answer, she says. He still doesn't want to, but she's so persistent it becomes evident the only way to end this would be to get his guitar and play, or slam his fist down. He's a pushover so he leaves and comes back with a guitar in hand. He clarifies it's the only luggage they let him bring.

Even from the simple act of tuning and running through a few warm-up riffs, I can tell he's not going to be awful. I brace myself.

I try to be civil, but I'm crippled with jealousy. He's good. Really good. Anna keeps making eyes at me like she thought he'd be alright, but *damn*, he's better than alright. He sings with a voice I wouldn't consider traditionally rich, but it has a distinct timbre that gives the music character, and his guitar skills are impressive. He alternates between quick fingerpicking and a percussive rhythm that makes it sound like multiple instruments as his hands jump all around the fretboard. The song is folksy and its hook, "I Will Return No More," jumps out to become immediately memorable. Anna starts swaying back and forth and closes her eyes.

"What song was that?" Anna asks when he finishes.

"That's one of mine."

I exhale and will myself to remember we have different mediums. "Play another," I manage to say and I realize I mean it. Anna scoots a little bit closer to Quinn. He plays another beautiful song and Anna and I applaud. "That was really great," I say and I excuse myself. Anna stays.

I'm too anxious to go write anything so I wander off to the lounge. Hector is there playing pinball and smoking as per usual. We've agreed the lounge is the smoking section. I ask him for a cigarette, and he cradles the pinball with one of the flippers before he uses one hand to fetch a cigarette. There's a singe mark near the neckline of his blue shirt next to a few bits of ash.

I've had cigarettes here and there, but never enough to have favored one brand. They're all the same, more or less.

It's not the taste that makes our supply of cigarettes distinct, though; it's their appearance. Rather than an all-white tube or white with tan filter, these have a red butt on them. The scarlet hue matches the color of burning ember, creating a peculiar visual effect. To my knowledge, Redlight Cigarettes never caught on as more than a novelty, even as it appealed to women smokers trying to conceal lipstick marks on the butt. Still, they're what we've been supplied here. It seems the facility was sold by their slogan, "Always Stop for a Redlight."

I exhale the smoke. "What do you think of Anna?" I ask.

"Gossip already! It's barely been a week," he laughs and resumes his pinballing, the chimes and lights focusing our eyes on the game. "I think she means well." I know exactly what is meant by the subtext.

"Quinn seems alright."

"Yeah, good kid." He's uncomfortable talking about them like this, I can tell. Or he's just really into pinball.

"Mind if I have the next game?"

"As long as you don't top my high score."

We alternate turns and chainsmoke, and I don't even come close to his high score. One of the flippers sticks ever so slightly and I haven't yet figured out how to manage the defect. He starts a new game, and the machine runs through a jingle I'm sure I'll be sick of all too quickly. Out of nowhere I say, "I'm a writer, I don't know if I've told you that." It almost feels like a confession that I needed to tell someone.

"Yeah? My wife was a writer." I open my mouth to ask more but… "Alright! Multi-ball!"

* * *

I feel the need to walk, but not on a treadmill, so I devise a route and start looping the hallways around the facility. Past the lounge, past the kitchen, past the dining room, past the gym, past the bedrooms, past the storage room annex, past the offices, past the labs, past the library and again past the lounge. It's on the third loop I realize I haven't been outside since the tour. The facility is big enough to feel like I'm getting out and about, but it's not like I have to head outside to run errands. The frost on the windows has been enough of a deterrent, but with impending stir-craziness, I decide it's time to brave the cold.

First, I plan a course. I go to the library, up the spiral staircase, and look out the domed glass of the conservatory. I spot a frozen waterfall tucked into a cliff face to the north, and it looks like a manageable hike that won't require any gear or much energy.

"Nice view, isn't it?" Peggy has appeared at the bottom of the staircase. She's holding a clipboard and makes a little tick mark on it. Part of her rounds. She pokes her head in each room from time to time, notes where we are, exchanges a pleasantry, and moves on.

"Amazing. I can't get over it." I think of asking her about a hiking path, but before I can, she smiles, ending the interaction, and moves on. Even without a route planned, I've delayed long enough. I suck it up and start heading for the tunnel. I'll brave the cold and step outside.

On my way, Peggy is ticking her clipboard as she notes Quinn and Anna in the dining room. She has a secret grin on her face. I stop to ask if it'd be alright if I got some fresh air outside.

"Of course. You're not a prisoner. Ha." I see her eyes stray towards the window in the kitchen door and my eyes follow. Anna is basically sitting in Quinn's lap.

"That was quick."

"I saw it coming. Anyhow, when you go outside make sure

you don't go too far or go to the ice field. There are crevasses hidden under the snow. And don't go too long. Frostbite." She smiles, ending the interaction again, and moves on.

* * *

It takes me at least ten minutes in the locker room to put on layers for the cold. I look like Ernest Shackleton by the time I'm ready. Fur-lined boots, fur-lined parka, heavy wool mittens, and big old goggles. I'm not going to go far so I'm not going to bother with snowshoes. I step into the tunnel to begin my expedition.

As it turns out, I'm overdressed. I'm sweating before I reach the end of it. In the sunlight it can't be colder than twenty degrees. It's cold, yes, but I don't need to be all Ernest.

The landscape is stunning in the clear sky. I take a moment to marvel at the majesty of the place. Clouds wisp through the nearby peaks, and the massive glacier nests into the concavity of the slopes, its aqua walls stretching hundreds of feet above our valley. We are enclosed on three sides by the mountains, making the valley feel almost like a crater. One of the lesser peaks opens into a bowl of snow beneath its summit before sloping downward into narrow chutes and channels. I can imagine skiers delighting in such a descent through the powder. There aren't many signs of wildlife besides the small birds. The landscape is frozen apart from a river beyond the runway that roars from the glacier's base and winds its way down the valley. It's the first I've noticed the sound of the water.

I trudge uphill through the snow toward the rear of the facility. My feet sink to the knee with every step, and, though it's not more than a hundred yards to the backside, I have to stop every few steps to catch my breath. The Medicament may or may not be having an effect on my endurance, but the tobacco sure didn't help as its taste swills in my saliva.

I make my way past several tinted windows which must be our bedrooms, and I'm almost to the lounge before I need to pause again. All this effort is silly. There's far too much snow for hiking, and I regret not strapping on the snowshoes, but I've come this far so I will myself onward and keep moving. Lift, step, crunch. Lift, step, crunch. Lift, step, crunch.

Around the corner from the lounge are Dr. Samesong's Office, the lab and the library. Beyond the library, nothing. I walk to the office windows to gaze in. It'd be kind of funny to startle Dr. Samesong while in my Nordic suit. When I shield my eyes to peer inside, I see no one. It's dark and there's no movement. There's a desk and office chair beside a filing cabinet; no loose papers or any decorations can be seen. I move to the lab and do the same. There are a few microscopes and digital scales and shelves of neatly arranged flasks, test tubes, and beakers. A few indicator lights blink on a refrigerator.

I've only seen Dr. Samesong during our checkups, and Peggy has been perfunctory in our encounters. I figured they were in the offices. But there aren't notes on the tables or empty coffee mugs or any sign of recent activity. I continue to scan the room and spot a door labeled with the common symbol I'd recognize anywhere. Stairwell.

They live underneath us. Simple architecture. Probably a basement that mirrors our own layout. They gave us the level with the windows because we're the guests. Actually, as I judge the depth of my path through the snow, I realize the basement is more likely to be a recessed garden level with a small strip of windows at the top; they're just buried in snow, which might be even worse than having no window at all.

The snowbanks ahead are even deeper, and with the wind picking up, I think I've done enough exploring for the day. I walk back, sweaty and even more overdressed now. I try to tug down the jacket zipper to ventilate, but my waterproof mittens are clumsy. I use my teeth to yank one off and accidentally drop it into the snow. The wind catches it and blows it down the hillside.

The mitten keeps drifting away, and I have to properly chase it. I'm bounding down the slope, on the verge of a tumble with each step but managing to keep the momentum in my favor as I gain on the elusive mitten. It's only a few feet ahead, and I lunge, snatching it as I plop into the snow. I roll onto my back and stare into the blue sky as I catch my breath and let myself feel proud of my modest victory.

My eyes wander the scenery, and again I'm mystified by the beauty. The sound of my panting and the crunch of the snow beneath me—I let it consume me and clear my mind. The dual sensation of the heat from my body and the bite of the snow soothes. I forget about the idiocy of my mission and laugh at myself. I needed this: to step outside to behold this place, to feel it.

I'm drifting between the ecstasy of a runner's high and a lucidity where this all makes sense. I am here. I am doing this. I couldn't leave even if I wanted to and that's perfect. No more excuses. I am happy to stay put.

My eyes stray backward and I find the icefield. Upside-down from my vantage, the sky appears as a sea and the ice as sky. A surreal painting by Magritte. Ice spires and formations jut down from the ceiling like stalactites, and I imagine them dripping into the sky-water below.

I'm snapped out of my reverie. On the far end of the ice field is a splash of purple that does not fit. I sit upright and then I stand. It's too far in the distance to make out clearly, but it seems to be a person in a purple coat. We're in blue, Peggy is in yellow, Samesong in white, but we haven't been introduced to anyone in purple. They're shifting back and forth, almost doing a dance. Whoever they are, they don't stay for long. The purple sinks below the horizon and disappears.

* * *

Back inside, I debate telling the other guests about the purple coat. It probably wasn't anything significant, part of a maintenance crew that de-ices the runway or something. The only reason I found it significant, I realize, was because of its stark contrast against the rest of the landscape. It was the purple that caught my attention as irregular, not the idea of someone in the distance.

It's also possible that there are people living nearby. People being people. Nothing weird. I'd assumed we were completely isolated, but that's not necessarily true. Isolated from our families and friends, yes, but the entire world doesn't need to be kept away from us. For all I know, on the other side of the nearest mountain pass is a bustling ski resort.

As I walk towards the lounge, Anna and Quinn pass by and try not to look at me. They stop in front of Anna's door. I quicken my pace, also acting like I saw nothing. I don't have to turn back around to know they both slink inside her room together.

Hector has stopped pinball but not the cigarettes. He's sitting in a recliner blowing smoke rings. It's the only thing he's doing, but he's doing it well.

"Saw you outside," he says as I walk in.

"Looked pretty silly, huh?"

He exhales another perfect smoke ring. "Determined." And another. "I haven't been outside, yet."

"Yeah, that was my first venture. Mind if I—" I reach forward and he proffers a Redlight, which he lights for me. I pause, trying to calculate the proper tone for my discovery. I go with mysterious, so I inhale deeply, philosophical like. "You know…" A coughing fit takes hold of me. My lungs are still frozen from the cold air, and they aren't liking the smoke at all. I work through it, but it's rough. I'm still coughing as I try again. "I had an itch to find something. It occurred to me," cough, "I haven't seen all the facility, because of the places we're not allowed to," cough, "go. Excuse me. By the way, did you know where the staff stay?"

"They're underground."

So much for my big reveal. "How did you know that?"

"Anna wasn't the only one paying attention in orientation." He stubs out the scarlet end of his cigarette. "It's even on the map. Look." He gestures to the map plastered on the wall. I move to read it. Sure enough. Ground level labeled with all the spots I know, and a lower level with living quarters for the staff.

"Ah. I guess I really did space out during that."

"It is weird we haven't seen the pilot since we arrived, though."

I'd forgotten the pilot. We were so out of it from the drugs I didn't even remember one existed. I couldn't really picture anyone—a groggy flash of an image crosses my mind of someone in an aviator headset after we hit the runway—but since the plane was still here, it followed that the pilot would be, too.

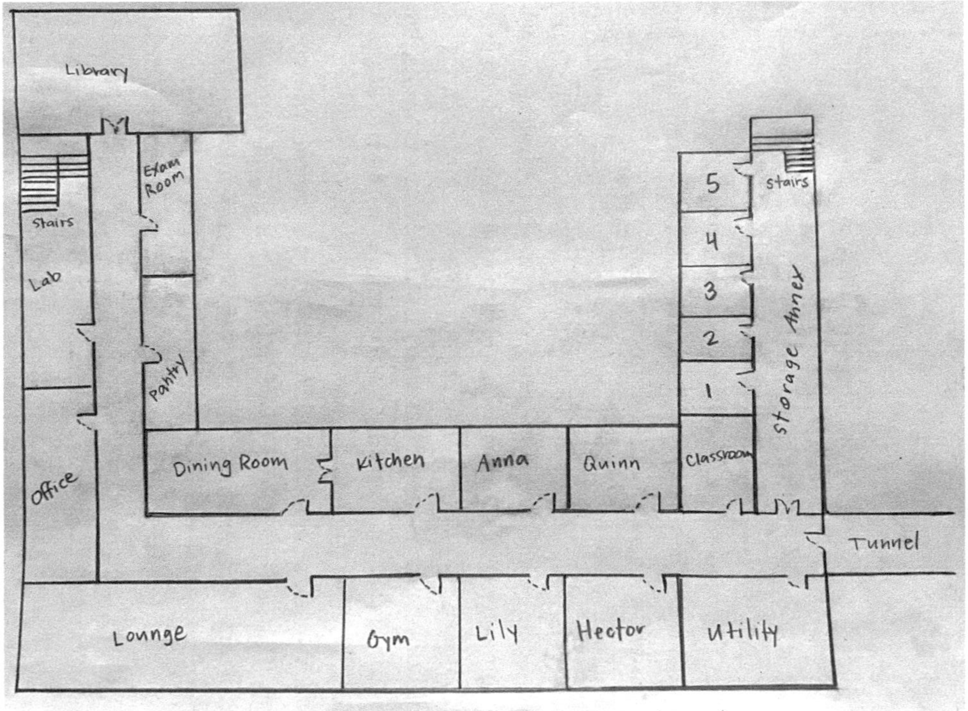
Library
Exam Room
Stairs
Lab
Pantry
Office
Dining Room
Kitchen
Anna
Quinn
Classroom
5
4
3
2
1
Stairs
Storage Annex
Tunnel
Lounge
Gym
Lily
Hector
Utility

Note From the Editor

The first step was to run the document through plagiarism software. When it came back negative, it eliminated the possibility it was a blatant reproduction.

Unfortunately, the text was terribly non-specific when it came to names, locations or anything I could research to confirm details. The last name Samesong, not Samsung, as search engines tried to autocorrect, though uncommon, yielded little of use. As far as the Internet was concerned, Peter Samesong did not exist. "Arthur Romaine" produced more results, but from what I could surmise from obituaries and LinkedIn profiles, none of them had any connection to the project.

A quick search of *The SL Corporation* gave me little to go on. The acronym yielded over a billion results ranging from a Korean auto parts manufacturer to Stockholm Public Transportation to a defunct Polish political party. Even adding relevant terms—pharma, medicament, research, medicine, Arthur Romaine—produced nothing. *The SL Corporation* may have existed, but it had terrible Search Engine Optimization.

If I was going to confirm the veracity of the document, my best chance was through geography. It probably wouldn't have been more than a hundred miles or so in any direction from where I'd found the cache, so I used satellite imagery, that is, Google Earth. It was mind-numbing work, and I'd often lose focus when poring over frame after frame that didn't look dissimilar from the last, but eventually I found what seemed to be a runway beside a glacier. The site was on the backside of the *Wrangell-St. Elias National Park*. Though I'd found the cache about twenty-five miles from the trailhead where I'd parked, the facility was beyond a mountain pass probably another twenty miles further. There was only one access road on its north edge, and the nearest gas station had been forty miles away. The only way into the facility was by foot or airplane.

From above, the facility looked to have been overcome by the elements of nature. The greenery appeared uninterrupted, and, at first glance, there was no sign of the steel of a wind tunnel or any other man-made structures. However, when a dome-shaped object appeared to reflect light, it could have been the remains of the conservatory. I took note of the coordinates and traced a path on a topographical map between the cache point and the facility. It would be difficult, but not impossible. If the document were a hoax, they had certainly done their research. For all intents and purposes however, I ruled out this possibility. That's not to say I abandoned the skeptical eye and read every word as truth, but in seeing the library, Lily became real.

The Routine

Quinn and Anna make sense, I guess. They're both attractive and probably a bit bored, so why not? The idea of coupling off so quickly irks me, though. It makes me feel like teams have formed. I suppose it's hypocritical of me. I'd been formulating the Everyone-Against-Anna alliance on day one.

Hanging out with a couple is different, though. They already have this couple rapport. Fortunately, they're not gross. I think I've seen them kiss once and they don't get all cuddly or anything.

I go back and forth on whether or not I like Anna. She's friendly and interested, and, yes, she does talk too much, but when there's not many options for socializing she's… fine. I wouldn't be friends with her in different circumstances. She is a good listener, but I can't help like feeling she's tracking any personal disclosure as ammunition for later. Or maybe that's not fair. I try to give her a chance, but her bubbliness makes me think of the backstabbing girls I knew growing up.

Quinn is cool, though sometimes a little standoffish. He's interesting and he's quite bright. It took me a while to figure that out because he's so quiet and uninterested in small talk. I was talking about books with him, and I couldn't remember the title of a novel I was giving a vague description of, but he remembered it then started to give me his take on it, pulling out details of the plot I'd forgotten and remembering characters' names. I asked him if he'd read it recently and he said it had been six or seven years, which would've been when he was fifteen or so.

He doesn't write, though. Doesn't have the temperament, he says. Music is different. It's natural. Writing feels like work.

I feel weird talking to Quinn alone now. Like Anna will swoop in and be like, what's going on here? Or, maybe she'd pull me aside later to ask how a friend could betray her like that.

Neither of these things happen. They aren't really a couple, I remind myself. They like each other, sure. There's something there, even if it's just sex, they've found some sort of compatibility. Some companionship. With eleven months to go, it might have been the smart move. Then again, if a minor tiff turns into an argument which turns into a fight... I'll enjoy my singleness.

2/2/1991

Mom,

You won't believe it, but they have a copy of "The Secret Goldfish." I didn't think it was real. I haven't read it yet, but it's from way before Salinger.

Remember how mad I was that summer when you gave me homework? You said we couldn't check out any more library books until I finished writing a story. I loved to start stories but not finish them. I'd start with a concept and put together a few scenes before giving up.

You gave me a prompt. Write "The Secret Goldfish," the (I thought) fictitious story referenced in *The Catcher in the Rye* about the kid who doesn't let anyone see his goldfish because he bought it with his own money.

If we already knew the moral of the story, what was the point in writing it? Well, I ended up rewriting it three different times, so I think that answered my question.

Love,
Lily

Peggy

One moment there's no one, and the next Peggy is poking her head into the library, or the lounge, or the dining room making checks on her clipboard. I don't notice most of the time. I half expect to see her popping into the bathroom to take notes. I've seen people wave to her, but by the time I turn my head, she's already gone.

She's not creepy. Especially in the Tweety Bird yellow. It's like a friend waving hello. I say it's *like* that, because she's not really our friend. We've been here for weeks and, though we see her multiple times a day, we've never exchanged more than the simplest pleasantries. We invite her to eat with us, hang out with us, whatever, but she always declines.

I'm sure she doesn't want to affect the study by bonding with the subjects, but it's a physiological drug. It's not like her playing cards with us will affect our cholesterol.

She's super friendly, though. Always asks if we need anything and does everything she can to accommodate. Hector asked her for another pinball machine, and she started to respond, not realizing it was a joke.

Half-joking, half-hoping, I asked her if I could get a typewriter. She didn't hesitate, even seemed excited by the request. There was one on my desk in the library later that day.

Someone changes our sheets. It must be Peggy, but I've never seen her do it.

I slice my thumb chopping an onion. I've never been a great chef, so I thought I'd take the time to learn technique. Hector shows me some knife skills, and I start to feel like a professional. Until I get carried away and slash my thumb. I was going too fast, thinking I had the technique down. Nope.

It doesn't hurt much, but my thumb is bleeding like it wants to see how quickly it can fill a pint glass. I wrap it in a napkin, which immediately soaks through as I put pressure on it, and I wander to the exam room to find Dr. Samesong.

"You know a bolt cutter would've been a much quicker way to cut it off," he smiles as he tends to the cut. "Because of the positioning, I'm not going to be able to use stitches. It might scar pretty bad, but this should do the trick." He squeezes a small gel-filled tube into the wound. The bleeding slows, then stops. "Super glue."

"Really?"

"More or less. Medical super glue it says on the label, but you could probably make a model battleship with it, too." He wraps my thumb in a bandage and then turns to his desk to write some notes. He's gotten a little stubbly and scratches at his cheek. Turning back to me, he yawns loudly, "Excuse me," he says, rubbing his eyes before they drift above me to the bulb arrangement. He shakes his head and gestures to the blinking lights. "By the way, the system has been glitching, try to ignore it. Anyhow, let me know if it starts to bleed again. I don't expect it will."

CHAPTER 2

Our main business district was so insignificant my mom refused to call it downtown. Even Main Street felt too formal for the collection of the four or five businesses where she'd run errands. Instead, she'd refer to the whole area as 'the store,' even if she meant she'd be poking in and out of each place.

The most frequent stop on her trip to the store was The Closet Shop, primarily a clothing store that also stocked odds and ends like cleaning supplies and basic hardware. Not only were its wares most diverse, but it also sat at the corner of Main and Elm, where foot traffic was heaviest.

When I was younger, The Closet Shop was the only store big enough to wander out of the sight of my mom. The circular clothing racks served as optimal hiding spots if you crouched down, spread the clothes apart, and squeezed into the dusty midsection.

If I'd been hiding in the racks for too long, I'd start to get bored and peek out. The surreptitious view of the store turned everyone into a spy-worthy target. Their secrets became clear to me, and I'd concoct their stories:

* * *

George Simons opened the shop the same way he did every day, fifteen minutes early so anyone could stop in before they headed to their shifts at the other shops. He made sure to read the newspaper before opening the store, so his small talk was always up to date. The town was big enough that he didn't know everyone who came in, but if he wanted to make a regular out of a first-time shopper, he'd have to impress.

After the morning rush, Mr. Simons made his rounds to check the shop's upkeep. The clothes left in the dressing room were the easiest to spot. He'd bring them to the folding table and crease them in the perfectly stackable way. The racks and shelves took more of an effort. Sometimes customers would refold an item themselves in a way that almost matched but didn't quite and created dissymmetry.

Clothes on hangers were the most tedious to inspect. Despite the plastic discs wrapped around the bar to divide sizes, there'd inevitably be a 32-waist where a 36-waist should be or even an XL shirt where a 34-waist pair of pants belonged. The inspection of tags and sizes was dull, but it kept Mr. Simons busy during the slow hours. He entered a near-meditative state as he rhythmically checked each tag.

* * *

A woman held a blouse up to herself in front of a mirror: her anniversary was coming up, and she wanted to surprise her husband with a new outfit, but as much as he'd like how she looked in it, he'd be mad she'd spent the money, so she'd only dream about buying it.

* * *

A man sized up a running shoe against the sole of his foot: after being a star athlete in high school, his dreams of making the pros fizzled out when he realized he wasn't as fast or skilled as the other college athletes, so he quit sports and hadn't thought about it since, except now he'd put on weight and everyone else seemed to be talking about health, so maybe he should try exercising again.

* * *

A teenager pocketed a wristwatch when Mr. Simons accidentally left the display case unlocked and went to fold shirts: his friends had dared him to steal something, anything, and he thought they'd be really impressed if he stole something valuable and not just a pair of socks, and when he saw the opportunity, he took it, and then when he was at the door, he wanted to change his mind, but the shopkeeper turned around again, so it was too late, and he left, and the bells hanging on the door jingled.

* * *

Pants didn't sell as well in the summer, but they still managed to get just as disorganized. 34-waist. 34. 34. 40. It was getting late in the season, and Mr. Simons was wondering if he should begin to rotate the displays or if he should do an end-of-season sale first. 34. 34. 36. 36. 36. 36. 32. Twenty percent off summer styles would definitely get them in the store, but he'd hardly make a profit on them. Then again, they needed to go sooner or later anyhow. 36. 36. 38. 38. 38. 38. 38.

Her eyes didn't scare him, but he was confounded by how long he'd been sorting through the rack without noticing the little girl. When he made eye contact, she giggled before freezing up. He played along and made a funny face back to the girl, but he wasn't sure if girls who hid in clothing racks were the same sort who would be amused by a funny face. Evidently not. She squirmed out the back of the rack, dislodging a few pants Mr. Simons would have to dust off and rehang. Even if she was too old to be amused by a funny face, she was definitely too young to walk out onto the street by herself. A woman exited the dressing room dressed half in store clothes and half her own. He made a joke about her fashion consultant having just run out the door. Then he noticed the empty space in the display case and watched the distraught girl flee down the sidewalk.

* * *

My mom didn't raise her voice often. She didn't need to. Her quiet anger did enough on its own. When she yelled at me, I didn't know how to handle it, I didn't have experience dealing with a yeller, so when she screamed at me outside The Closet Shop, I mirrored her and screamed right back. Passersby may have stopped to watch or done anything to pretend like they weren't watching, but I wouldn't know; the other people disappeared. She was sure I had done something terrible.

"How could you do something like that!?"

"Like what?!"

"Stealing!" Her teeth were gritted now.

"I don't know what you're talking about."

"Are you calling me a liar?"

"The kids took it, I saw them."

"I thought you didn't know anything about it! Which is it, Lily?"

And with that verbal trick I was stuck. Whatever way I answered, I'd only be in more trouble. I dropped my voice and answered in the only way I knew how to in such a situation, with a mumbly "I don't know."

She spoke deliberately, articulating each syllable in that

way I hated, "Come. You're going to give it back, and then you're going to apologize." She made a move to grab my wrist, but I retracted. She repeated the motion, but again I slid away. I'd found my advantage. She might yell at me in public, but she sure wasn't going to physically overpower me. I slumped onto the ground and crumpled into a little ball. It was my last defense.

"Get up, Lily."

I shook my head and rocked side to side. Small ants clustered next to my mom's feet, attracted to a sticky residue on the sidewalk.

"I'm not doing this."

I put my hands over my ears and tucked my head between my knees, erasing myself from the world.

"Alright. You win." This was her ploy. A way to guilt trip me into an apology. Normally I'd have given up at this point, but this time I hadn't done anything wrong. So, I stayed planted on the corner sidewalk, waiting for something to end this terrible moment—a police officer to ask if there were a problem, or a traffic accident that caused everyone to gasp, or a meteor strike at the corner of Main Street and Elm that would swallow up 'the store' in a fiery blaze.

* * *

"It took a lot of courage to do this," Mr. Simons told the teenager who was picking at an acne scab on his cheek and couldn't meet his eye. "I respect that." He made a quick inspection to confirm the watch was undamaged, "And even though I admire your honesty, I never want to see you in my store again, is that clear?"

"Yes, sir," the teenager replied.

Mr. Simons led him to the door and stepped outside to

scan the town. The group of teenagers waiting for their friend ducked into the alley, not wanting to be recognized as accomplices. Kids always hung out in bigger groups during the summer, and bigger groups meant bolder behavior. Adults avoided them, not because they were afraid, but because their dumb activities might turn into something they couldn't ignore, and then they'd have to stand up and act like the adults they'd sworn they'd never become when they'd been teenagers.

A couple shoppers walking by on the other side of the street waved to him, and he waved back, "A fine day, isn't it?" but his words were swallowed by the traffic. They shouted back, "Thanks! You too!" and Mr. Simons smiled.

At the corner, the girl from the store was curled up on the ground while her mom seemed to be wondering if she could just leave her there if she was going to act like this. Mr. Simons took a step towards them, then a step back. A shopper was heading for the entrance. He opened the door for her, the bells jingling, and turned to follow her into the store.

The Typewriter

It's become an addiction. I don't mean that figuratively. I crave the sound of the keys, the ping at the end of each line and the shift back to the start. There's a cadence to it as maddening as it is soothing. When I'm out of rhythm, when I'm stuck, the silence mocks me, but when I'm producing, it's cheering me on, pushing me to keep going, keep the keys hammering, the cogs cranking.

I need to pry myself away, or else I will become so entranced I don't realize I'm producing junk. The slap of the keys gives me the fix, and I keep feeding the reward center of my brain with each stroke. Rhythm doesn't make good writing, though. I convince myself I'm writing brilliance, but I haven't written anything decent for two pages. I rationalize a pedestrian sentence "The wine tasted good," as deliberate, perfectly underwritten to communicate the ordinary. But it was lazy, because my brain was being fueled not by thought, but by the high of the clack clack clack and ping and crank. Then there's the crumple. A terrible page. Crumple. Reload.

It's not writing. Not really. But it's thinking. It's an exercise tangentially related to writing, and it's intensely gratifying.

Dragging myself to the library desk is another story. That's where I write. Actually write. Where I look at the pages I brain-spewed and cut and mark and scribble and annotate and loathe myself for thinking any of it was good in the first place. It's a chore, but it's necessary. I have something close to a process.

There are days I have nothing. But even if I sit and make pages of garbage, it's okay because I was probably going to make that garbage at some point anyway, so it's better to get it out of the way. Or maybe it was a mood.

I've always resisted the term "writer." Anyone who is literate is a writer. It's like calling someone a breather or an eater or a thinker. I prefer the term "composer." Everyone has thoughts and opinions and stories, but the composer is the one who puts them in order, arranges them for clarity or a specific reaction. They don't have access to anything more insightful or relevant or interesting than anyone else; they've only managed to compose the erratic flashes of thought into a series of letters that will translate to someone else.

Music runs through my head constantly. Somewhere in the background but always present. Sometimes the music has been written already, but sometimes it's something no one else has ever heard. I don't have the tools to put that music into the world, though. I still hear the music, but either I have to dance to it or ignore it.

What I can't ignore are the words in my head. They are too loud. I'll transcribe them into a composition or into writing. Once they're on the page, someone else may hear them if they want, but even if they don't, at least they're a little quieter.

2/26/1991

Mom,

What? Why? How?

I had that note over my desk for years and years but never thanked you for your advice.

What do you want to say?
Why do you want to say it?
How are you going to say it?

If the answer to any of these questions is, 'I don't know,' you said, you need to do some brainstorming. It'll help you tease out your intention. Writing for writing's sake isn't going to please anyone. Breeze past any of those questions and you'll be left with a mess of ideas that doesn't add up to much.

I can't approach the written word without seeing that note. It helped me through school. It put my story in that journal. It kept me from screaming at the page when I was stuck. I'm loathe to admit when you are right, but you were right about this.

Love,
Lily

The Routine #2

With 168 hours in a week and only about one of those hours of real obligation, I have 167 hours left to myself. Subtract fifty-six hours of sleep, and I'm at 112 hours awake. Ten hours eating. Another five bathing and the like. Even if I'm hustling on the typewriter, I can't go for more than six hours a day (and even that's a stretch) before my mind turns to mush and I'm composing drivel, so that leaves fifty-two hours of free time. And that's just in one week. We've been here four weeks with forty-eight to go. Sometimes I get bored. I create a daily schedule for myself to ward off the monotony.

8:30 a.m.–9:30 a.m. Wakeup / Shower
9:30 a.m.–10:00 a.m. Breakfast
10:00 a.m.–11:00 a.m. Writing
11:00 a.m.–12:00 p.m. Weekly Checkup (Exercise / Walking when no Checkup)
12:00 p.m.–12:15 p.m. Medicament
12:15 p.m.–1:00 p.m. Lunch / Social Break
1:00 p.m.–2:00 p.m. Library / Reading (fiction)
2:00 p.m.–3:00 p.m. Exercise / Walking
3:00 p.m.–4:00 p.m. Writing
4:00 p.m.–5:00 p.m. Designated Screwing Around Time (DSAT)
5:00 p.m.–6:00 p.m. Library / Reading (non-fiction)

6:00 p.m.–6:30 p.m. Editing
6:30 p.m.–7:30 p.m. Cook Dinner
7:30 p.m.–8:00 p.m. Eat Dinner
8:00 p.m.–10:30 p.m. Designated Screwing Around Time (DSAT)
10:30 p.m.–Bedtime

The schedule is good for my writing, too. When I didn't schedule it into a day, it was just something in the back of my head I'd eventually get to. Shutting up that nagging voice was my primary motivation. After the guilt reached overload, I'd sit down, spew out a page of garbage and shout at the voice, saying, "There, are you happy?"

When it's built into my schedule, I actually do it. I don't cheat and write "This is a good sentence" or end a session with a terrible run-on that meets my word quota but will definitely be scratched out the next day. I use the hour to write. Like, actually write. Since I'm going to be there for an hour just sitting, I might as well write well. It's more fun that way.

Just as important, I do NOT write during my non-scheduled hours. I'm as strict about that as I am about the writing hours. It keeps the guilt at bay. The *shoulds* don't nag at me about the writing I should be doing. I know when I will write, so I'll do whatever I damn well please in the meantime.

As it turns out, my commandeering of the library works out fine. Everyone else has placed a flag in their own separate area. Anna spends most of her time in the lounge, almost always watching movies. She's always liked movies, she says, but you know how everyone has a list of movies they've been meaning to watch but never get around to, and the list keeps growing. Well, she's going to be the first person ever to have checked off every title on the list of movies to watch before you die.

She indulges in both popcorn flicks and the canon of cinema. In a very Anna-like way, she's made a meticulous list of the movies available, sorted them by genre, and prioritized them. In her system, she ranks movies based on two different criteria: those she wants to see and those she knows she should see. She then gives each a ranking on a scale of one to five. For example, she's never seen *The Godfather*, which is a five on the "knows she should see" criteria, but she's only level three excitement about seeing it. Eight total. She wants to see every Disney movie there is, but she knows *The Aristocats* doesn't deserve more than a one in its cinematic importance. Six total. The tens on her list she's placed in PRIME SCREENING slots every Friday night. These include *Close Encounters of the Third Kind*, *Gone with the Wind*, and *Cool Hand Luke.* Sometimes she'll throw on a two while she's eating lunch.

It's further complicated by the viewing calendar. She's not going to want to watch all the top-ranked movies first, and she doesn't want to power through the lesser-ranked ones just to get to the others, so she's made a graph that looks like a sine wave. She'll build up to a climax then slow down for a while until another climax builds and the cycle repeats.

If you're watching with her, she'll talk a lot more during the movies low in point totals.

Quinn spends most of his time in his room working on his music. Muffled songs bounce around the hallways enough that I feel the need to keep up with my own creativity. As far as the common areas, though, he's put his claim on the kitchen. Specifically, the oven. Not unlike Anna's movie quest, he's committed himself to an epic and methodical task—baking his way through the Betty Crocker cookbook. He didn't have much skill at first. I'd politely taste his cakes and breads and pies, but "oh, I couldn't possibly eat more." They weren't terrible, just unnecessary; politeness wasn't enough to have me take seconds on dry cornbread. But he's stuck to his hobby, and it's paid off. Both the guests and staff find themselves near the kitchen right as something pops out of the oven. It's like a tendril of smoke appears in the form of a cartoon hand, its finger crooking back and begging you to follow.

Hector is the most ambulatory of us. Most often, I'll find him wandering the halls puffing a Redlight or sitting in whatever chair is nearest when he gets sick of wandering. To my mind, his time looks pretty dull, but he's far less bothered by the need to occupy himself. He tinkered with the hardware in the pinball machine and managed to disable the sound effects to everyone's relief. The dead bumpers and warped boards are still a problem, but it's tolerable.

I need a hobby besides reading and writing. Quinn has his baking, Anna has her movies, and Hector has his smoking. I'll leach onto their hobbies, but I need one of my own.

There's a cupboard in the lounge with art supplies no one has touched. I'm a terrible artist. Actually, I'm a terrible drawer. So representative art (art that tries to actually look like something) was out, but I could still paint. I don't call it abstract, because there's not enough quality to categorize it. To label it such would be insulting to abstract artists over the age of five. Some people will look at an abstract painting and say, "I could do that." Turns out I can't.

It's cool, though. It makes my mind work differently. When I'm struggling to write I begin to daydream about color combinations and shapes and forms. I made a green one that has the word "blue" written on it in white paint, a blue one with two horizontal rectangles that look like an equals sign, but aren't an equals sign, and a hodgepodge of brushstrokes of hundreds of colors that took hours to feel balanced. I am not thrilled with how it turned out. I tried to paint the mountains. It looked like a first grader did it. I lit it on fire and tossed it in the oven. Then it was back to colors and shapes.

Unintentionally, the hobby gave my bedroom character. And color. The minimalist design worked for me in the early days, but it needed something else. I'll keep making paintings until there's no space to hang them.

Effect

The drain in my shower is clogged. The basin backs up to my ankles. It's almost like the plug is in; nothing is draining. I crouch down and fish into the drain and my fingers wrap around something soft and slippery. It's not easy to dislodge, especially with my fingers, who aren't happy with the grossness.

Eventually, the wad comes free, and the drain suction resumes with an emphatic, satisfying slurp. In my hand is a nest of hair roped around a used bandage. It's from when I cut my thumb. I didn't even notice it falling off in the shower. You never think much about cuts after they've healed. But when they're still healing, it's a preoccupation. Especially on my thumb. I would have noticed the pain every time I held something or had to replace the bandage when it was wet.

I don't remember any of that.

I retrace events to think about when I cut my thumb. Days tend to blur together here. There have been times I've been dead wrong about what day of the week it is. I'm sure it happened the night we watched *Ghostbusters*. I remember fiddling with the bandage the whole time. But that was just yesterday. Tuesday night comedy.

That can't be right. I sliced it up so badly Dr. Samesong had debated using stitches.

As I look at my hand now, there's not even a scar.

The Purple Coat

I'm walking across the runway. Just as bundled up as last time, but this time I've slung a pair of crampons over my shoulder. I'm less overheated, though; the wind is strong, and snow flurries sting my face. I'm walking with pace, deliberately, almost expecting someone to run out and stop me. No one comes. I'm nearing the end of the runway, and I'm still not seeing signs of people or a settlement near where I saw the purple coat. I step off the runway and into the snow, looking for any signs of something irregular. There's a small hill. I think the purple coat must have disappeared on the other side. I crouch down to strap on the crampons and climb, fighting the wind and snow, angry at it, and ready to reach the peak.

Nothing but snow and ice. The bulk of the ice field is level, but it's filled with cracks and treads that stem from the glacial flow to my left. I try to avoid the uneven sections where the ice has formed crevasses, and the wind has swept the snow into dunes. At the far end, the ice pack looks to turn to snow as the terrain slopes upward to a minor peak and ridgeline. I don't really know what I'm looking for, but I'm not finding it. My eyes aren't focusing in the punishing weather, and I vow to return when it's sunny. That could be days, but it'll give me something to look forward to. I'm preparing a mental list of items I'll pack—shovel, snacks, extra gloves—when my feet tangle and I fall forward. When I hit the ground, the snow is looser than expected, and I sink down headfirst. My arms and head plunge deep into the snow.

I'm hardly in danger but still feel like an idiot. My feet poking out of the snow with my body submerged must look ridiculous. Somehow, it's worse that there's no one here to laugh with me, or even at me.

Still, I'm stuck. It's not panic inducing, mostly just annoying. Soft light penetrates the mini cave my arms have created. I shift back and forth with my legs swinging above me, and I'm able to kick the air and create backward thrust. It's working slowly. My face is pressed against the snow, and, as I sweat, a frozen burn starts to aggravate me further.

The struggle is nearly over when I feel something brush against my foot. It's a light enough touch that I'm not sure if it was a phantom sensation or something more. Instinctively, I try to turn around to see, but still stuck, my face only turns into the wall of snow. I kick out trying to propel myself with a final thrust, but the heaving is insufficient. I'm more buried than I'd thought. My energy sapping, I pause before intending to give a concentrated burst of energy.

My pant legs must have rolled up with my flailings. I know this because the skin of my ankle is exposed to the cold air and each gust of wind cuts deep. And because of the hands wrapped around my legs to tug me free.

I call back to the stranger, but my voice is muffled. The fingers grip my ankles and tug me backward. I let my body go limp as the stranger retrieves me. Whoever it is, they're strong. They don't have to heave or jostle, just a steady pull as I watch the cave recede.

Then assistance ceases. I'm not free, but with only my shoulders and head still trapped, it only takes a few more squirms. I exit into the cold air, prepared to sheepishly thank my rescuer. None is there. I don't have the best viewpoint, so

I'm expecting Hector or Quinn hiding nearby, waiting to pelt me with a snowball. When none comes, I begin a cautious search, still prepared for a bombardment. Climbing atop the small ridge gives me a better vantage, but there's no one around.

I look down to find a trail of footprints next to the mini cave. The snow and ice are packed down, but there's enough of an impression to follow a path. They're spaced wide apart, suggesting whoever it was had scampered away. The extent of the practical joke seems excessive, but with so little to do out here, I understand the amusement.

With my eyes downward, I'm so obsessed with following the trail I don't notice it's leading downhill. As the wind abates, I realize a wall of ice is now shielding me, and the path becomes hollowed out, as though entering a cave. The trail becomes less distinct as it's joined by more footprints. With the howl of the wind dying, a quiet sets in, and I'm wondering if I should turn around.

A door appears before me. The ice and earth meet a concrete framework buttressed like a mine adit. I'm staring at a few steps leading downward to a steel door. Not wanting to fall victim to another practical joke, I prepare before testing the door handle. I cluster up some snow and form a proper snowball and a few additional ones for backup.

After checking the area again to make sure I'm not being tricked, I move to the door. With one hand clutching the snowball, my other reaches for the steel latch. It's lighter than expected as I haul it open. Without waiting to react, I hurl the snowball straight through the opening. When no one cries or laughs or makes a sound, I discover the reason. Inside, the concrete room is the size of a small closet without any passageways or doors beyond. It's empty apart from a coat rack and purple coat.

Note From the Editor

To properly research, I'd need to return to Alaska and see what I could find on the ground. I arrived in Fairbanks in June and outfitted for the excursion. Looking at maps and surveys, I charted a course from where I found the cache to where I'd located the facility in satellite imagery. It would take me five days to reach the facility and five days to return. I brought enough supplies for fifteen days to be safe and, in case of emergency, a satellite beacon.

Germany (the dog) didn't come with me this time. Between the moose and bears and mysterious research facility, I thought it best to leave him with family while on my quest. It was uncomfortable being away from him. While in Fairbanks, I checked to make sure he was okay, but once I headed into the bush, I was well out of cell range and had to trust all was well.

My pack was brutal. Since I was covering a lot of mileage, I crammed in the calories. I was covering twenty miles a day, fifteen if the trail went up and down, which meant I needed at least four thousand calories each day to stay healthy enough to continue on. Four thousand calories is a lot of freeze-dried.

I'd done part of the route in my original trip, but once I reached the cache site, I'd have to head over a mountain pass rather than continue through the valley. On the inward route, the scenery was magnificent. Hiking up switchback after switchback was exhausting and gave me plenty of time to rest and gaze. I couldn't help but pause for pictures constantly once above the tree line. The spring snowmelt had the rivers rushing and provided a constant roar to the ambience. Not only was there the majesty of the peaks and rivers, but also the vestiges of abandoned mineshafts tucked into hillsides. From my elevated vantage I spotted a family of moose soaking in a bog down in the valley. I didn't see any bears but stepped over more than one set of droppings. Thankfully none looked fresh. I had no trail to follow, so I kept snowcapped Mount Hastings in view as much as possible to orient me on the topographical map. I didn't see a single other person.

It may have been beautiful and serene, but walking all day is still walking all day. There were little challenges: Should I walk this way or that way? Is the brush easier to walk through or the mud? Is it better to stop and eat two small meals or one big one? Enough to keep me from thinking too much about the oddity of my mission, even though I did that plenty.

After five days of walking and talking to my own brain, I ascended the final crest. Even though I'd eaten through some of the calorie weight in my pack, my legs and lungs were still really feeling the mileage. I became certain I'd find nothing, or I'd find everything, depending on when my brain asked my brain. Nature had been uninterrupted in every direction. No sign of human life whatsoever, which made it jarring when I summited the crest and saw the runway—its painted lines and arrows drew my attention as though an invitation. A part of me wanted to turn around, but knowing a sense of regret would never leave if I bailed, I fought through the nerves.

The scree of the downslope soon led to heavy brush as I descended into the valley. Each time I paused to chart a path, I took photos, noting each of the landmarks in Lily's account. The effort gave the mission a documentarian aspect, like I was doing simple research, not exploring a haunted house. The ice field was not the glacial blue behemoth I'd imagined but rather a dirty gray expanse extending from the mouth of the opposite valley. At its base, a river roared into a gully before switching back on itself to wrap around the steep faces of a mountainside. Thankfully I was on the right side of the river, as it would have been impassable.

The runway had been weathered—there were cracks in the tarmac, the lights no longer illuminated, and the painted lines had partially faded—but it still looked functional.. Skid marks from landing were concentrated on one end, indicating the approach would come from over the pass I had just descended.

As I approached the facility, I first examined its structural integrity, fighting through brush and bramble to do an inspection of the perimeter. The concrete exterior had been worn by the extreme weather, but no walls had caved in, and the roof showed no signs of damage. I couldn't see through any of the windows since they were covered in a layer of filth on each side. In the mud surrounding the building were a few animal tracks, but none from a human boot or foot. To the facility's rear, a gated section contained the generator and other mechanical components. The machine was painted a faded yellow and stained with chemical residue. Pipes feeding the central component were rusted, and one section appeared to have been crushed by blunt force. The lack of power would have made the building uninhabitable long-term, but with the facility's structure intact, I decided it'd be safe to enter.

In the entry tunnel I called "Hello," only to be answered by my echo. I called again, trying to find a tone that sounded more authoritative and less terrified. As I wandered the passageway, I'll admit, I was hoping the door would be locked. Then I could try some fruitless options and leave. The handle turned and the door opened without resistance.

My headlamp provided the only light in the hallways which were windowless. "Hello," I called, finding the terrified tone again. There was an odor of mildew, and the walls dripped with damp. Apart from the water damage, there wasn't much sign of deterioration. The space was dusty and filled with cobwebs, but the rooms were rather tidy. It had been abandoned but not abused; rather, it had been undisturbed for years. None of the doors were locked anywhere. Faint light shone through the grimy windows of the bedrooms.

* * *

There were no traces of The Medicament. I did an exhaustive search. Since I made good time on the way in, I was able to check every room, shelf, drawer, and panel. During this search, I gathered documents that might have been relevant. As I sifted through, I covered my face with a scarf to protect from the dust. Most were damaged beyond readability and could be ignored, but if I wanted to be thorough, I'd have to extend my stay.

Each time I registered something I'd read in the manuscript—the bumper pool table in the lounge, or the spiral staircase in the library, or the pantry still stocked with food and liquor—it felt uncanny. The most haunting relics, however, were the nameplates still left outside each bedroom. Anna, Hector, Quinn, and Lily were no longer characters, but real people who had slept and walked and bathed and eaten and lived in this very place.

I don't know why I had the urge to sleep in Lily's room. She'd left stray clothes, some books on the shelf, and a writing desk with slim notebooks that'd had pages removed. It might have been the desire to sleep in a bed and not my tent, it might have been an attempt to make the facility more utilitarian and less nightmarish, or it might have been something less rational, an unreasonable desire to feel close to her. That night as I fell asleep, even though I didn't bring her manuscript with me, I had read through it enough that I could hear her voice.

A Game

"Not Scrabble. You'll destroy me," Hector says.

The pinball defects have become too frustrating, so we've emptied out the game cabinet. There are only a few things left in the maybe pile. Most were discarded immediately. We needed a game, Hector decided. With Quinn and Anna doing their, whatever, we need something for us. A game. Something neither of us knew but could learn. And fucking master, he joked. It proves to be a harder proposition than we would have thought. Most of the games require more than two players to be any fun: Pictionary, Monopoly, Trivial Pursuit, Risk, Scattergories. Or we're mismatched; he's played chess a lot, whereas I'm better at backgammon. And we both think checkers is dumb. Chinese checkers is our fallback, but we're not too excited about it.

"I've got it." He pulls out two boxes from the top shelf. "I know you had your heart set on a game—but—Notre Dame or Yosemite Valley?" he displays the 1000-piece jigsaw puzzles to me.

"Notre Dame. Plenty of wilderness around here. Let's get some culture."

"When's the last time you did a jigsaw puzzle?"

"Can't remember."

"Same."

"This will be fun."

"Will it?"

"It better be. There's at least a dozen more for us to get through."

Spreading out the pieces and flipping them over one by one is oddly gratifying. Clear objective and purpose. This feeling continues as we proceed and find the edge pieces. There is a process. It's simple and can be completed.

I'm fixated on the upper left corner, a cluster of one bell tower and blue sky above, when Hector breaks what has been about ten minutes of silence. "I think we're going to need more puzzles."

I look to the cupboard, look at our progress, make a quick calculation and say, "I never thought I'd be wishing there were more jigsaw puzzles in my life, but you're right."

It's comfortable. Easy. Mindless. Or maybe the opposite. Mindful. Thinking, but not. Focus. That's what it is. Steps I can focus on. And there's the passive teamwork, too. Without having to verbalize, we are communicating and producing something.

"It really is impressive," he says as he works on the flying buttresses. I think he's talking about the cathedral.

"I want to go back in time and shout at my younger self for wasting all my time not doing jigsaw puzzles."

"We're going to have to ration. We'll be finished with this by tomorrow."

"I'll bet they have a supply room full of them."

"I wouldn't doubt it."

He pulls out a Redlight and before I ask, he pushes the pack in my direction. I've convinced myself it's okay as long as I only smoke with Hector. And I've kept to that rule. I have been spending more Designated Screwing Around Time "hanging out" with Hector even though I know I'm looking for rationale for a cigarette. But it's good to be social. The mental health of socializing counterbalances the negative effect of the smoking.

A former smoker once told me if you pause to think about having a cigarette, it's not just automatic; you're not addicted.

"Have you been outside yet?" I ask.

"Briefly."

The time doesn't seem right to mention the purple coat.

Trouble

The day begins with an inconvenience. Quinn and Anna "break up." It's unwelcome news. Ten months left and the tension of a split-up couple to underlie it all.

Quinn walks past me in the hall. He doesn't say anything. His eyes are fixed forward like he doesn't see me. When he's passed me, he sighs as though conceding a point to an argument he's having in his head. Something is amiss, and I wish I were invisible.

In the kitchen, Anna looks angry or sad, it's hard to tell. She has a clenched jaw and intense stare. I was planning on just dipping in for a coffee and slipping out, but she needs to talk. She hasn't said anything, but I feel her tracking me as I move around the room. Instead of the distant body language of Quinn, her puppy eyes are saying, please, please ask what's wrong.

"Everything okay?" I ask in a tone I'm hoping is ambiguous. I want to sound sensitive, but not too sensitive. I don't want to be her shoulder to cry on. Not because I'm cruel, but because such a gesture might mean I've taken a side. There aren't enough of us for sides.

"He said he needed space. Seriously. Space. We're in the middle of nowhere. We have nothing but space." I don't follow her logic entirely, but she continues, "It was just supposed to be a fun release anyhow. A distraction. I mean, he's thirteen years younger than me. And not to give you too many details, but he's hardly the first person I've been with since I left my husband."

I'm not sure if she's serious or just trying to reassure herself after the breakup. I think everyone likes to console themselves with small wins in these circumstances. I'm a little surprised she's upset, though. Like she says, I always saw it as a relationship of convenience. As for the space, Quinn might have a point. They basically spend all their time together. At least from what I've seen. He's got his moments of music or baking, and she'll sometimes watch a movie alone, but they are usually together. They sleep in the same room, they have their meals together, they spend time in each other's bedrooms during the day, and they even kind of wander around the facility together.

Now that I think about it, it'd be hard to use the normal social cues to have alone time. There'd be none of the normal excuses. I need to blah blah, whatnot. We don't have any obligations here so any expressed desire to be alone would be blunt. Even a soft, "I need to lie down for a bit," basically translates to, "I have had enough of you." I don't know Quinn too well, but I know him well enough to know he's an introvert, and one prone to the occasional bout of standoffishness, so he probably was less than delicate when indicating a need for solo time.

I do my best sympathy work and offer the rationalization, "He probably just wants more time to work on his music." She seems unconvinced so I add, "Artists, you know."

Tears now. Like she's processing the change of arrangement.

"I'm going to be so fucking bored now."

I've never heard her drop an f-bomb before.

So, there's a broken-up couple in our midst. Whatever

social dynamic had been in the balance is askew, and I can't imagine it being better now. Anna is sure to cling to a new companion, and who knows what Quinn will do. Broody and moody, I suspect. Being around either one of them will be difficult, and being around both of them will be insufferable. There are only four of us here.

I need to further my one remaining alliance. Or I need a cigarette. Either way, I go to find Hector.

He's not interested in the gossip. Not because it's improper, he just doesn't care. I try to explain how stressful it's going to be now, how we'll have to be tiptoeing around, preserving peace and order. He stubs out a Redlight and tells me I think too much.

It's hard to imagine Hector as a young man. His calm wisdom makes sense because life has hardened him, made him contemplative and sage. Or maybe I'm hoping I'll have mellowed out by the time I'm his age. But probably not. In fact, I'm sure he was all Zen when he was my age, too.

After my third Redlight in succession I announce, "Let's get out of here."

He nods to the window like he's asking a question.

"Yeah, outside. I want to show you something."

"I suppose it's about time I had some fresh air." He doesn't want to go, I can tell, but he doesn't protest. He's doing me a favor, but he doesn't want to let me think he's doing me a favor. He bounces onward toward the locker room as though going into the bitter cold is a great idea.

***

It's not just cold, it's windy and snowy and completely overcast. Textbook terrible weather. Stepping out of the tunnel, I start to reconsider, but Hector says, “Aw, come on, we’re bundled up now. Let’s see what’s worth seeing.”

“It’s on the other side of the runway,” I shout over the wind.

We squeeze our arms close to our bodies to preserve warmth and kind of waddle across the runway. The clouds whip past the sun. It’s midday, but it feels dark as twilight. I panic when I realize Hector is no longer beside me. In the chaos of the weather, I didn’t notice him trail off or possibly stumble. I turn around and a snowball pelts me in the face. Hector roars with laughter. Well played. I scoop up a cluster of snow and hurl it back, but it dissolves pathetically midair.

We continue onward. I don’t mention what we’re looking for since I don’t know what to make of the purple coatroom, and it’ll be better if he sees it for himself.

We’ve made it to the far end of the runway, and we stop. Hector waits with his hands in his pockets, not exactly sure what we’re waiting for. He almost looks like a stranger when not wearing the same blue garments I’ve seen him in every day. The chill stings, but he’s still polite. I lead him toward the hidden entranceway. He’s impressed, I think. He’s under about five layers of clothing—body language is vague.

When I tug the door, it’s locked. Even with the hidden body language, I can’t imagine he’s pleased. It’s freezing, and we’re standing in front of a locked door.

“There’s probably another entrance,” he shouts as we duck into the alcove of shelter in the doorway.

“I don’t think so. I’m sorry. We can just head back. This is crazy.”

“Where’s your spirit of adventure?” he asks as he steps back into the weather. At this point, he seems genuinely curious and not only humoring me. Or maybe after eight weeks indoors, he’s not too eager to head straight back. We’ve done the hard part and forced ourselves out here.

We trudge up a small hill to get a better view of the area. I crouch down to put on my crampons. Hector had declined in the locker room, saying he'd be fine. The snow starts to come down more heavily, so it's difficult to see. "What's that?" he shouts, pointing over the ice field.

By the time I turn my head, whatever he's seen is gone. "What? I don't see anything."

"It was this purple, like, flag or something."

"Where?"

"A couple football fields in that direction. Pretty close to where that rocky outcrop meets the ice over there." He starts walking without waiting for me, leading the way across the snow and then stepping onto the ice field. It's rocky and uneven, and I hold a hand in front of me so I can brace if I slip. Hector is more confident, and his distance ahead of me grows. I'm walking with both arms extended now. My teeth are clenched, too, like that will somehow help my balance. It does not.

I stumble. Even with the crampons, my foot slips right out from under me, and I flail around trying to land with some grace, but my bottom crashes into the ice so hard the shock reverberates through my body. My jaw slams shut, and, unfortunately, my tongue is the victim. I taste blood immediately and spit red into the snow and ice.

Recomposing myself, I stand and shout, "I'm going back!" figuring he'd turn around and follow. But he can't hear me. He's walking like a man possessed, intrigued by the phantom purple just as I was and determined for answers. I shout again, but still he marches onward across the desert of ice.

I see it, too. It's being hoisted up and down a pole. Up and down. Up and down. Mechanical and hypnotic. It disappears from my line of vision below an ascending hill of snow, then reappears moments later, reaches the top, then descends out of sight again. It signals to us like a semaphore or Morse code. The flagpole may even be beyond the ice field, but it's difficult to tell in these conditions. I can't see the flag bearer, but someone must be in control. We're closer to the flag than our facility, so I follow.

Hector snaps from his trance and finally turns around to check on me. I wave. He points to the flag to acknowledge that we've both seen it. Thumbs up. He stays put and waits for me to catch up.

I take each step deliberately, not wanting to fall again. I'm staring down, plotting each step and watching as my foot finds its way. It's slow, but I think if I fall again, I'd bite my tongue clean off. I don't look up. I don't want to see how slow my progress is. One step at a time and eventually I'll be there.

Step. Step. Step.

Step. Step. Step.

Hector is gone.

There's not a trace of him in any direction. Maybe he's made it to the flagpole, but even at a sprint, that seems impossible. I taste the blood in my mouth again and feel my pulse through my tongue. I shout out, but my voice is swallowed by the wind. Blood spurts onto the snow as I shout again, more frantic this time.

I stagger forward, abandoning my surefooted technique and almost run. I fall and my knees smack the ice. I rise and continue to rush forward, giving in to each stumble but powering through to maintain pace. Still no sign of him and I'm nearing the flagpole. I pause to scan the horizon again. Cupping my hands around my mouth, I shout his name, but I'm losing hope. I take a few steps and shout again. Nothing. A few more steps. Nothing.

The cold blows through me and I feel misguided rage

toward it. I collapse to the ice, helpless and trying to compose myself. There is no sense in this. I try to think clearly but fear has me overwhelmed. The once beautiful scenery is now my tormenter. The wind and snow brutalize me. The endless sky dwarves me. And the mountains only stare at me.

He could not have disappeared. I breathe and try to think, try to find the rational explanation for what has happened. First, I come up with nonsense. He has actually disappeared. Like spontaneous combustion or some such supernatural occurrence. I try not to linger on this possibility.

Only slightly less nonsensical is the idea of him being smuggled away by someone. Perhaps a secret passageway opened and he was dragged inside. We were looking for another door anyhow, so it's not completely outrageous.

Maybe he's playing some sort of practical joke. He buried himself in snow and is hiding from me. But even if he had been pranking, he wouldn't have been cruel enough to keep it up when he heard me panicking.

I punch straight down into a snowdrift with fury. I punch again. My hand sinks in so deep it swallows my mitten. I curse and struggle to reclaim it from the compacted snow, my hand burning with cold. I'm shoulder deep when I finally fish it out. I look at the hole, and it registers.

He sank into a hidden crevasse.

Most of the ice is solid, but pockets across the field have a thin layer of crusted snow at the top with gaps beneath. The one beside me isn't too big and looks to be filled with loose powder snow, but some of the gaps must be massive.

I stand to scan the ice field again. Now that I know what to look for, I might be able to spot a recess in the ice that might be concealing a crevasse. There are small pockets of loose snow amongst the ice cracks throughout the field, but I notice a larger crater-bowl depression nearby where snow has amassed. With the weather, I'll have to come right up to the rim to see any gaps or crevasses.

It takes courage to tread across the ice now. A crevasse could swallow me just as easily. It was dumb luck that kept me on the surface during my scramble moments ago. At least now I feel purposeful. My steps might be slow, but they have intention.

I near the edge of the crater-bowl, and it's looking promising. Indeed, the snow is deep, and much more of the surface is snow than ice. With the snow falling, it's still hard to see clearly, to make out if there are any holes he might have plunged through. There are gaps everywhere, but most are too shallow to disappear into. My own footprints vanish almost immediately in the snow and wind, so it's foolish to look for his.

On my hands and knees for safety, I enter the snowy gap of the crater, pushing into the snow with each motion forward. If my hands reach ice, I proceed; if my arms sink to the elbow, I find a new path. With this method, I scout the snow-covered gaps in the ice. One by one. My knees still hurt from falling, but pressed against the ice, they're beginning to numb.

I see him.

The elation from the discovery does not last. I am peering over the edge of an ice sheet into a crevasse less than a meter wide. One arm extends over his head, motionless. He is wedged between the walls of a narrow canyon of ice, a couple body lengths away and out of reach. If I leave the safety of my ice perch and descend, I might be able to get to him. The snow could easily swallow me up as well, though. I don't have any ropes or equipment to aid a rescue.

I shout his name. Still, he does not move. That could mean anything. I hope.

Make a plan. It's worked since I stopped panicking. I sit upright to think. I assess the options and formulate a strategy. But I don't have to. When I stand to survey my surroundings, I see a rope. A rope held by a figure in a purple coat.

The Facility (Part Two)

Hector survives. He hasn't woken up yet, and they're treating his extremities for frostbite, but they're not worried at all. They are confident he'll wake up in the next few hours. We leave him to rest on the bed in a room that looks like our exam room, except isn't our exam room—there's no window.

I was so relieved to find help from the figure in the purple coat I didn't even stop to question it. Help is here. Next.

Now that he's safe, I'm allowing myself to process. There are four of us. Three in purple and me (in blue). We are sitting in a parlor, distinctly, a parlor. A chaise lounge, bookcases filled with leather-bound volumes, teacups on saucers, and a historic globe in the corner with sea monsters in its ocean. The room resembles our lounge but is outfitted with intellectualism in mind rather than leisure. There are no windows in here, either.

Though the strangers are color-coordinated, their attire is less sterile than our blue kits. The man who found us is the youngest, about my age, and dressed in a plum sweater-vest and trousers with a lavender button-down shirt beneath. The other man is probably in his fifties, has a white mustache, and wears a cable-knit sweater; I'd call it mauve. And the woman, aged in-between, wears a purple cardigan and rather bold purple jeans. Each one of them seems to be waiting for something. Sweater-vest fiddles with his cuff buttons before he rolls up his sleeves, Mr. Mustache is doodling on a pad of paper in his lap, and Ms. Purple Jeans is sitting cross-legged, dangling her shoe off the end of her toes as it bobs up and down.

I'm still a little distraught and coming from the cold puts me in a bit of a haze, adding a surreal quality to their introduction. They appear as my audience, not only because of their position seated at the opposite end of the room like a panel of judges, but also because they are silent. They watch me and wait for me to speak with friendly eyes. But it doesn't feel uncomfortable, it's like they're trying to be polite.

"Who are you exactly?" I ask.

They exchange confused glances with each other. "It seems Dr. Samesong disregarded protocol," the woman in the cardigan says quietly to her associates. "Our presence should not be a surprise."

"What do you mean?"

"We're the professors," says Sweater-vest as though this clarifies everything. Sensing my confusion, he adds, "For the study." I must still look perplexed, because he then says, "Would you excuse us for, well, one moment?"

I gesture with a flat palm for them to please take a moment. They don't leave the room; they merely shift their shoulders to face one another and speak in muted voices. Their tone is difficult to decipher. Sweater-vest seems more upset than the rest, but I can't tell why. He raises his voice as he shakes his head saying something about protocol. "I'll handle this," Sweater-vest says as he turns to address me. "You see—"

"—it seems—" Mr. Mustache interrupts.

"—someone should have—"

They all speak at once. No one leads this trio, which makes it all the more confusing. After some stammering and talking over one another, the woman, Ms. Purple Pants, eventually takes control. She crosses the room and sits in the chair beside me, resting her hand on the arm of my chair as she speaks.

"I sincerely apologize for the confusion. As you can tell, we're not all on the same page here." Her eye contact doesn't lapse as she speaks, though my eyes do drift to scan her face. It's hard to gauge her age; she comports an air of wisdom, but her skin is unwrinkled, and I wonder if she's had work done. She speaks with a Mid-Atlantic accent, placing irregular emphasis on her words like an actress from Hollywood's golden age.

"Would you like to look around?" Sweater-vest offers, stepping forward, trying to soften his previous tone. He looks a bit familiar, like an actor I can't place, or maybe I'm thinking that because he over-enunciates every word.

"We can call Peggy if you're worried they'll wonder about you," chimes in Mr. Mustache from the other side of the room.

I'm starting to feel warmer, but I'm still chilled, or maybe I'm warming up too fast, and my nerves don't know how to feel. The sensation draws my focus, and I have trouble listening, and my mind starts to wander. They have more decorations. Personal touches, it seems. But they are not tidy people. It seems they've positioned me in the parlor to face away from their mess. Behind me are dirty dishes left in odd places, and purple clothes are strewn across the furniture. An easy chair looks to be where they pile notes they don't know what to do with. Books lie everywhere. Open or stacked oddly. The word eccentric comes to mind more than once.

"I'd like to check on Hector, if you don't mind," I assert, standing up.

"Of course," responds Ms. Purple Pants with her drawling vowels, "Let us know if you need anything."

In the hallway I find the wall map and note their facility's layout. It's similar to a portion of ours—four bedrooms, a dining room, kitchen, lounge, exam room, gym, and storage—but there's no library, office or additional level. The corner of the map is labeled B, which I interpret as basement and explains the lack of windows. It's hard to imagine their stir-craziness. I peek into the exam room and am heartened to hear Hector snoring. He's trying to pull up his blanket in his sleep but can't grip it with the bandages on his frostbitten fingers. I tiptoe to tuck him in. When I raise the blanket, the snoring stops momentarily before resuming, and I retreat to the hall. There's not much to explore without barging into their private rooms, so I return to the professors.

They've returned to their research it seems. Sweater-vest is flipping through a stack of documents, Mr. Mustache sits cross-legged with his nose in a book, and Ms. Purple Pants is scribbling on a legal pad. She pauses, and her eyes scan upward, though not in my direction, nodding her head while muttering to herself as though she's willing a thought to compose itself. Her pen returns to the page, and after noting a few words, says, "Dr. Samesong is on his way over to escort you back," without emotion. "Don't worry, you're not in trouble." She gives me a half-smile and begins to write again. The electric kettle finishes boiling without notice.

None of them tells me their name.

Chapter 3

I've only hit someone once in my life. Twice if you count the time the kid dared me to hit him as hard as I could. He didn't think I could hit hard, and he tried to act like it didn't hurt even though he left minutes later saying, "I'm bored, you're all so lame." He didn't make it out of sight before he rubbed the welt on his elbow, but I was the only one who noticed.

The other time, though, the punch came out without me willing it. My fist found Allison's face so quickly I didn't do it right. My thumb stuck inside clenched fingers, so it got pretty messed up, but not as bad as Allison's face. Her braces snapped off some of her teeth and had to be fixed with all the money I'd saved up in my life, even though they had insurance that paid for it anyhow. Knowing all that, I'd still have punched her.

* * *

I didn't have many friends growing up, but I had Allison. She was the only one who lived close enough I could ride my bike to her house. When I'd get a block away, I'd unclip the helmet from my handlebars and strap it on my head to ride the last stretch. Allison had given the helmet to me for my birthday, and my mom thought it would be a good idea to wear it when

I went over there, even if it hurt when strands of hair got stuck in it after riding only a single block.

Sometimes Allison came to my house, but she wasn't allowed to ride her bike over, so someone had to drop her off and pick her up. Her mom liked to talk to my mom at the beginning and end of the visits, which was really her way of making sure my mom was home the whole time.

Allison tried out curse words she'd just learned and would make fun of me for not knowing what they meant. I'd get dared into shouting them when I was at her house, but I wouldn't fall for the trick, and then she'd lose interest, and we'd play with her cat or something.

Our moms decided a homework group was probably a good idea. I already got straight A's, so I didn't think I needed a study partner. My mom told me it was called being a good friend, and I shouldn't let it bother me if Allison wanted to copy my homework; it would only hurt her in the long run. Our teacher, Mrs. Pearson, didn't notice the work was the same. She didn't think we were friends.

Allison said she had slept over at her cousin's place plenty of times, so it was no big deal when she came to sleep over at our house. She brought a sleeping bag and some toys, and her mom said it would be okay if we stayed up until midnight, but no later. The phone didn't usually ring after nine o'clock, but when my mom answered, she reassured the voice on the other end everything was going well, no, no there's no need for that; that's okay.

Mom said it would be nice if I let Allison take my bed. Each time she rolled over, the bed squeaked. The shadows must have been different than the shadows in her room. I was worried we'd get into trouble when I saw her go downstairs after midnight. She whispered into the phone, and I couldn't hear what she was saying, but ten minutes later headlights appeared in the driveway, and her mom came to the door and walked Allison to the car in her pajamas. The next morning they came back and picked up the sleeping bag and toys and apologized for the family emergency that interrupted the sleepover.

On Monday at recess the kids were doing that thing where they keep looking at you and whispering, and when you ask them what they're saying, they giggle and say, "nothing." It happened all day; kids kept looking at me and whispering. One of my classmates came up to me later and said she didn't know if she should tell me, but Allison was saying I totally freaked out during a sleepover at her house and had to go home early. I tried to explain what really happened, but she just ducked away and muttered under her breath.

* * *

Allison was the first kid I knew to get braces. Her mom said she would be thankful when she got to high school and didn't have metal glued to her teeth anymore. For the first few weeks she didn't smile much, and when she did, she'd start to blush and close up her mouth again. Then she developed this odd habit when she laughed where she'd wrap her upper lip over her teeth. You could still see her braces ninety percent of the time, but she needed to believe they were invisible. When it was taffy apple day in the fall, Allison couldn't believe we would eat that junk.

She got a doctor's note excusing her in gym class from playing games like dodgeball or volleyball or anything that might end up hurting her braces. Other kids started getting braces, too, but Allison was the only one who stood to the side. Her braces stayed intact, as did her new clothes.

When we got to junior high her clothes really started to

change. Gone were the jeans and T-shirts and generic dresses. She wore clothes like people wore in magazines. If she wore a sweatshirt, it had a logo on it. Other kids followed her trend, too.

Rumors circulated that Allison kissed some guy. Like, a full-on make out session. Apparently, he was older and went to a different school, so a lot of people doubted if it was true. But it was confirmed. My mom told me she thought she saw Allison holding hands with an older boy in town, but she looked so different she didn't even recognize her at first. She asked if we were still friends, and I said we weren't ever really friends, and she didn't ask any more about it.

Her dad wasn't living at their house anymore. He left one night and didn't come back. Everyone knew it. Our teachers were sensitive to the situation, so when she acted out in class or started to get bad grades, they didn't make a big deal of it.

At the end of seventh grade, we had a big book report where you had to pretend you were a famous character and write what they'd think about a book. You could write Winnie-the-Pooh's take on *Little House on the Prairie* or Johnny Tremain's opinion on *Alice in Wonderland*. I decided to write a review of *A Midsummer Night's Dream* from Tinkerbell's perspective. It was about how Shakespeare got it all wrong about fairy life; there was much less romance and much more mischief.

My teacher didn't think I wrote it. She thought the play was too hard for a seventh grader. I confessed that my mom had helped me with it, but that wasn't good enough because she had more evidence that I'd cheated—Allison had the exact same essay.

I wasn't the only one who was accused, at least. I guess Allison had tried to rat me out after she got caught, and they were doing due process by bringing me in. Obviously, Allison's mom was none too happy. She drove over to our house and screamed at my mom, who just stood there and didn't say anything. It wasn't until she had left that my mom started to cry, but she told me she was only sad for Allison.

Allison didn't yell like her mom; instead, she lied. This time there were no whispers and turned heads and giggles—the lie spread right in front of me. Worse than that, it wasn't really a lie, even if she thought she was lying.

"Lily, your mom is totally crazy. Seriously, she belongs in the nuthouse."

If I'd been thinking, I would have taken the higher ground and shrugged it off or been sympathetic and known she was lashing out because of what was happening at home, or noticed there were teachers, like, right there who could see everything even if they couldn't hear everything. But I wasn't thinking. The fist had a will of its own. I got blood on my T-shirt and jeans, and my thumb got messed up, and I lost all my savings, and I got suspended from school for a week, and they said if I just told them what made me snap like that, maybe they would understand.

Sleep

"I hear you met the professors. An odd bunch, huh?" Dr. Samesong makes a light joke as though this will be sufficient commentary.

"Why didn't you—"

"I do apologize for the mystery. Their research is best conducted if they stay detached and don't form relationships with you and vice versa."

"You're making us sound like lab rats."

"No, no, no. Not at all. No." He pauses. "It's just that they're interested in data and figures. Not people. And we don't want you eavesdropping on their conversations about sensitive health concerns."

"Such as?"

"Look, I'll be frank. They lack certain social skills and might not be as delicate as Peggy or me when we ask you personal questions. You know, about bodily functions and such. You say you don't want to feel like a lab rat, but, well, answering their inquiries about calorie intake and waste production might be a bit much. And it goes the other way, too, I'm afraid. We hired them to be data processors, not counselors and friends."

I wonder if Dr. Samesong got this job based on charisma alone. His explanation makes some sense. They were awkward even in my brief encounter. Dr. Samesong is clearly brilliant, but, after meeting the other side of smart, well, I'm thankful for someone who can hold a conversation.

"How have you been sleeping?" he asks, transitioning. He's looking through data on a continuous dot-matrix sheet with holes and perforation on the side.

"Great, actually."

"Looks like you're getting about six hours per night." He pens a note in the margin of the printout.

"How did you—"

"Monitors," he interjects, not looking up from the data. "Don't worry, they're rudimentary. Simple sensors on the beds." Before I can ask more, he adds, "And it looks to be uninterrupted sleep, which is even better. No getting up for the bathroom. Doesn't even appear to be much stirring. It's on the shorter side. Six hours per night on average. Are you feeling tired at all during the days?"

"Not really. Quite a bit of energy."

He looks through a few more printouts. "Would you consider abstaining from caffeine or switching to decaf? It would be ideal if we could isolate the source of the energy."

It sounds like a command rather than a request, but my curiosity is piqued anyway, so I don't mind agreeing. He asks a few more questions, mostly about my diet and daily routine. He's satisfied and puts the printout away in my file. I'm about to leave when he clears his throat and asks in a softer tone, "Forgive me for asking, but did you previously dye your hair?"

I laugh. "Yeah, actually. Prematurely gray. My mom and all my grandparents, too."

"I just noticed the roots coming in. Science." He smiles an odd smile, and I move to look in the mirror. I hadn't noticed my roots recently, to be honest. Haven't been doing much of anything in the way of grooming or maintenance. It's been a nice break, in fact. But when I study my hair, he's right. My roots aren't gray, and they aren't red either, well, at least not the shade I'd been using for dye. No, they're natural. Younger.

The Thaw

Hector is out of the infirmary. He's a little mellow, but he's largely unfazed by the whole experience. I apologize profusely, but he tells me if I say sorry one more time, I can't have any more of his cigarettes. It's the sort of joke that makes me glad he's back.

I expected him to look worse somehow. Less color in his skin. Or walking with a limp or something, but he's exactly the same. He's still having his late breakfast, his afternoon walks around the facility, his extensive pinball sessions, and earnest no-pressure chats with whoever he encounters. He doesn't even smoke less. There's a perpetual buildup of red butts in every ashtray. I'm not sure he's obeying doctor's orders, but I don't want to pester. And I'm just happy to have him back, so I don't really care.

I wrote nothing of consequence while he was away. I was too anxious. Anytime I started something, it would turn into a crumpled piece of paper moments later. It was hard to focus on reading, too. I'd read words, absorb nothing, but continue to turn pages anyhow. Even a children's chapter book about a warring group of mice and rats in a medieval realm proved too difficult for my mental state.

I found salvation in mediocre movies. It was like a sick day for myself. I had an excuse not to be productive, so I let myself indulge.

* * *

Hector and I do a jigsaw puzzle as a way of catching up. We don't talk much. It's pleasant. We're working on a photo of a red Lamborghini. It's basically impossible because of all the pieces with similar coloration and texture, but we're powering through.

I'm working on the wheel in the foreground and spot a piece I need on the opposite side of the table. I walk around, my eyes focused intently on the piece, so much so that I lose track of the ash from the Redlight dangling in my mouth. An ember falls, catches the draft and lands on Hector's wrist. He doesn't notice.

"Hector. Your hand."

He doesn't react. I watch as the ember singes the hairs on his wrist, wisps of smoke rising. I reach over to brush it off.

"Sorry, I—"

"What did I say about that word?"

Apparently starting a fire on his skin isn't worthy of an apology. "Oh, I mean…" I stop, puzzled. The ember is gone, but he still hasn't reacted. There's a blister beginning to bubble on his skin. I point it out. "Doesn't that hurt?"

"Huh?" He holds his wrist to his eye like he's trying to read the time. His expression is no different than if he learned it were three o'clock.

"Must be a side effect. They increased my dosage."

"That's weird."

"They said my body needs to be kick-started again. I don't mind."

"No, not that they increased the dosage. The side effect. Look at your wrist. You can't tell me you didn't feel anything."

He looks at his wrist again and shrugs before joking, "Science."

Amiss

Something's wrong with Hector. Since he's the one I talk to most, I'm not sure where to turn. My first instinct is Peggy and Dr. Samesong. They are the authority figures. But after the encounter with the other facility and the professors, they don't feel as reliable. I trust them in general—they helped Hector recover and have been accommodating in every other regard—but something wasn't quite right about their lie of omission, which leaves me wondering about what else they may be withholding.

Which leaves Quinn or Anna, neither of whom are optimal. Since they broke up, Quinn's been aloof, spending most of the time in his room. Anna has been friendly, but also needy and chatty and emotionally unpredictable. Still, she'd be willing to listen, someone to whom I could verbalize my concern about Hector. She could tell me if I'm crazy or not.

* * *

She's mid-movie when I find her. A couple days after the breakup she pushed an exercise bike in front of the screen. Now, she won't watch a movie without pedaling. In the daytime, at least. That's her rule. She must have sores from the bike seat at this point.

When she greets me with enthusiasm, it's obvious it's the

sort of movie that won't keep us from talking while we watch. I don't have to check the point scale. Either it's trashy, or she's seen it before, or both. An actor I recognize from a rom-com just told an actress ten years younger than him it's about time she, young actress, grows up. It's the fight that will set them back before they reconcile in the third act. The scene fades, and a montage begins.

I take the moment to interject, "They increased Hector's dosage."

She keeps pedaling but faces me. "Is that normal?"

"What's normal?" I jest, half-heartedly.

"Right." She dismounts the bike and pauses the movie, strictly adhering to her daytime TV rule.

"I think it's having a weird side effect on him. I was just with him, and a cigarette burned his arm, but he didn't feel it. It looked painful and he didn't even react." Anna looks less concerned than understanding, so I add, "That's strange, right?"

"Well, you've noticed some changes yourself, haven't you?" she asks with an almost condescending tone.

"Like not realizing my flesh is burning?" I'm not mad, really, but I'm upset. She's got this look on her face like I'm being dense. Like I'm missing something. It's this wry smile. The type you have when you wait for the joke to sink in, for the person to react to the punchline they don't quite understand, but it's a good one, so they're eager for you to get there.

"Nothing at all? Your body hasn't acted at all differently?"

I look at my finger. Not even a scar after such a deep cut.

Anna recognizes my epiphany. "I first noticed my migraines were gone. I used to get them all the time. Every couple weeks or so. They were awful. But since we got here, I haven't had a single one." She moves to a seat, spreading a towel over it before sitting on the edge as sweat runs down her body. "At first, I thought it was good luck. Coincidence. Then when I was helping Quinn bake one day, I burned my palm badly on an oven dish. I was in tears over the pain. Parts of the skin swelled and blistered. I iced it all night and went to bed with an ice pack the pain was so bad." I finally take a seat; I'm feeling wobbly on my feet. "Then, in the morning, the pain is gone, but I know it will still look awful. I don't want to, but I force myself to inspect the burns." She holds her hand up, reliving the gesture. "Nothing."

I process what she's telling me and what happened with Hector and my own experience with the cut and my hair. I know it's The Medicament, but it's still surreal. I really hadn't thought of it as much more than a vitamin. Good for the hangovers, right? "So, what? It's a drug that makes you heal really quickly?"

"I guess so. But I don't think that's all. I don't know about you, but I'm sleeping like a rock. And with what you told me about Hector, it sounds like he's not even *feeling* pain now." She scoots forward like she's going to tell me a secret, even though it's just the two of us in the room. "I don't want to make you blush, but, well, when Quinn and I were together, well, his..." I squirm. "Well, he could keep going and going." I squirm again. "Like, he didn't need to take any time to recover."

"That sounds—"

"Exhausting?" she laughs before turning to the doorway. Peggy has poked her head in.

I expect her to make a note on her clipboard and move on, but she says, "Sorry to interrupt, but we were hoping to speak to everyone. I know, it's not on the schedule, and this is your free time and all, but—" We're already standing, waving off her further apologies.

Note From the Editor

After having slept in a tent for days and acclimating to daylight at nighttime, Lily's room, with its blackout curtains, felt impossibly dark. At certain points, I heard a roar coming from outside, a disturbing mechanical sound, which I eventually realized was the calving of the nearby glacier. With a rumble and crush, pieces would fall and jostle me awake, but in my exhaustion, I'd nod back to sleep. I slept better than I had any business sleeping, considering I was in an abandoned mystery lab.

To add light to the facility, I drew every curtain I could and propped open the doors so light would bleed into the hallway. It was still dim, though, and I relied on my headlamp to conduct a search. To my surprise, the blinking red bulbs above the doorways still illuminated. The units were attached to a converter that led outside to a solar panel beside the generator. The lights didn't blink in each room as I explored it, though. Instead, the motion sensors would trigger the dim pulse in other rooms.

Because of the cave-like atmosphere, I gathered documents to review outside in the daylight. Most of what I found was unhelpful. Official-looking papers revealed nothing beyond the professional letterhead. In filing cabinets, thousands of pages of business letters and invoices and everything else were filled with Latin-filler-gibberish, i.e., *ipso lorem fac-*

totum. Along with these forgeries, notepads were filled with illegible scrawl and doodles. Even the notes I could make out appeared to be nonsensical musings such as *Pterodactyl v. Bear?*

In Anna's room, I found a few useful leads. A neatly organized folder on her desk revealed meticulous notes in legible handwriting. Many of these were comments about the movies she'd been screening, but there were details regarding the orientation as well. At first glance, it was difficult to figure out what would be relevant (there was a lot of technical information and a shorthand system I couldn't decipher), so I kept the entire folder. Most thrilling, however, was the brochure she kept. She was obviously the sort of person who kept all her school papers when she was a kid because they might come in handy.

Of note in my last inspection was the food in the pantry. The expiration dates ranged from 1993-1995, indicating the facility had been abandoned sometime not long before.

The packaging evolved as I dug deeper. Apparently, they never threw anything out, even if expired. One of the boxes of Frosted Flakes offered a sweepstakes with an entry deadline of March 1991. In a different section, Tony the Tiger looked more slender than the cartoon I'd known. Less upper body strength and a longer tail. Next to him was a brand of granola bars which must have gone out of business.

In addition to food, there were shelves supplied with various media. Plastic container boxes were loaded with VHS tapes—a wide selection from B-movies to Academy Award winners to animated children's movies to foreign films. Books and music were similarly varied across genre and prestige. The random assortment was curated to resemble something that might have come out of somebody's basement. A few VHS tapes were labeled by hand, "Orientation." I could make room in my pack.

There was hardly any medical equipment.

SL Corporation

Our perpetual endeavor is to redefine what is possible.

Who Are We?

The SL Corporation pharmaceutical RESEARCH DIVISION, FOUNDED IN 1952, is a team of expert scientists focused on generating unparalleled advances in MEDICINE. AS We enter the final stage of our most recent medication's development, We are seeking eligible candidates for trials.

During your stay, our doctors and scientists will monitor your response to the trial medication daily, ensuring optimal comfort and security. In exchange for your participation, we are offering a generous compensatory package:

Extraordinary Benefits

$100,000

As simple as that. For only one year's efforts you will be paid $100,000.

NO LIVING COSTS

During our program you will be accommodated in a modern private bedroom with attached bathroom. A shared state-of-the-art kitchen will be available in addition to full access to our cafeteria. Weekly allowances of alcohol and tobacco will also be furnished.

FACILITIES

You will have unlimited access to our multimedia library, private movie theatre, fitness center, and recreation room.

Our facility is located amongst beautiful mountain peaks, lakes, and forest, making outdoor recreation convenient and easy.

WHO ARE WE LOOKING FOR?

Anyone between the ages of 18 and 65 with proof of United

States Citizenship.

WHAT DO WE WANT FROM YOU?

If selected, you will need to live at our facility for the duration of the one-year study. Aside from daily health exams and brief written reports, you will be free of any other obligations.

WHAT'S NEXT?

Fill out the application form and return before September 20th, 1990. We will contact you promptly if your application is successful.

The Announcement

We gather in the dining room. Hector is already there and Dr. Samesong is fiddling with some equipment in the corner, tapping buttons on a computer and adjusting cables. He's cursing to himself and apologizes for the delay, obviously thinking setting up was going to be easier. Quinn finds his way in and sits behind the rest of us without saying anything. He plops down with his legs spread and the look of a bored teenager on his face. He's gone beyond aloofness, deep into moodiness and verging on shittiness. We have ten more months.

Dr. Samesong speaks into the computer, "Are you there? Can you hear me? Testing?"

Whoever he's trying to communicate with doesn't respond, and he keeps fiddling with the dials. A sudden pop of static from a speaker makes us jump. He twists a knob to lower the volume and a voice comes through "—yet? How about now? Anything?"

"Hold on. We only have audio."

I'm not the only one excited by a video call. I look around and everyone else perks up a bit when they realize what's happening. Even glum Quinn shows some emotion. We've only seen these in movies. The computer screen flickers and an image comes through. It's pixelated and choppy, but it's a video call. The person looks vaguely familiar.

"I'm seeing you now, Arthur. Picture looks great." I recognize the mustache now. It's the guy from the Orientation video. He's leaning towards the camera, not quite sure where to focus his eyes. Anna waves at him. "He can't see us, actually. Only audio on our end. But it's pretty cool, right? Anyhow, we brought in Arthur today because we have a special announcement. We were going to wait to share these results, but we've determined that it's important to the health of the project and your own peace of mind that you be given the same information we have. Now, before you get excited, know that these are only preliminary findings and that additional—"

"Come out with it already," interrupts Hector.

"Of course. Arthur, would you like to do the honors?"

There is a delayed reaction from Arthur, an evident lapse in the feed, then he proceeds, "Now, I'll try to keep the prelude short: human beings may be categorized by two different ages—chronological age and biological age. The chronological is the one based on your birthday. The number of candles on your most recent cake. All you need to determine it is a calendar. Biological age, on the other hand, is how old your body seems to be." Anna takes out a pen and paper to begin scribbling notes. "If you're an Olympic athlete with a healthy diet, you'll probably have a biological age a few years lower than your chronological age. Conversely, if you're a heavy smoker, your biological age is probably a few years older. We are able to measure biological age through DNA testing, hence all the blood tests."

The monitor static has become distracting. It's flickering in and out and the audio is clipped, too. Instinctively, we've leaned in closer, but it's not helping. The magic of the teleconference has worn off. I want Dr. Samesong to take over.

Nevertheless, the pixels continue, "Anyhow, without further preamble, we are happy to announce that The Medicament has lowered each of your biological ages by at least two percent. And we expect this trend to continue. Your body will feel younger and younger every day. It's like you're aging in reverse. Congratulations!" I'm not sure if the congratulations are for us or for the team, but no one claps. Dr. Samesong and Peggy are watching us, gauging our reaction to the perplexing news. It's a muted reaction from me and the other guests. Quinn looks like he's wondering if he still has to be here, Anna is waiting for more information she can add to her notes, and Hector snaps his fingers over his lighter to ignite the flame for another Redlight.

Dr. Samesong breaks the silence, "Thank you so much, Arthur," he says, getting to his feet. "We're all still processing over here, but we appreciate you taking the time to share this fantastic news with us." The pixels mutter a sign-off salutation, and the screen goes blank. "Any questions, folks?" Anna's hand goes up.

* * *

As I contemplate today's revelation, I can't help but feel underwhelmed. Two percent younger? If I'm thirty that means my body is only about six months younger. That's not entirely remarkable. I don't remember feeling particularly different six months ago. Even Hector would only be a little over a year younger. And if a hundred-year-old suddenly started feeling like a ninety-eight-year-old, would that really be revolutionary? Enough to isolate a team of people in the middle of nowhere for an entire year?

I look at my finger again and remember the incident with Hector and the ash and what Anna said about her burns. Something doesn't make sense. When I was six months younger, I could still feel pain.

The Professors

My encounter with the professors feels like a dream. I know I'm not supposed to have contact with them, but I want to give them another visit. It makes sense there are other researchers here, but I'm not buying the excuse of their suboptimal social skills. Everything has been painfully comprehensive. Every detail, whether we were interested or not, was covered ad nauseam. Even Anna, our diligent notetaker, has no memory of a second facility having ever been mentioned. It doesn't add up, and I'm not sure why they kept them hidden, so I'll go ask the professors myself.

Anna decides to join me. She's eager to go outside and uses the mission as an excuse. "I'll admit, it'd be good to talk to some fresh blood, too," Anna adds. "Sorry, I don't mean anything by that. You guys are great and all, but this is strange, right? Only talking to the same five people for weeks."

It is. Though, oddly, I have come to find our dynamic soothing. I know everyone well enough at this point that I'm comfortable. Bringing other people into the mix gives me a small sense of anxiety, like I'm worried they'll mess up our equilibrium, especially given the professors' awkwardness. I feel like if I asked them for a sandwich they'd first have to look it up in the encyclopedia to know what I was talking about.

"I don't want you to get your hopes up. They're pretty weird. And I'm not even sure they'll want to talk."

Anna shrugged. “It’ll still be fresh air.” She brushes her hair out of her face with her hand, and I spot a smudge of makeup on her forehead. I keep my eyes on it, a smear of concealer overtop foundation.

“Are you wearing makeup,” I ask. “I haven’t touched any in weeks.” I’m realizing Anna hasn’t been wearing any, either.

“Oh, um. Yeah. Clumsy me tripped on the treadmill this morning. Gave myself quite the bruise. Guess I didn’t want to admit it.”

“Ouch. You must’ve really done a number on yourself if even this miracle drug won’t patch you up.” I say, half-joking. She lets it drop.

* * *

We’ve bundled up fully. Long underwear, scarf, hat, snow pants, parka, wool socks. When we open the boot cabinet, however, it’s empty. Every pair is gone. While still bundled, we go to track down someone. We find Peggy peering into the kitchen with her clipboard. She’s startled, perhaps because our footsteps are muted by our socks.

“Yes, they’re being cleaned. I apologize. It’ll take a few days for them to dry. You see, we can’t put them in the dryer, and we don’t want to risk…” and she continues on with a detailed explanation of their boot drying procedure. I start to peel off the layers before she’s finished talking. In a few days the boots will be dry.

Chapter 4

If it had been a weekend, there'd have been other cars around. It was a drizzly Wednesday, though, so the lookout was quiet.

He'd missed the sunset, and there was nothing to look at while he smoked his cigarettes except the rain on the windshield. It was a bad idea to go to bed angry, so he drove out to clear his head. Even if he still fell asleep angry, it wouldn't be in their bed.

Standard disc brakes rely on hydraulics to transfer the pressure of the foot on the brake pedal into a much more powerful frictional force on the wheels. In this way, a weak human becomes enough to stop a machine. The emergency brake system, however, relies entirely on Newtonian physics. If a car rests on an incline, the emergency brake pulls a steel cable, which, in turn, locks a set of wedges against the rear wheels. The handbrake locks into place and cannot be dislodged unless it is manually shifted. When a car is parked on a slope, it's recommended to steer the wheels toward the curb so if the wedges slip, the car will roll into the curb and not begin to speed downhill.

He didn't angle his wheels. There was no one around, and, anyhow, he was sitting in the driver's seat.

* * *

My mom stood over me as I tried to find room to sink further into the couch. She held her eyes steady, not wavering. If I got sick of looking at nothing and let my eyes wander, I might have accidentally looked in her direction, at which point she'd pounce. Since she was tear-free, it was better to talk now, while she was still in the angry stage. When I couldn't resist her beckoning eyes anymore, I was reeled in and began sputtering out my defense, by which I mean, shifted it back to her.

"I don't know why you're so upset about this."

"This isn't about me," she swatted away my ploy. "This is about your future. Your life."

As I rolled my eyes they strayed across the photographs atop the mantle—the two of us on the beach at sunset, me being pulled in a red wagon, that horrifying school photo when she'd guilted me into showing my teeth even though I had braces, her holding me as a newborn with a candid smile that photographs never capture when you're trying for it.

"That's exactly why it should be my choice." I exhaled, sure that would stump her for a moment.

"You're too young to make these choices," she breezed through. I hated her. "If you did whatever you wanted, you'd be..." The rhetorical gambit backed her into a corner. If she finished the sentence with a preposterous scenario, she'd weaken her stance, "The point is—" she said, bailing. "I want what's best for you." She sat next to me, anger giving way to self-pity, the most contagious emotion.

"All I said was that I was thinking about it. I mean, why does everyone assume I even want to go to college?"

"If I have to explain that—" she trailed off as the tears started. She tried to distract herself by fiddling with a section of wallpaper that had been peeling for years, but the tears still came. I hated her.

* * *

Once the frictional force on the car gave way to gravitational pull, the car began its slow descent. The steady incline ensured constant acceleration, and by the time the car reached the shores of the lake, it had enough momentum to propel it through the water's resisting force. As it did so, the change in equilibrium created a vacuum enveloping the car's rear.

It is unlikely, given the force of impact or the eruption of sound, that the car's driver (more accurately described as the car's occupant) remained asleep.

* * *

I wasn't listening anymore. Not really. Once it turned to tears, I did my best to ignore her. If she was doing it on purpose, it wasn't fair, and if she couldn't help it, then she should have left the room. My arms were crossed but there was still a lump in my throat.

"If I do decide to go, and that's a big if, what would you do?"

"Don't worry about me."

"You know I will."

My mom crumpled. A silent cry and gasp for breath. I didn't mean for it to cut like it had. It was the truth of the words that made it hurt most. She didn't know about my plans yet. I'd only told the first part, the part about skipping college. I'd let her think she was the reason I wouldn't go. That I needed to stay and take care of my poor, pathetic mom. Maybe then she'd realize why I desperately needed to leave. She shouldn't be the only one allowed to wield guilt.

A bit more composed now, she stood up and made like she was going to leave, but she paused in the doorway, finding courage to speak, even if she had to face away from me while she did.

"I didn't ask for this, you know. I'm doing the best I can."

"I know, Mom," I said with just a hint more disdain than I'd intended.

She stood in the kitchen and dialed the phone. The punch and tone of each digit familiar as if a poem recited from memory. After the line connected, a brief pause, "Dr. Forester, please."

During the call, I only half-listened as I packed up a few items. I was optimistic and only packed a few days' worth of clothes. It wasn't like I wouldn't be visiting either way.

* * *

If it hadn't been raining, he might have had the windows open. If the windows had been open, the water would have rushed in and the pressure differential between the outside and inside of the car would have stabilized. With the windows up, however, the doors became unmovable. No human could overcome the strength of the water. He left the windows up, wanting to preserve the air, to give the impromptu watercraft some buoyancy, any small amount to keep it afloat. The water leaked in through the vents, slowly, trickling in to submerge his feet, then his knees, then his upper body.

The radio was off. When the water rushed over his head, his death came silently.

* * *

They always made you sign in, even if you came every day and knew everyone on staff. There were probably whole filing cabinets filled with old sign-in sheets.

The nurse behind the desk made the same joke she always had about my mom and I being sisters, as though she'd never met a young mom before. Dr. Forester debriefed me on what I needed to know. He talked to me like I was an adult. There may have been a time when he talked to me like I was a child, but I couldn't remember it. She'd been sleeping most of the time, but she'd gone to a lot of the group meetings, too, he told me, tagging on a positive. They were going to try a different medication and see how she responded. They'd like to keep an eye on her. She might seem drowsy when we talk, but that was just a side effect; they had to keep her on a high dosage at first. He was glad I was there. She'd be glad, too.

When I came in, she was knitting a maroon and white scarf. She didn't ever knit at home, but here, she'd knit scarves I never saw finished but that she said some poor kid would appreciate come winter. They trusted her with the knitting needles, which was a good sign.

The hug was one of those gentle, forceful ones where she held on without putting much weight into it, like she was giving every ounce of strength into the effort even if it wasn't much strength. There wouldn't be tears today; she was past that for now. I got the blank expression that was either the drugs or a different numbness. These were procedural, matter-of-fact days, when I'd ask if she was hungry and then convince her to eat something even if she didn't have an appetite, and maybe we'd watch a game show.

"That Dr. Forester hasn't aged a day. No wonder the nurse is so grouchy," I jested, and she gave me a closed-lip smile. I didn't bring in any photographs for her this time. It would be better if the room stayed bare and didn't feel like home.

* * *

He didn't leave a will, but his only major asset drowned in the lake, too, so there wasn't any fight over it.

The baby wouldn't stop crying at the funeral, so she stepped outside into the summer air while the pastor spoke the words that would later be described to her as very nice. Guests took turns poking their heads out to offer to relieve her from baby duties, but she declined each time. They'd sad-smile in consolation before returning to the church to give the pastor a shrug-nod that the service should continue.

Her friends said they would help with childcare; they'd make it work. She said that was a kind offer, but unnecessary. When they insisted on watching the baby for a weekend, she was so anxious she got even less sleep than when she was up crying all night.

They tried to give her both space and support. Sometimes they gave her too much of one and not enough of the other. She told them she didn't need them to do this anymore, and they insisted, and she told them, flat out, she didn't want them to. Then she had plenty of one but none of the other.

An insurance man came to tell her the driver/occupant wasn't responsible and there was going to be a recall on the emergency brake system. The car company was going to pay a huge settlement, so that was something.

* * *

The drive home would be full of optimism. I'd listen without listening while thinking about my recent trips home alone, the days when I couldn't wait to get out of there, but then would get home and not know what to do, so I'd clean the already clean house while Mom stayed in the hospital to nap and knit scarves the staff would keep from getting too long to cause trouble.

There would be promises and a new outlook and apologies I didn't want to hear because I knew it wasn't her fault, not really. And she'd thank me for putting flowers in her room. And she'd tell me I could close the door, even though she knew I'd leave it open.

Except this time, she was quiet on the ride home. Not silent, she responded when I mentioned the prescriptions I needed to pick up and the food I'd stocked in the fridge, but she was quiet. Even when a motorcycle swerved in front of us and I slammed on the brakes, she didn't display a hint of a reaction.

Doctors had always waffled between physiological and psychological explanations. At first it was ulcerative colitis causing the pain, then it was a psychosomatic reaction to trauma after my father's death, then it was neurochemical instability treated with a regimen of mood stabilizers, and then Dr. Forester was assigned as case manager to monitor all aspects of her physical and mental health. His treatment would work for a time, but there'd be setbacks. A new set of abdominal pains or fits of emotional dysregulation would send her back to the hospital until a new treatment kept her well enough to return home. Overnight stays were rare when I was younger, but they'd pull a cot into her room for me, even though they weren't supposed to. Before I'd learned to drive, the hospital provided me a discount bus pass.

We stepped inside the house, and with the door barely shut, she began, "I think we should talk," which she followed with something she hadn't said, no matter how much she apologized or how much she promised it would be different in the future, she always omitted the next part: "You're right, Lily."

I instinctively opened my mouth to protest, expecting this to be a ploy to set her agenda, but she waved me off and continued.

"I've attached myself too much to you. It's just been you and me for so long, I forget you're your own person. I took care of you and raised you by myself, and have loved you as much as it's possible to love someone." Some of this was coming from her psychologist, but she wouldn't have said it if she didn't want to. "You needed me, but you didn't want me. And now I need you, but I don't want you." She paused to rephrase. "I mean, I want you to go. I want you to be able to make your own mistakes."

* * *

There was never a more beautiful child. Everyone agreed. And such a loving, caring mother. They went everywhere together.

Quinn's Darkness

At first, I thought Quinn was moody because of his breakup with Anna. Their relationship might not have made much sense in the first place (besides convenience), but that didn't mean the breakup wasn't upsetting. Especially with our situation. He might not have thought it through. Ending things with Anna meant cutting off a third of our group from pleasant interaction. But Anna doesn't seem to be the problem. They're fine when they're together.

Anna even confesses they've had sex a few times since the breakup. Don't spend the night together, she was clear about that, but they could be adults about enjoying each other physically. Sexual gratification must be worth the tradeoff of his mood swings.

At times he's perfectly pleasant, if a bit removed, but at other times he's a brooding pain-in-the-ass that no one wants to be around. Unfortunately, you can't just ignore him either. He'll be within earshot and make snippy comments under his breath. I was telling Hector an admittedly mundane story about how I used to have a lot of nosebleeds as a kid, and I hear Quinn mutter "fascinating" as he exits the room. None of us are confrontational, so we don't want to escalate a pretty harmless situation, but it's become tedious. He wears this scowl-pout on his face at all times. It's like he's trying to broadcast his foul mood and bring the rest of us down.

No one wants to talk to him about it. Hector doesn't really care, and Anna is afraid of offending him and reigniting an old fight.

* * *

I'm steeping tea in the kitchen when a new face appears. He's dressed in all black and wears a hat labeled "Security." He nods toward me without a word and fills a glass of water. There's a tattoo of a dragon on his arm that might've once looked cool. He adds a lime wedge to his water and nods again to me before he departs.

I give my teabag a few more lifts and sinks before sipping the too hot liquid. The door opens again and this time it's Quinn who enters. I smile and don't engage further. He nudges past me and starts the coffee maker. It looks like it's been days since he's showered. I move to the tap to add cool water to my cup. While the coffee pot gurgles, he breaks the silence, "How's the writing going?" It's an odd tone. I sense he's hoping I'll say I have terrible writer's block and haven't written a thing in weeks.

I choose an ambiguous response. "There are good days and bad days," I say, which is true. Though I have been in a bit of a slump, I don't want to give him the satisfaction of knowing. "How's the music?"

He hears me, but he's preoccupied with the coffee preparation, practically hand counting the grains of sugar. I'm about to ask again when he says in a defeated voice, "It's my ears."

"Is something wrong?"

"No. I don't know how to put it. They're different."

"Have you talked to Dr. Samesong?"

"Yes. He did some tests. They're too good," he says like

I should know exactly what he means. "That's the problem. They're perfect. I'm hearing things I haven't heard before. And I'm realizing I'm shit."

I stop myself from reassuring him. He's opening up, and I'm guessing he's not fishing for faint praise. I don't know him well, but I can tell he's the sort of talent who's good enough to know he probably isn't exceptional. I've known plenty of delusional talentless types who disguise their narcissism as self-deprecation. The ones who make excuses for why it doesn't sound good, "I just learned this yesterday," and wait for you to say, "No, it was amazing." Quinn, however, is good. He's just not a virtuoso.

I let him continue. "I'm picking up on things I didn't before. I realize how off-key my voice is." I'm fascinated. And thankful that my own creative medium won't change because of what's happening with our bodies. But he's been such a moody bastard, I'm less inclined to sympathize. "It makes me appreciate, no, appreciate isn't the right word. It makes me envious of real musicians."

This part does cut a bit. I haven't been working in the library as much because the books like to mock me. Whatever a real writer is, it's not someone who has to run away to the middle of nowhere to force themself to write.

Now that he's brought me down, too, he pours some milk into his coffee and as he leaves adds, "What the hell are we doing here?"

The Draft

Quinn can go fuck himself. Whether he was trying to make himself feel better or make me feel worse or somewhere in between, I don't care. Well, I did care for the rest of the morning. And afternoon. Pretty much the whole day I was stewing about it. He's right that we're not the artists we want to be. To answer his bullshit rhetorical question, though, that's exactly why I'm here.

I debate carrying a notebook with me at all times to put my creative process on display. I check my ego, however, and deny the spiteful (however gratifying) exhibitionism. This isn't about him. Even though a lot of good can come from a rivalry, I'd be way too self-conscious to do any quality work in the public space.

Instead, my room is now my official writer's office. Whatever creative rivalry is brewing between us, it'll have to transcend the walls of Residential Facility A.

I've tried not to think about the bruise on Anna's forehead last week, but now that I've seen this side of Quinn, it's hard to ignore. Anna hasn't mentioned it so I don't want to advocate on her behalf, but I worry about what he might have done. It's not my business, I tell myself. I'll shutter myself off.

I lay out a chart of daily word count goals. Next to that I compose a detailed outline, so I don't feel intimidated. Writer's block is for the lazy. I've heard that before. Or maybe I made it up. Either way, it's written in bold letters on the wall in front of my desk.

I make a calendar and count out daily goals, add some editing time, and make a big circle on June 21st. The first day of summer. I have three months before the deadline for my first draft.

For the next few days, I don't see anyone. Not really. I don't have any conversations, at least. I've bumped into people in the dining room as I've retrieved food, but after a brief, "hey," I bring my food back to my room. More than once, I've been about to leave my room when I hear someone in the hallway. I postpone my exit for a minute or two. I'm standing on the opposite side of the door looking at nothing, waiting for enough time to have passed so I won't have to exchange a simple pleasantry with whoever. It's not antisocial; it's so I can keep all of them out of my headspace while I'm writing.

This is my logic for the first few days of self-imposed solitary confinement. It's when I'm running through the logistics of having a TV moved into my room that I realize I need to snap out of it. I might be content on my own right now, but the desire will eventually subside and, presumably, I'll want to have human interaction again. I'll force myself out and have some face time now, so I don't burn any bridges. Or else it'll be like when friends stop inviting you out because you always say no. I'll make time to be social. With Hector and Anna at least. Quinn, well, Quinn can still go fuck himself.

To keep my writing routine going, I rewrite my schedule. I figure I need at least three hours of HIT—Healthy Interaction Time—each day. If one were a meal and the other were a movie, I'd already meet the quota. Quantifying it in raw numbers makes me realize how anti-social I've been since the conversation with Quinn. It was only five days ago, but even so, that's been a lot of time staring at a typewriter and taking baths. I made a couple paintings, too, but they're barely worth mentioning. They were little swirls of color that never felt right. Setting them on fire would've been cathartic. But instead of raising alarm, I ripped them into strips and flushed them down the toilet.

My original schedule, the one I'd written in my second week, has made its way to the bottom of a pile of notes. It had been so earnest when I'd written it, but it didn't last more than a couple weeks. The thought was there. And it'll be there again, too, with the new one I'm composing. I start to revise the original schedule by crossing out and revising with red marker before I realize I'll have to start over entirely. Maybe I'll stick to it this time if the schedule has a bit more pep. A piece of college-ruled notebook paper was never going to be inspiring.

* * *

I haven't had a good writing day, so I want to avoid Quinn during Healthy Interaction Time. Instead, I'll try the second facility and see if I can chat with the professors. They did extend an open, if empty, invite. I might as well see if I can interrogate them a bit and try to unpack whatever details they can offer.

Before bundling up, I confirm the boots have been dried and returned. Once outside, the weather isn't ideal, so I walk with pace to the hidden entrance. To my relief, the door is open. I shout inside in an exaggeratedly friendly voice to announce my presence and give them a moment to make themselves presentable. In my mind, though, they're always finely dressed and sitting with perfect posture. I continue to call out as I move from room to room. There are no sounds but my own. Everything is tidy and orderly, as though an empty hotel awaiting new guests.

Though the rooms are well lit and the walls are colorful and adorned with artwork, the windowlessness gives it a feeling of captivity. It's like a movie set, designed to approximate real life, while being entirely contrived and lacking any true feeling.

It's becoming clear no one is here, so I stop announcing my entrance into each room. The sensation of being home alone gives me a nagging urge, an urge to snoop. The bedrooms leave me without anything juicy. All the drawers and closets have been emptied and not a single personal artifact was left behind. In the parlor, there's little evidence of people having been there besides a scorecard notating the running totals of their gin rummy games. The pantry and kitchen are still stocked, and the laundry room looks like a laundry room.

My guess is the professors will continue their work remotely; analyzing data from afar since they don't interact with us anyhow. The seclusion probably got the better of them. I don't want to linger. Snooping around is one thing, but I'd be pushing it if I started full-on lounging.

I'm walking across our runway when I spot the open door of the hangar. I don't need to be closer to see that it's empty. The plane may have left days or even weeks earlier, but no one had taken notice. The small hangar couldn't be seen from anywhere inside the facility, so it wasn't a landmark of our panorama.

Instinctively, my pace quickens as I am eager to share the discovery with everyone. I'd like an explanation from Samesong and Peggy, and if that doesn't suffice, I'd like Hector or Anna to reassure me it's not a big deal.

I end up not sharing the news with anyone. It's overshadowed by what else has happened.

Quinn

As I remove my outer layers I'm greeted by Peggy. I expect her to check the mark on her clipboard, but she isn't carrying it. She speaks before I can say anything, "Lily, we didn't want to disturb you, but it's important that we talk." It's a tone I haven't heard before and it's not easy to read. "Something's happened."

The chairs in the dining room are arranged into a circle. Between each chair is a small end table with a glass of water and a box of tissues. I take a seat between Hector and Anna, who look like they are waiting to be lectured for something they did wrong. Neither Peggy nor Dr. Samesong is taking notes. Dr. Samesong begins, sparing euphemism and speaking with a sympathetic, controlled voice.

"Quinn is dead. He killed himself. We found him this morning. There was nothing we could do."

"We have already contacted his family and are making arrangements," Peggy adds without pause as if to anticipate our questions and fill all silence. "Counseling sessions are scheduled. We would love to have you join us, but we know and respect that everyone processes tragedy differently. These sessions will be optional."

"Your safety is more important than ever before."

"We understand this may be difficult."

"That this *is* difficult."

"We ask that you come to us with any concerns you have. If you're having any trouble coping with difficulties here—the isolation, the solitude…"

"Even the weather. We're glad to talk."

"We encourage it," Dr. Samesong says before pausing. "No one is to blame for Quinn's death. He chose to end his life for reasons we may not understand. He hid his pain. We may not have been able to help, but—"

"But that doesn't mean talking isn't therapeutic."

"In light of this tragedy, the intent of this project is no longer as important as it may have been before. If you would like to reexamine the nature of the contract, that may be negotiated." Dr. Samesong distributes a copy of the contract to each of us. "We have failed you; we have failed our agreement. It would be unfair of us to expect you to uphold your end. That being said, we still believe in our project."

"We still believe in you."

"And, I know this may seem inappropriate, crass even, but we are willing to double your compensation should you choose to stay." Dr. Samesong waits for our reaction, but we remain silent. "But please take your time."

"Of course, take as long as you need. We respect that this is not an easy decision."

"However, until you make your decision, we do need you to keep taking The Medicament. It's imperative. It's for your own safety. It's more of a precaution than anything, but we don't want there to be any withdrawal symptoms. If you choose to leave, we'll employ a weaning off regimen."

"Again, take your time. We will respect whatever decision you make."

"Though, of course, we'd love it if you stayed." He pauses. "I do need to mention, however, despite the change of circumstance, for security reasons we still cannot allow you to contact family or friends back home.

"Out of respect for Quinn's family as well."

"Let's try to stay strong in this difficult moment. Now, please take whatever time you need, and again, don't hesitate to reach out anytime. We are here for you."

The tissues beside me remain untouched.

Chapter 5

Boys crushed en masse on three of the lucky girls (or unlucky, depending). Since no one actually admitted they had a crush on anyone, it was normal if, say, twelve boys liked one girl. They weren't officially in competition because they denied it if they were accused of liking anyone. Still, the girls who were crushed upon were the obvious choices. Allison, of course, and two others who had nice hair and acted mature earlier than others. One of them was kinda plain, to be honest, but she hung around with the cool girls, and she had cool clothes, so, voila, Crush Subject #3.

When Tommy started calling me Lily Pad, I didn't get it, and I still don't. It's not even an insult really, just word association, but the nickname caught on. If my name was called out by anyone, it'd be echoed by "Pad" and sometimes a "ribbit." Then Tommy started picking dandelions, which he'd hand to me and say, "Every Lily Pad needs flowers." Tommy didn't pick flowers for any of the Big Three.

If no one else was around he might ask me about what music I liked or if I liked swimming in a pool or a lake better.

On Valentine's Day we had to bring valentines for the whole class. Tommy was sick that day and didn't come to school. Someone said he was probably busy making a huge valentine for Lily Pad. He didn't come to school the next day either. Or the day after that. Our teacher rearranged the desks so there wasn't a hole in the middle of class when Tommy moved to another town. Ribbit.

***

Junior high was my ugly phase. I wish it weren't as simple as that, but, for junior high boys, it was.

***

I had no intention of going to the dance. My mom thought it would be nice if I participated in school activities. If I had been the one to answer the phone, I might've avoided wearing a dress for the first time since I was nine. As it was, I tried to lie.

"He was just wondering about homework. That's all."

"Homework makes you blush now, huh?"

"Um…"

"So, what did you say? No, what did he say?"

"To what?" I'd already lost, but I was still clinging to playing dumb.

"Come on, Lily."

"I said I'd think about it."

I don't know why it was important to her, but I saw it on her face. Of course, I didn't let her know she'd just won.

We took photos at my house, and he was already sweating in the layers of his suit. He did his best not to be embarrassed about having his mom drive us to the dance. When he opened the car door for me, there was a brief hesitation about whether he should turn his mom into a chauffeur and join me in the back. In the daylight, on the way there, the seat next to his mom won out.

It was more fun than it should have been. We were both

terrible and self-conscious dancers who danced goofy to act like we weren't really dancing.

"Aren't you hot in that jacket?"

"Roasting."

"Take it off, ya goof."

"Thank God." I felt his eyes on me and the whole-body smile he sent toward me, too. "You, um… you—" Whatever he said, it was swallowed by music.

"Thanks!" I shouted. He looked confused, and I blushed. He might have been asking if I wanted to fight for all I could hear.

As silly dancing switched to earnest dancing, we turned into opposite poles of a magnet. When I got too close, he was repelled back, and when he got too close, I was repelled back, thus maintaining the invisible field. Even without his jacket, he was sweating like mad. I was sure I was wearing my dress wrong somehow, or it was about to rip, or I'd burst out, or I'd succumb to some other disaster that seasoned dress wearers were aware of but I'd never known.

Then the music slowed, and the girls cheered, and a previously unnoticed disco ball cast its spell to command us all to touch each other. To our left were his hands on her waist and her hands on his neck, and the couple to our right had the same, and yet, we still fumbled to find the proper position. His sweaty hands on my sweaty neck were somehow not unpleasant.

"Phew, I needed to rest," I said in my normal voice.

"Me too."

"Seriously, I could fall asleep," I said in a cuter voice as I lay my head against his chest in a fake sleepy way.

His crotch brushed me, and I felt the protrusion. I knew this could happen, that it was supposed to happen, but only to characters in books or sex ed film reels. We hardly knew each other, and I wasn't attracted to him, but the moment didn't disgust me, or arouse me, or startle me. It fascinated me. This was one of those moments everyone knew about, but no one really talked about, and here it was, happening in my actual life. I moved closer to him and continued dancing while he rubbed against me. He said my name in a whisper, and then he shook and recoiled and said my name again, except in a different tone, and then his sweaty hands were off me, and they turned into a shield as he escaped the dance floor.

When his mom picked us up later, he opened the door for me, but this time he sat beside me in the back seat. With his hands on his lap, he told his mom the dance was fun, yes, and there were lots of people there, yes. At my house, he sat planted in the back seat while I scooted out of the car. Forgetting himself, his mom needed to prompt, "Don't you want to walk Lily to the door?"

He didn't want to, but he took my arm, and before a kiss could come that I didn't really want but would have accepted, he said, "I think we should just be friends." I watched out the window as he sat in the back seat and his mom drove off.

* * *

It wasn't hard to ignore guys in high school. Their undeclared contests to see who was the King Cro-Magnon, competing to see who could be the most nasty, brutish and tall. When one separated from the pack, they weren't quite so terrible, and I had sex with a few without fanfare, but didn't feel anything resembling pleasure. Sex became something to be experienced and appreciated in the same way you'd appreciate Gilbert and Sullivan: whimsical and with trace amounts of a hidden depth. But, like Gilbert and Sullivan, there were better ways to occupy oneself.

Still, sex was what everyone seemed to be talking about. The talk didn't make me uncomfortable but simply bored me. The sex I'd had was underwhelming. I couldn't help but think everyone had been marketed to by *The Joy of Sex* and didn't want to admit to being a mindless drone who'd bought the same shoddy product. Either that, or they knew they were lying. It wasn't that great, but if we said that, the human species would cease to exist.

In the same way other people found the new self-help literature empowering, with the focus on you and your pleasure, and you, you, you, I found it condescending. If you're not enjoying it, there's something wrong with you, you, you.

***

As I began to meet more interesting people, I realized I craved the intimacy of a relationship, if not physically. At the age of twenty, determined to have a boyfriend, I found a boyfriend and made him my first and only boyfriend.

Even though I didn't go to college, I didn't deprive myself of the college experience. There was a college bar and a college coffeehouse and a patch of grass people hung out on in the center of campus to wax philosophical about doobies and the patriarchy and shit. Everyone assumed I was a student, and I didn't correct them.

By this time, I was used to being noticed, but it was easy to write off when coming from a Cro-Magnon. When interesting people started to notice me too, well, I liked it.

The guy who would become my first and only boyfriend didn't try very hard, but not in that sort of way where he was trying by acting like he wasn't trying. He drank from a flask and smoked cigarettes even though people were quitting the habit more and more. I never saw him without his beat-up denim jacket, which functioned as a de facto purse with all he'd carry around. In the front pocket he'd stuff a paperback of whatever existentialist he could find at Goodwill— Kierkegaard, Camus, Simone de Beauvoir—and carry it around until it became a tattered mess. He must've read some of it, too, because his vocabulary was littered with philosophical jargon.

He asked me out on what I interpreted to be a date, but which turned out to involve eight other people with flasks and cigarettes. To be fair, he focused his attention on me and closed the evening with the straightforward, "Do you want to go on a date?"

We were three official dates in before he made an attempt to kiss me. Even then it was a lackluster I-guess-we-should-do-this type of gesture. His hands stayed as stilted as a manikin. At least it made us officially more than friends.

His was the first male body I saw unclothed that wasn't immediately obscured as it was pressed upon me. Neither tantalized nor repulsed, I observed him like a nude in an art class. There were patches of thin hair in unexpected places like his shoulders, acne and scars from blemishes on his back, and somehow his muscles managed to be toned in certain places and flabby in others. The penis was still a puzzling conundrum. Its ability to change shape, while scientifically explainable, still seemed a magic trick all the world's magicians had sworn not to reveal. He hadn't mastered the illusion, however, and most often needed to practice the levitating trick while I waited. We seldom had sex as a result. He wasn't into it much either, it seemed, a dynamic I didn't object to.

It wasn't a great relationship. He liked his friends, people I thought were thoroughly okay, but he tried to include them as much as possible. The thing I liked most about him was that he wasn't boring. I might be annoyed or anxious or even a bit mad when around him, but I was never bored. Whatever he liked about me, I couldn't be sure; whether it was my personality, or wit, or my looks, or my body, I don't know, but he touched me more when other people were around.

We had our first fight when he found out I wasn't enrolled in college.

"I never told you I was," I stated.

"So, it's my fault for assuming?"

"I didn't say that."

"Impressive," he huffed.

The second fight wasn't so much a fight as it was a long overdue conversation, followed by a breakup. I didn't catch him cheating, per se, he just admitted he'd started having sex with someone else.

I wasn't jealous, honestly, confusion gave me the aggrieved tone, "I didn't think you were that into sex?"

"I could say the same about you." And so, our sexual stalemate, which, apparently, had never been the compromise, became untenable. When he said we could still keep seeing each other, I gave it legitimate thought.

Guilt

Earlier that day, I wished to never see Quinn again. I didn't cry when they broke the news, but someone I knew was gone, and it hurt. Even if I didn't miss the individual, the absoluteness of death, its suddenness, made me sad. I'd never see him again. I'd never catch the faint aroma of one of his baked goods and decide it was a good time for a break. I'd never have to avoid him when he was being moody. I feel guilty for wishing him gone. Worse is my sense of relief at the news. I'm glad he is gone—maybe not that he is dead, but glad that he is gone. I feel guilty for wondering how he killed himself; I feel the impulse to know how it happened, but feel gross for wanting to know. I feel guilty for not feeling the sadness the others feel. Anna's hysterical sobs have lasted for hours, and Hector has entered into a nearly catatonic state. He looks blank and empty and has been staring at the same few pages of an old *Popular Mechanics* magazine for hours. Their sadness is genuine. Mine is borrowed from them. It is secondhand sorrow—I am sad because they are.

I feel guilty for doubling my money. I feel guilty because I wonder how this change will affect me. I feel guilty for wishing Anna would stop sobbing.

* * *

It's a few days before anyone smiles again. We're in mourning, or, at least, being respectful. I tell them I am staying. Hector, too. Anna hasn't made her decision. The counseling sessions have been useful. For her, at least. She's able to work through her emotions, and we're supportive. She talks of Quinn's temper, too, and I'm reminded of the bruise on her forehead.

To my surprise, Hector has a lot to unload, too. He regrets being so private, fears that he didn't make an effort with Quinn. From what I saw, they didn't have much of a relationship. They're both introverts. They didn't force a connection. It was easy. Hector regrets that he let it be easy.

I'm pretty reserved. As cathartic as talking might be, I don't want to divulge my conflicted emotions, so I half-heartedly fake some. I talk about death in the abstract. I mention his musical talent. I try not to let my mind wander when discussion turns to coping strategies.

In our free time we let a documentary series fill the silence in the lounge. We spread out on the couches and watch animals hunt each other and flowers bud in time lapse while a British voiceover anthropomorphizes. *This curious creature has a secret. His tail not only gives him balance and keeps him from tumbling—it's just what he'll need to land a date. This magnificent display of courtship leaves the female unimpressed. She leaves the suitor to try his charm on the next pretty thing to catch his eye.*

It lulls us into a state of hypnosis. The three of us bond through collective trance. The narration echoes in my head throughout the day, though. I can't take a shower without hearing a pleasant British man describe my *ingenious grooming patterns*.

Anna has started smoking. She pinches a Redlight awkwardly between her thumb and index finger, and she hardly inhales, but she needs something to do with herself. If her biological age breaks even, so be it, she says. Often.

After a week, Anna can't rationalize declining the extra money. We are all going to stay.

Quinn's Room

Realtors do what they can to hide when a house has a violent history. It's not the best selling point when there was a bloodbath in the kitchen. It's not about ghosts or curses or anything. People don't like to think about death, especially grisly death. Even if the linoleum has been replaced, you tell someone there was a murder where they're cooking dinner, and they'll want to start scrubbing like Lady Macbeth.

I wouldn't mind. I'd try to haggle a discount out of a death house.

There couldn't have been much cleanup in Quinn's room. I didn't see them go in there a single time after breaking the news. Must have been a tidy death.

When I ask Peggy if I could use Quinn's room as a studio space, she's incredulous; she begins an inquisition.

"Why?"

"I could use the extra space. One room for writing, the other for painting."

"Is everything alright? You haven't been going to counseling recently."

It's true. I couldn't fake it anymore, and whatever conflicts I feel, I'm not going to hash it out in front of everyone. "I'm ready to move on. It doesn't bother me. It's just a room."

"I don't like the idea." It's the first request she's ever dissuaded. Usually, she'll accommodate me as quickly as possible and apologize that I had to even ask.

I debate playing the victim, that given the circumstance they should do all they can to make sure we're happy. The more I push though, the more suspicious she'll become. She'll think I have some morbid curiosity, which I do, but it's not worth it.

"I'll have to talk to Dr. Samesong." She turns to leave. "But I don't think he'll like the idea, either."

I don't get the room. It would show favoritism, or so they say. Nevertheless, they all seem to look at me differently for the next few days.

Note From the Editor

The open space of nature was solitary. It was a disturbing solitude, though, different than the one I normally felt outdoors. I wasn't the only one to have ever set foot here.

* * *

For those that had come before, it didn't end well. I knew the truth, and I saw it with my own eyes. Still, I was trapped by the optimism of the story. It made me want to believe, even though I knew better. It was like rewatching a movie I'd seen several times and still rooting for a different script.

* * *

I had put off searching for the second facility. Based off Lily's descriptions, it was near the opposite end of the runway, but there was not much else to go on. Tromping through the ice field would be unwise while on my own, and even then, stumbling upon it wouldn't be easy. Still, I needed to investigate properly.

It was early morning as I crossed the runway and paused at the hangar. Apart from the grime that had amassed on the corrugated iron of the structure, there were no signs of deterioration on the exterior. Unlike the facility, it was securely shut and there was no way to pry open the steel entrance. Defeated, I continued onward to the glacier.

In mid-summer, the ice field was slushy but still a behemoth. The river rushed underneath as the melt churned into itself with force. Beneath the top layer of slush, though, the ice's solid core extended for miles. I walked around the rim, scouting the area and looking for signs of human impact.

There were clear skies, and by midday the sun hastened the melting. Each time I ventured into the field thinking I may have seen an entranceway, my feet sank into the slush and soaked my socks as I plodded onward. After hours without any luck, I began to reconsider the separate facility. It may have been Lily's hallucination, or perhaps a metaphor I misread. Since the text felt literal, I hadn't given this due consideration. But in my trance and march, I became convinced the notion of a hidden passage in the ice was ludicrous. It was a strange sense of betrayal. She had lured me into a false belief by being carried away with her imagination. It might have been my exhaustion or my cycle of thoughts that fed on one another until I couldn't think of anything else, but for the first time I was mad at her. The story had always felt fantastic, but now I had my first evidence that it may have been embellished or simply untrue. If the second facility didn't exist, what else was to be questioned?

Confident I'd searched enough to declare the facility non-existent, I turned and headed back with pace. I'd wandered farther than planned and it would be some time before I returned to the relative security of the first facility.

The return of an out-and-back hike always seems to take longer. The landscape becomes annoyingly familiar, and each marker passed for a second time reminds how far there is to go. I was passing a distinct iceberg that had broken from the field when the obvious occurred to me. The boulder of ice had been the natural result of glaciation. As the ice melts or refreezes, masses calve and separate from the glacier.

Though the ice field would still gain mass in the winter, climate change would make its losses greater than its gains. On the Kenai Peninsula, the Exit Glacier has receded several miles in the past century. As you approach, signs mark the glacier's previous extent, beginning with a 1920 sign about three-and-a-half miles from the current glacial face. Even the 1990 sign is a few hundred yards away.

It was foolish to have spent all day tracing the rim of the field. When Lily was there, the field was probably fifteen percent larger. My path would have been deep in the field, and the previous edge would be farther out on dry solid ground. If there were a secret passageway, it would be nowhere near where I was looking.

Reenergized, I directed my view outward and looked for evidence again. I cursed myself for having spent the whole day looking in the wrong direction, but at least my aggravation could be directed at myself and not Lily.

In the end, it wasn't too hard finding the entrance when I wasn't being an idiot. Outside the rim of ice, the landscape remained rocky for a few dozen feet before plant life found purchase in seams of soil and shrubs and grass had sprung up. From a hillside, I scanned the area and could easily spot a gap in greenery and a small concrete recess descending into the earth.

I rushed to the entrance, again feeling uneasy about what I might find on the other side. The entry sat embedded in the earth like a bomb shelter with a concrete archway overhanging the doorframe. Soil and plant life had intruded on the margins of the concrete, and a steel grate covered a section of the ground outside the door beneath which lay a drainage system. A security camera stared downward from the corner over the door. To my surprise, its red indicator light was illuminated.

The unit may have been connected to a solar panel like the red bulbs in the other facility, but that wouldn't explain the clumps of discarded mud I now noticed clinging to the grate at my feet. I no longer felt alone. Since locating the facility days earlier, I'd felt a range of emotions—mostly a combination of curiosity and puzzlement, with occasional apprehension and unease—but with the sight of the camera crept in something new: dread. I checked my watch and noted there was still plenty of time left in the day, plenty of time to see beyond the other side of the door.

When I opened the unlocked door and called in, I hoped to hear nothing in response. Instead, a voice responded, "Give me a moment," in the tone of someone who was coming to answer the door of their suburban bungalow. The dread now mixed with astonishment. My sense of etiquette kicked in, and I found myself saying: "Oh hi, I didn't know anyone was home," as my host slowly climbed the stairs.

The man was probably in his late fifties, and he stood in the doorway, skeptical-like, as though he were gazing out at a solicitor or Jehovah's Witness. I extended my hand and introduced myself. He accepted it but then stood motionless. His brown eyes stared at me through thick eyeglasses, and his nose wiggled slightly as if to coerce me to speak. He must have been fresh out of the shower; he brushed his wet hair off his face, pressing the water droplets onto his olive-toned skin. There were wrinkles around his eyes and plenty of gray in his hair and beard.

It took some time to convince him I didn't wish him any harm. He was certain I was going to steal something or at least evict him.

I'm not here for you, I kept telling him. I'm just curious. I held out my business card as a credential, hoping it would be enough. When he looked it over and was persuaded I wasn't a government agent or worse, he invited me for a cup of tea.

I was surprised to find the place orderly, and for that matter, to find him so presentable, too. There wasn't debris strewn about like in the other facility, and care had been taken to make the living space habitable. He'd led me straight to the parlor, which had become his multifunctional living space. While fully packed bookshelves lined the room's exterior, the rest of the room had been partitioned like a studio apartment. A camp stove sat in an ad hoc kitchen of pots, cutting boards, and utensils in the corner, and on the room's opposite side a cot lay with bedding folded neatly at its foot. The room's central element was a wooden desk layered with books and loose-leaf pages of notes. Its swivel chair had been worn so severely that stuffing poked out from creases where the leather had burst.

Even though the electric lighting was on, the room had been filled with unlit candles. Every ledge and table had clusters of candles. He cautioned me away from an open flame on the bookshelf candlestick, noting he always left one burning for when the solar panel stopped working, which must have been often enough. It looked as though he'd shaved that morning and might have even ironed his shirt.

The only seating was the solitary desk chair, so we stood as we talked. Neither of us found our words too well.

* * *

Back in 1990, he'd been hired after a line-reading audition for what was described as an avant-garde performance piece in two phases. First, they shot a few corporate training videos. A costumer globbed him with makeup and prosthetics, and he read from a script in a studio. The second phase was more comprehensive and required a months-long commitment. It would be mostly improvised, they said, but the most important thing was never to drop character. Room, board, and travel would all be taken care of, so when they offered him the spot, it seemed an obvious choice.

Actors are common in behavioral sciences. It's one of the only ways to make it successful. Since a study needs to be contained and can't be conducted in public with variables to skew results, actors are a way to exert control. I pressed him for details on who he met with, a name, a description, and if it was at a permanent office, but he couldn't remember any of that. "It was a while ago. I mean, could you describe someone who gave you a job interview twenty-five years ago?"

As for the project itself, information was equally fuzzy. Most of his memory was about his failed attempt to sober up. He imagined there would be no access to alcohol and was going to use the time to detox. When he arrived and found the nearly endless supply of booze, the temptation became too much, and he eventually cracked. As he told it, he spent most of his time semi-drunk, rationalizing his intake as a means to occupy himself. "There was nothing to do," he recounted. "Seriously. Nothing. We took turns going outside. Once per day. Besides staying in character, that was our main instruction. It might not sound like a lot, but when it was your turn, it sure wasn't pleasant braving the cold. You'd have to wander around out there for an hour. On top of being bitter cold, it was boring, which only made you think of the cold more," he gave a false shudder. "They never told us much about what was happening. It was a psych experiment, I think."

I asked if he had been the one to have found Hector in the crevasse. He hadn't.

It was hard having him stay on topic. To be fair, it was

twenty-five years in the past, and, even though we were at the same site, his life was in a much different place. He couldn't remember anything about the participants. He wasn't sure they'd even met, and he didn't remember anyone named Lily or Hector.

His social skills were obviously rusty, and he seemed eager to return to his solitude. He'd humor me and answer questions as best he could, but I got the sense that, if it was all the same to me, I could show myself out at any point.

When I asked about the other professors, I had to clarify. "The other actors, that is. Who were they?"

"I never cared much for the others. If you've hung out with actors, you know how quickly they can irritate you. They're always performing. Trying to one-up each other's jokes or making everything theatrical."

And he continued on like this, musing about the dynamic between him and his colleagues. He had the habit of gnawing on a knuckle after speaking. His fist would find his mouth, and he'd give it a little bite, not enough to break the skin, but pronounced enough it probably hurt. There was no favored finger or hand, a random rotation ensured each digit was equally gnawed.

He said little about his current state. It was a free place to stay, and he didn't much like people anyhow. He had been spending his summers here for a few years while he worked on a screenplay and ate old supplies from the pantry. It saved money and let him clear his head.

It was a sensible enough story, but there was an unreliable quality to his narrative, stemming from the fact of who was telling it. On one hand, he was an articulate, thoughtful person with a tidy place and well-groomed physique; on the other, he was a recluse squatting in an abandoned research facility in the middle of nowhere. When I pressed him for his reasons he regurgitated standard hippy-dippy rationale. "The civilized world has become too hollow, you know. It's all about what you can sell. Selling a product or a lifestyle or an idea. Anything people will buy. And then those become consumed by what they buy. So, I wanted to go somewhere I could be away from all of that." Blah blah.

He made no mention of his acting career. My guess was it had stalled.

I wanted to continue interviewing him, but I could see I was beginning to press my luck. I stood to signal my intent to depart before asking a final question. "You said you left abruptly. Would you talk about that?"

"We weren't supposed to be put at risk. That's why we left. It wasn't my choice."

"So, you were forced to leave. How did you find your way back here?"

"I could ask you the same question."

***

I didn't spend another night in the facility. Sleeping nearby the stranger would've been unsettling, so, satisfied with what I'd uncovered, I packed my items and retraced the path out. In the days since my entry, blueberries had ripened along the trail. I gathered a handful and stood with the snack in my palm as I took a final look at the facility. The sky was overcast, and the shadows were getting long as the glacial breeze swept toward me, howling through the valley and rustling the trees. I turned and departed, making sure I'd be a few hours' walk away when I set up camp. The berries were too tart. I tried a few more to be sure, then abandoned the rest.

The Proposal

"It seems you're adjusting well?" I extend my arm so Dr. Samesong can wrap a rubber tube around my bicep to bulge a vein and extract blood. As he goes through the physical exam, I anticipate each step in the process and am shifting my body before he even has to ask.

"I'm fine, really. Honest."

"I believe you. Look away, please." The needle punctures my skin and slides in. He still tells me to look away even though I never do. "Peggy and I are still working through it ourselves. We feel responsible." He sticks a Band-Aid on my arm. I lean forward so he can press his stethoscope against my back and listen to my lungs. "All sounds good."

"Really? I've been smoking like a chimney." I fake a phlegmy cough.

"Could've fooled me." He pauses. "I'll be honest with you. You're in the best physical shape here. Now that—" he cuts himself off before he can say Quinn's name. "Well, anyhow, you're showing such progress, such a positive response to The Medicament, that we'd like to make a proposal." Normally he'd have moved to the door to open it for me. I'd been edging in that direction already. Instead, he sits and crosses his legs, casual-like. "Now, results show the reverse-aging abilities of The Medicament. To be honest, that was fully expected based on animal trials. What is less predictable however, is how the human body, while being treated with The Medicament, will respond when confronted with disease."

I breathe in and straighten my posture, not sure what he's proposing, "Do you mean—"

"Nothing serious, of course. We're not asking you to inject yourself with smallpox." His tone and pause suggest this is a joke. I don't react and he continues. "No, something much more common. Influenza."

"You want to give me the flu?"

"Try to. If The Medicament is as effective as we think it'll be, you won't even have a headache."

"I don't—"

"A-a-and—" he stutters, interrupting me, "—of course, you'll be compensated additionally, since this wasn't part of our contract."

"I'll have to think about—"

"An additional twenty thousand dollars."

After reading it through twice, I sign the new contract. Even if it's the worst flu imaginable, I can suck it up for twenty grand. He pulls a test tube from the refrigerator, spins it around in a centrifuge and administers the injection right then.

"It's just like a flu shot, really. Only stronger." The needle goes into my shoulder so it's tricky to watch this time. Instead, I stare ahead and wonder what other liquid diseases are stored in that fridge. "Don't tell the other guests about this. We don't want to play favorites."

* * *

As a celebration for my new earnings, I want a drink. When our compensation doubled, I was elated, but given the circumstance of Quinn's death, I had to keep my glee secret.

Enough time has passed. Even if it hasn't, I'm going to have a special drink, dammit.

The top shelf of the pantry is lined with hard liquor, but we've hardly touched it. We've mostly been on the wine. It starts with a glass at dinner that turns into the rest of the bottle afterward and maybe more depending on the mood. On some subconscious level, I think we've resolved to stay away from the hard stuff, because without hangovers as a deterrent, it'd be pretty easy to tie one on anytime. We don't want to be real drunks. Just social winos.

I pick a bottle of Scotch with a name I can't pronounce. The label describes the nose, color and finish with hyperbolic terms that make the liquid seem less distilled than divined. With the opportunity for a crisp, radiant, yet mysterious finish, I'll be able to feel both fancy and drunk.

It smells like I've unbottled a campfire when I pour it. To feel sophisticated, I swirl it and hold it to the light. It's hard to rate it, since I don't know what I'm looking for. I sip, and the fire moves from my nose into my mouth. If it's delicious, I can't tell; the flavor must be hidden underneath the bonfire. I intend to find it, but I'll need help.

* * *

The three of us are tanked. Thank God. Snapped out of the fugue state. We're passing the bottle back and forth and drinking straight from it. What once had made me wince now feels like an elixir. Like a smile in a bottle. Hector and Anna are smiling, too, so, yeah, that has to be true.

We're still working on a jigsaw puzzle. Apparently, you can redo jigsaw puzzles. It's not like you've cracked the secret of a puzzle after doing it once. It's the second time I've been fishing through pieces looking for the white foamy ones to complete Yosemite Falls.

I didn't last more than two pulls from the bottle before I spill the news about the flu shot. Super flu shot. They don't really care.

Anna confesses she didn't like Quinn too much. He was alright, she guesses, but really, he was a pretentious shit. He acted like she should be grateful for his presence. The sex was good-ish. Sex is always good-ish, right? Anna goes quiet. The venting had been helpful, but now she's remembering the rest. We raise a toast to the pretentious shit, each of us with a hand on the nearly empty bottle.

"I wanna show you something," Hector says, rolling up his sleeve. He's got a cigarette dangling from his mouth that's been unlit for at least five minutes. He relights it like he needs its power to do whatever he's gonna do next. With the lighter's flame still going, he waves it back and forth under his arm like it's a little trick. Then, wait for it, he mumbles, he holds the flame still beneath his forearm and lets the skin crisp up. Anna shrieks, and I jump right up. Just wait, he says, not losing focus. The flame goes up, and he plops his elbow on the table, giving us a full view of the damage.

It's sooty and black... but it's hard to... he wipes away the ash. I clutch the bottle closer to me, then take a big drink. Anna's eyes don't leave Hector's display as she motions for me to pass the bottle. Well, damn, now we have to finish it.

* * *

A sleepover, that'll be fun. We'll all sleep on the couches. Or, like, pass out cuz we canna be botha to move. My eyes dinna focus. I'm nearing the spins. I canna fall asleep. The lights over the doorway wone stop blinking. One of dem.

I canna ignore it. On and off. On and off. A rhythmic

pulse. The others are out. Hector snoring and Anna curled into a ball like a cat. Annacat. I wanna turn off dat light. On and off. Ima gonna toss a, a sock over it. I get up. Stare at the offending bulb. Get right up in its face. I'll show you, Mr. Lightbulb. Second from the left. Quinn's room.

4/27/1991

Mom,

Remember when Mrs. Pappas gave me a C+ on that short story because I didn't follow the instructions? She said my story needed a beginning, a middle, and an end. Well, you were the one who told me to start in the middle. It would be a lot more interesting to let the setup come after I'd thrown the reader into the middle of the action. I tried to blame you, even though you didn't care about the C+.

Plenty of people follow the instructions, you said. It's the fastest path to mediocrity. You might pass the class, you said, but no one will remember a word you wrote. I do wonder if Mrs. Pappas remembers that C+ story.

Love,
Lily

Storage

The lounge doesn't have blackout curtains like my bedroom, so morning comes in with aggression. I know better than to still dread hangovers, but I'm grateful none has come. Even so, the daylight has me awake earlier than desired. I lie still, groggy eyes looking out the unshaded window when Anna walks past outside, resolute for the early morning. It's unexpected, but not enough to rouse me up to investigate. It's not as cold these days, and the snow has begun melting as the days lengthen. In the perma-shade of the mountain peaks, the snow remains, but elsewhere the once total whiteness has changed to a wet earth complemented by sprigs of green. The deciduous trees have started to bud, and I've spotted some squirrels and other critters dotting the landscape as they've emerged from hibernation. I should follow Anna's example and take a walk outside. Instead, I refuse to rub the sleep from my eyes, and I try my best for more sleep.

I toss and turn with a combination of exhaustion and restlessness. My body wants to sleep but my mind is wide awake. This could be the start of the flu. Fatigue is a symptom for everything. Probably didn't help that my immune system took a slap in the face from a half liter of whisky.

Giving up on sleep, I rise to take a shower. My body is different. It might not show change like a before-and-after diet photograph, but I'm not the same. When change happens gradually, it's hard to notice. However, Hector's showmanship with his flesh was impossible to ignore. Not only did he do it without pain, he healed instantaneously. I'm not bold enough to ignite my skin, but I can test myself with less drama. Apart from the cut, I haven't noticed physical change. It's happening inside me. I'm becoming younger and healthier. Maybe I don't feel pain either. I don't remember the needle pricks hurting before, but maybe I just wasn't thinking about them.

I want to feel pain. Something light. I can't bring myself to intentionally stub my toe even though it might not hurt at all. Or whack my funny bone. And cutting myself is too gory. The shower runs around me as I picture my blood dripping down the drain.

My hair droops in front of my face. I isolate a single strand and, before I can think about it further, I pluck it from my head. Nothing. No pain. Didn't feel anything. I try again, and in my haste, I rip a whole clump out. Nothing.

But it's not like I'm numb. I can still feel my body. The warmth of the shower, the chill of the air, my feet on the tile. And pleasure. My hand wanders downward. I breathe in. I can definitely still feel pleasure.

* * *

Anna insists it's warm out. There's still snow in places, but it's soft and slushy. She wants to show me something. When we're out of view of the facility, I ask, "I didn't just imagine what Hector did last night, right?"

"His freak show? No, that happened," she says with a hint of disdain. She's walking quickly, and she's right about the warmth; I'm beginning to sweat.

"Slow down a minute. I want to try something," I say. She stops, and I look around to confirm no one is watching us.

"I'm going to close my eyes. And I want you to hit me."

She looks away. Suspicious and a bit disgusted. "What?"

"I don't think we feel pain. None of us. Haven't you noticed?"

"Yes. But—"

"So, what happens when we should feel pain and don't. I want to see if I feel anything." She faces me. Curious now. "Slap me. Seriously." I close my eyes. "Try and make it sting. Don't tell me—"

I'm interrupted by her hand across my face. Except, it's not a slap. Her fingers gently drift over my cheek in an odd and slow caress. It's soothing as each fingertip glides over me, but I'm annoyed she didn't hit me. Not to mention substituting a slap with an awkward face massage.

"I told you to hit me."

"I did. Don't make me do it again."

"Once more. With my eyes open this time."

"No," she turns and keeps walking. "Come on. This is important."

I follow silently for a few minutes before I think to ask, "Did it hurt your hand?"

She shakes her head. Then tilts her head onward, "We're almost there."

We step across a footbridge above a small stream. The spring thaw is evident as chunks of ice float over the rushing water. In another month, the melting snow could double its depth. The once massive icicles have slendered but still dangle from the bridge as they drip rapidly.

The facility is at least a mile back now. We haven't been following any discernible path, so I puzzle over how Anna found her way here. She hasn't been taking many trips outside that I've noticed. It's unlikely she stumbled upon whatever it is she's about to show me.

It's a calm day, so the wind doesn't overwhelm the sound like it usually does. The air passing over the top of the mountains produces a striking and distant pitch that makes our position in the crater feel secure and protected from the extreme force beyond. Birds whistling from the cliff faces and the timbre of the creek combine to produce a pleasant ambience. It's the sound of a nature I've known before. A nature we choose to escape into, not the one of the unforgiving ice field.

Anna snaps me from my reverie. "Here it is."

Hidden in the mountainside is a small opening I would've missed had she not pointed it out. Two rock slabs lean into each other to form a natural overhang. We crouch beneath to peer into the rear of the semi-cave. Anna pulls a flashlight from her coat and focuses the beam on a square frame of wood. The light doesn't penetrate too deep, but I recognize the structure as a mineshaft. It's not much larger than a person; one could squeeze in if they wanted.

"Have you been inside?" I ask.

"Yes."

"And?"

"You'll have to see for yourself."

"After you," I say with wobbly sarcasm.

Beyond the narrow passageway, we crawl into a larger room, buttressed by struts that look as though they may splinter and give at any moment. Anna senses my unease and reassures, "This will only take a minute." There are additional tunnels leading out from the room deeper into the mountainside. She directs my attention to one. It's difficult to see with the minimal light, but the cave-like room is packed with a disordered array of metal. My attention is first drawn to the mess of computers and monitors haplessly clogging the entrance. Stethoscopes, IV stands, and other medical equipment are scattered about as if they have been thrown in without care.

In the room's rear, the beam of light focuses on the familiar shape of a wheelchair. Except it's not made of modern steel. No, it looks to be mostly wooden, like an antique. The tools adjacent to the wheelchair look of a similar vintage—rubber tubing and rusted wide-bowed forceps and calipers.

But it's the clothing that provides the most evident timeline. Mixed in with the miscellaneous equipment are lab coats, smocks, and hospital scrubs. The white coats don't follow any progression apart from their wear; but the nurses' uniforms progress from the familiar modern scrubs—like those we see Peggy in every day—to plastic aprons and smocks to closed-neck dresses and caps.

"Do they want us to find all of this?"

"What do you mean? They showed me."

* * *

Outside the claustrophobic mine, we sit on the hillside while Anna debriefs me. After Quinn died, she began spending more time with Dr. Samesong and Peggy. She would linger after the counseling sessions and continue to talk. It was their authority she found comforting, and she knew she might exhaust my and Hector's sympathy tolerance.

During these after-hours sessions, Dr. Samesong and Peggy began to open up, shift from the doctor/patient relationship to more of a give-and-take friendship. They showed her their living quarters, which she admitted were underwhelming.

"To be honest, I thought they might be propositioning me. Like, readying me for some *ménage à trois*. Their demeanor. It's so hard to read, though. I mean, I still don't know if they're an item." I nod along, urging her back on topic. "Anyhow, when they took me out here, I was nervous. We'd strayed so far away, I started thinking about how I didn't really know them at all and maybe I'd misplaced my trust entirely. But then, they showed me this storage room. That's what they called it. They said they wanted me to know. But if I could keep the secret, I'd be compensated."

"Twenty thousand dollars?"

"Exactly."

Either this has happened before. Or they want us to think it has.

"So what is Hector keeping secret?"

* * *

On our way back down the mountain, Anna and I form a plan for talking to Hector. We had spilled our secrets voluntarily, albeit I did so when drunk and Anna in response, but Hector might not be forthcoming. His behavior made us uneasy. To be fair, we might be coping differently. There's no proper way to respond to something like this. Still, his cavalierness and glee were unsettling.

We resolve to question him directly. He's normally a straightforward person, or was, so he'd respond best if he didn't feel like we were trying to trick him. For a moment, we are concerned about privacy, that we might be interrupted by Peggy or maybe even surveilled. We laugh off the fear. We're not in control, regardless, so fuck it.

Before we track down Hector, I stop in my room to rinse off. My notes and pages laid out on my desk seem so trivial. Months of work, of emotion and effort, looking meaningless and empty, like a forgotten wheelchair. I want to punch the wall, to feel something, but I know pain won't come. Something has happened, is happening. The person who wrote those pages is gone.

I resist the urge to destroy them. It's an intense urge, like it needs to be done if I'm going to embrace this new version of myself. Instead, I read the opening page, sit and revisit the thoughts I had when I'd first arrived. The complications and confusion are there and they still are, they've just altered. I don't want to erase her. I want to preserve her.

I recommit to finishing my project. Something is wrong here. I cannot deny that. As my body continues to change, I want to cling to what I can control—my voice.

* * *

The ashtray is overflowing red in front of us. To stub out a cigarette, I need to use the butt to push aside the old ones. It's gross, but none of us want to leave the table. Anna and I have explained what we know. What we've been told. Hector listens, his expression interested, but not giving anything away. He's neither surprised nor cagey.

Eventually he responds, "I'm not sure I have anything for you. Not like that, at least." He speaks with a friendly tone, like the one from before the thaw and the change. "I mean, I think I know what's happening. But I couldn't bring myself to ask them. And I can't bear to say it out loud."

Anna and I exchange glances.

"Hector."

"I can't," he says, shaking.

"Please," I urge. "Whatever it is. You can tell us."

"No. I don't know anything for sure," he lights another cigarette. "I have ideas, but I try not to think about it."

"You're being awfully vague."

"Well, there's one thing I can tell you. They offered you twenty thousand, you say?"

"Yes. Twenty thousand. Each."

"Okay." He stubs out his Redlight. "I'm being honest when I say I don't know why, but they offered me fifty. Fifty thousand."

"For what?"

"They seemed to think I knew already. They said I had been recruited."

"What's that supposed to mean?" Anna asks.

"I wish I could tell you. They went through a questionnaire with me. Not too different from the ones they've been giving us in our weekly exams. I answered honestly like I always do and they offered the money."

"Okay, but you must have said something different than usual," I say, trying to tease something out of him. "Think about what you might've said that would've had them offer you a new deal."

He rubs his chin, contemplating. "I don't know. I told them there was a moment in the crevasse I didn't think I was going to make it. I hoped I'd make it out, of course, but it was there, a flash of a thought that I was done for. Like when you're nearly in a car accident. Or wobble on the edge of a cliff and can see how it could play out. That's what it felt like right before I passed out. Like I was on the precipice." He pauses, grabs his pack of Redlights but decides against it and places them back. "I guess they felt sorry for what happened. I don't know why, though. I told them I felt fine. Great even. I was kinda embarrassed for thinking I might die out there." He stands and moves towards the pinball machine, signaling he is done with the conversation. "Oh, and they asked me if I were angry with them. I didn't understand what they meant and they asked again. I laughed to myself. They saved my life, of course I wasn't angry."

Next

With Hector giving us nothing but cryptic responses, we have few options besides confronting Peggy and Dr. Samesong. They'll know we revealed our secrets to each other, but if they rescind the money offer, so be it.

They aren't upset. In fact, they seem vaguely proud, and they're happy to talk to us. They're so accommodating in hearing our concerns it's almost irritating. Still, the conversation is no more revealing than the one we'd had with Hector. Like a psychiatrist, they answer each question with another question. Their statements are contorted and prefaced: "Do you think…" turning it into a hypothetical question.

"What aren't you telling us?"

"Do you think we would keep anything from you?"

"Yes."

"Why would you think that?"

It's like having a conversation with an M. C. Escher drawing. Every time you're about to grasp its meaning, it slips away into a paradox that leads nowhere. I pause before framing each question, trying to head off a slippery response. The key is not answering their questions either.

"Do you have our best interests at heart?"

"Is there any reason you think that we wouldn't?"

"If you don't, you've gone through an awful lot to convince us that you do. If you do, all the secrecy makes your motives suspicious. Do you have any idea what you're doing?"

A long pause. "What do you think?" Dr. Samesong says, making direct eye contact.

There's something in his stare I haven't seen before. He is usually so confident, breezing through misgivings, like he's done so many times before. This time though, it's like a plea, like he's asking me for help. I work it out in my head. They aren't playing dumb. They're as clueless as we are. They aren't being elusive because of any strategy. We've had faith that one of them was in control here, but that was misguided.

"Who's in charge?"

"Do you think you might be asking the right questions, now?" Dr. Samesong says before letting out a sigh and turning to his notes.

Anna begins to waver. She abandons the questions and unloads. It's a long monologue, full of fear and sadness and she isn't particularly articulate. The same scramble of words is happening in my head too; I'm just not verbalizing it. They nod and sympathize and reassure, but she's starting to unravel and become hysterical. Peggy retrieves a blanket from the cupboard and drapes it over Anna's shoulders. She clings to it as she continues, making a fist around its edge. I'm frozen as I watch her pour out raw emotion in stuttered speech. "I don't, I mean, I'm not—" she inhales a sharp audible breath. "—please let me talk to someone. Please. I wish I'd never…"

I'm perversely calm. I find myself rising and walking out. They do not attempt to dissuade me. I mutter something about needing a moment to breathe. Banding together with Anna had felt sensible but witnessing her fall off the edge makes me feel like I'm going to be dragged down with her. She's working through it, however she can; I'm not abandoning her, I'm respecting her process.

It's quiet.

As I close the door to my room, questions swirl in my head. With each one, the imaginary Dr. Samesong in my mind responds with another maddening question. If they were trying to unnerve us, they have succeeded. After whatever The Medicament has done to my body, I do not fear physical harm. From them or anything else. It should be a relief.

I still have my wits. Searching for answers might drive me crazy, but I can't help myself. Anna is trying to cope through talking, but it's making her sound mad. Hector is retreating into blissful ignorance.

I'm going to work through this with writing. Even if the words don't make sense. I'll scribble down until a theme emerges.

After three pages and an aching hand, I have calmed slightly. I edit and organize. My thoughts circled around the underlying questions—What couldn't Hector bear to ask? What is it they won't tell us? What do I need to figure out for myself?

I draw a giant T on a fresh piece of paper. On the left Side I write: What I know. On the right: Why?

***

What I Know
I feel no pain.
There is equipment from decades ago.
They aren't telling us anything

Why?
This has happened before.
They don't know anything, either.

I abandon the chart and take out a new piece of paper. I write down the only thing I know to be true in giant letters.

I am alive.

And I cross it out.

Stable

They aren't actors. Actors aren't that good. When Hector makes a joke, it's real. When Anna sobs, it's real. When Dr. Samesong reacts, it's real. They might not be actors, but they're playing roles, like we all do. We become different people when the moment demands it. Whether that means being the leader, or the empath, or the stabilizer, we all shift into these roles without thinking about it. Without acting.

Peggy and Dr. Samesong have better practice in their roles. They're well-rehearsed because they've done this before. Anna and Hector and I are still learning; we're still feeling our way through our part. We're on stage in front of an audience, and we don't know our lines.

I'm too afraid to stop taking The Medicament. I want to take it. It's the key to what's happening here, all the horror and uncertainty, but I worry what might happen if I stop, what I might lose.

Before, I used to have bad days, times when I felt sick or slept poorly, yes, but also days when I was just kinda bleh. A malaise would set in; it wouldn't linger, but I'd feel uninspired and would drift from one activity to the next until the good days returned. Now, it's only good days. If I had made a daily word cloud since coming here, there'd be no mention of words like frazzled or worried or bored. Even with the isolation, I'm iquisitive and sharp and determined. I'm optimized.

I'm a human incarnation of an inspirational poster, the best goddamn version of myself.

It's not an addiction. I don't feel cravings or withdrawal before my dosage. It's an automatic process, like breathing or swallowing. Once a day, they'll hand me a pill in a paper cup and a glass of water. And I'll continue to take it. That part I can handle.

* * *

The hysteria has dissipated, and we're treading back into normalcy. Dr. Samesong and Peggy continue to guide us, but it's become clear they don't have all the answers. There's no other option, so we lean on their support even if it's fantasy.

Escape is as much an impossibility as refusing The Medicament. We are surrounded by wilderness without access to any lines of communication. Even if we could escape, that would mean the end to the treatment, the end of The Medicament.

Routine and patience have become allies in survival. Managing each day without fear means clinging to the familiar. It's counterintuitive, but the mundane has become the goal. It's the relief from madness.

I talk with the other guests, with Dr. Samesong and Peggy, keeping the conversation light and simple. I exercise and go for walks, read and write, watch movies, and make pleasant meals. The urge to act has given way to quiet resolve. I am pacing myself. My calendar has June 21 circled. The deadline still approaches.

The Tour

It's our weekly appointment. We're still following the schedule. Dr. Samesong is impressed with my progress. He says I'm in "perfect" health. He asks how I've been sleeping, but he already knows I've been sleeping well. I point to the light bulbs above the doorway. He smiles and says, "I'd almost forgotten they were there."

"You don't monitor them?"

"We don't have the resources. Or motivation." It's a startling admission.

It prompts me to ask the question I've been wavering over the past few days, "Are you a doctor?"

"Yes, yes. Of course. But you need to understand something about medicine. Most of my job involves being the most confident person in the room, even when I'm clueless. A lot of being a doctor is guesswork. Looking at odds and narrowing possibilities." The manner in which he speaks makes me think he's reciting his lines. He starts using his hands to gesture for the rest of the monologue. "For example, you're in perfect health, like I said. But I don't have any idea why. Science. If patients knew how clueless doctors are, they'd never trust us. That's what the white coat is for."

"Okay," I try to pivot, unsatisfied with the confident pitch, "But you basically admitted you're not in charge here. So, let me ask, who is?"

"Ha. Everyone has a boss, right?" He reads my unamused face. "I wish I could say, but I couldn't tell you even if I wanted to. NDA's and that sort of thing." He swivels back to a filing cabinet and retrieves a paper with SL Corporation letterhead. "I know it might be an unsatisfying answer, but corporate politics, you know?" He hands me the paper, which, at a glance, is rife with legalese.

I say nothing, hand it back, and turn to leave.

"Oh, I almost forgot," he says, rising from his chair. "Your thumbprint will not restrict access anymore. You will be able to enter any room in the facility. Even our rooms. Just make sure you knock first." The last bit is an attempt at humor I let fall flat. "We want to restore your faith in the project. If it seems like we've been keeping things hidden, that's only been for your safety. Or, safety isn't the right word. Comfort. Though it might be hard to see, we are trying to do good."

My hand is on the door handle now.

"If you do decide to explore, try to have an open mind." He places extra emphasis on "if," discouraging exploration while also infecting me with curiosity. He wants to make it seem like it's my choice, but really, I've been given instructions.

I might as well turn the tables, "Would you come with me?"

* * *

He lets me lead the way through the annex. "A lot of storage rooms," I say after the third consecutive door reveals rice, pasta, and canned goods. We've also opened closets filled with toilet paper, linens, and cleaning supplies.

"An entire year's worth," he says matter-of-factly.

Peggy passes us in the hallway, says hello, and makes a

checkmark on her clipboard. "She's still at it, huh?" I ask when she's out of earshot.

"It's something to do."

I move methodically: walk to each door, place my finger on the plate, watch the indicator turn green, open it to observe the unremarkable contents, and proceed to the next one. If Dr. Samesong is bored, he's not showing it. He's polite and charming as usual, making a running commentary as I complete my inspection. "When I first arrived, I thought I wouldn't last a week. The cold and the sterility and everything. But you adjust, am I right? You start to wonder how people back in the real world put up with going to work eight hours a day. How does anyone have the time to read a book? A twenty-four-hour day feels so constricting. I mean—"

I'm so wrapped up with the efficiency of my search, I almost don't react when I discover the room of filing cabinets. It's dull and utilitarian, but it's different than the others. I notice each cabinet labeled with one of the guests' names. I pull open the one labeled "Lily" and pull out a folder. Dr. Samesong stops babbling so I can read.

The subject displays a positive reaction to The Medicament. Progress is as anticipated.

This is the only commentary on the page. That and a bunch of scribblings that look like words but aren't legible. Like someone trying to look like they were taking diligent notes. On another page there's nothing but a doodle of a smiley face wearing sunglasses. I place the folder back into the file, and Dr. Samesong shrugs sheepishly.

When I open the door leading to the basement, Dr. Samesong makes a face I can't interpret. Nevertheless, I proceed and he follows. I expect it to be darker in the basement, but the lighting is identical. Soft fluorescence. The layout, however, is not the same. While a portion matches the upper level, a network of hallways tunnels farther into the hillside. Checking each door would take hours. Now, I understand Dr. Samesong's indeterminate look, which conveyed, "If you must, I am willing."

"I think I'll have lunch first," I say as he holds his breath, "before I come back and explore on my own later." He suppresses a sigh of relief.

***

If I'm going to navigate the basement, I'm going to be exhaustive. Whatever secrets the facility might hold, they'd be kept underground, I tell myself. I bring a notebook so I don't reframe my reactions later. My notes are sincere and immediate.

***

Notes… Labeling the stairwell (Door 0) and to its right (Door 1), I proceed in sequence along the right side of the hall unless otherwise noted. See diagram.

Door (0) - Stairwell to upper level and laboratory.

Door (1) - Storage. Canned goods. Vegetables. Beans. Sauces.

Door (2) - Laundry. Washing machines. Dryers. Linens.

Door (3) - 4 Bunk beds. Empty.

Door (4) - 4 Bunk beds. Empty.

Door (5) - 4 Bunk beds. Empty.

Door (6) - 4 Bunk beds. Empty.

I make it to Door 18 before abandoning the mission for the day; I'm not even close to halfway. Either they're expecting more people to come or more have been here already.

* * *

At night, the silence in my room is suffocating. I find Peggy and ask her for a record player. As always, she's apologetic that I had to even ask. Like room service, she's back at my door within minutes, a phonograph and speakers tucked beside her on a rolling cart.

"You didn't tell me what records to bring," she apologizes. "I didn't want to insult you with my poor taste, so I brought a mix of everything. I hope you'll find something."

"That's alright. I'll manage."

"Are you sure? It's no trouble for me—"

"Goodnight, Peggy. Thank you."

The record plays through side one, though I'm not conscious of it. The needle traces the innermost groove, nodding as a metronome and rocking me to sleep like a boat in harbor.

Chapter 6

I didn't like him, not really. I mean, he was kind of attractive, I guess. Whatever looks he did have were hidden under a dopey baseball cap. Still, after weeks of conversation when I didn't speak much Spanish and everyone else didn't speak much English, I appreciated a dope in a dopey cap more than I should have.

He ordered his drink like he wanted me to know he spoke Spanish, or, at least, knew exactly as much Spanish as could be read off the cerveza poster behind the bar.

"Have you found that beach that's free of tourists, or is that just a fantasy?"

Not a terrible opener. "Well, if I'd been there, it wouldn't be tourist-free anymore, would it?"

"You don't look like a tourist."

"That's because I left my fanny pack in the cab."

"Good one. Sorry, don't let me interrupt you. You're reading." If he hadn't sounded sincere, or if he'd made a pseudo-intellectual comment about my book, or if he hadn't looked content sitting on the stool watching the fuzzy soccer game on TV, or if I had spoken more than ten consecutive words to a person in the past week, I might have just returned to my reading.

But I found myself folding my book across my lap and even re-initiating conversation. "Who's playing?" I couldn't have cared less.

"Well, it looks like the static giants and the dark blurs."

"That's racist."

"The, the uniforms," he spat out quickly, not sure if I were joking.

"No, I mean, giants. You wouldn't say midgets, right? So why is it okay to discriminate against giants."

"Not really racist, though, is it? More like height insensitive."

"I think Tolkien identifies giants as a distinct race."

"But they're the same species? Like a giant and dwarf could produce offspring? Or maybe just infertile offspring like a mule."

"My name's Lily," I said, hoping to steer away from a conversation that had become both oddly sexualized and bestial. This was the human interaction I had been craving.

"I'm Mat. With one t." He gestured the one with his index finger.

"I'll try not to walk—" I stopped mid-sentence, realizing he'd heard whatever lame joke I was going to make, and better ones, many times before.

"Hey, don't tread on me," he saved me with the lamer joke and offered me the chair next to his. We talked and drank cervezas and sometimes glanced at a screen with static soccer, which we sometimes called soccer and sometimes called football. The bar began to fill up, and we started to shout to each other as the fuzzy TV soccer turned to crackly-speaker music.

Next, he would move in so he could hear me better, then he'd tilt his head so his ear was next to my mouth, then he'd touch the small of my back, for balance, of course, and if I didn't recoil, he'd keep his hand there and move it just a bit while he looked me in the face, then he'd ask me to dance, no, if I could dance, to shift the pressure onto me, and then another drink wouldn't even be a question, but a statement, just like when I would say I should get going, but that wouldn't really be a statement but a question.

Except that didn't happen.

He excused himself, saying he needed a smoke. When he left, I looked around the smoke-filled room, an ashtray on every table. His dopey cap stayed at the table and waited for him with me. After it became clear he wasn't coming back, and I'd had enough of the *ruido* and the cervezas, I left the cap and the bar.

* * *

The heat made me sweat out most of the alcohol during the night, but there was enough left to make my head swell come morning. I checked at the desk to see if any mail had come, but still nothing.

"*Uno noche mas?*"

"At least. Yes. *Sí.*"

Guest house life meant I had to eat out for every meal. Food didn't sound so good, but I wandered over to the restaurant for a morning coffee. I heard my name seconds before I saw the dopey cap. I wasn't the only one looking for a caffeine jumpstart.

"I see you got your cap back."

"Oh yeah. Sorry for disappearing last night. I should have said something."

"It's not a problem," I said, not sure if it was. There were plenty of empty tables, but he didn't make an issue of his weird departure, so I didn't either, and I joined him.

"I was thinking of going to see the ruins today. Have you been?"

If there were ruins nearby, I didn't know about them. I

didn't show my ignorance, "Not yet."

"I've heard they're great, like, not touristy or anything, you know, real authentic."

"Can ruins be inauthentic?"

"You know what I mean."

"I know what you mean," I'd given him enough of a hard time. "Sure, that sounds good." I was too hungover to do any writing, anyhow.

"Oh, yeah. Um, we could probably convince a taxi to take us or something."

"If it's—"

"No, of course. Would you like to go?"

"Sure. Sounds interesting."

"We'll go after breakfast, or, er, coffee."

We finished our coffee and made small talk about the surrounding area. I repeated everything I told him from the previous night. He complimented my memory for remembering his itinerary.

"I'll take care of the bill if you want to get ready and meet outside in a minute."

"Thanks," I said with a mixed tone of gratefulness and begrudging. It would have been awkward to insist on paying the equivalent of fifteen cents for the coffee, but I didn't want to establish the trend of him paying. He strolled to the counter and, as I left, he mumbled something to the waitress in Spanish. She apparently didn't understand him either, so he had to repeat himself; she nodded and retrieved a bottle from the shelf and added it to the dregs of his coffee. While he swirled it around the cup, I ducked out.

There was bad news and good news. The bad news was taxi drivers didn't want to take people anywhere apart from downtown or the airport.

"And the good news?"

"Ever been on a motorcycle?"
"That's good news?"
"It's authentic."

* * *

The roads were dusty and bumpy, but the breeze and smell of orange groves made it hard not to romanticize. I was grateful my moto-driver hadn't been zipping around with the recklessness of Mat's. We agreed to pay them half when we arrived and half when they took us back. They didn't look like the sort to ditch us out there; they looked like the sort who had slightly altered their plans to hang out all day, but it was still good to feel in control of the situation.

Dismounting the motorcycle proved more difficult than expected; I stumbled toward Mat to give him a wobbly high-five when we arrived. There wasn't much around. A few shanty-like structures sold snacks to people in plastic chairs under the shade of Coca-Cola umbrellas. Some chickens fought for scraps. The moto-drivers joined a group of other moto-drivers who were expertly reclining in reverse position on their seats, arms slouched on the handlebars, feet dangling over the tailpipe.

"Shall we?" he said with a dramatic open-palmed gesture.

"Why, yes. Oh wait, I'm almost out of film. Shoot."

"They probably have some you can buy," he pointed to the shanty-kiosks. When I looked skeptical, he added, "I'll check it out." Without waiting for affirmation, he wandered over and shouted back to me, "Hey, do you want anything else while I'm at it?"

I shook my head.

He talked to the shopkeeper and, to fill in the language gap, he began to mime camera and film. The shopkeeper wrinkled his face and shook his head, and Mat turned around to give me the thumbs down and shrug. Still, he stayed and said something else to the shopkeeper, holding up two fingers. Moments later, he returned to me holding two cans of cerveza, offering one to me.

"Hydration for the walk."

"That's not how it works."

"Then, cervezas for the walk," I instinctively checked my watch, "Oh, and here, they had postcards, since you can't take any pictures."

"Thanks," I said, taking the gifts and cracking the can open. "Gross. It's warm. Basically hot."

"That's how they do it here. I'll take it if you don't want it."

***

The ruins didn't look like the postcard. When the photographer had taken the picture, they'd waited for perfect conditions to create mystique—a twilight mist with the vines freshly blossomed. Now, the summer heat had roasted all the greenery to a burnt yellow. With the bright sun overhead, the ruins possessed little magic, and the tumbled pillars and stone steps resembled an abandoned construction site of stray concrete masses. We dutifully walked through with reverence, trying to appear less underwhelmed than we were. The shade on the far edge of the clearing gave us an excuse to stay a bit longer. His dopey cap started to look like a good choice.

We weren't the first to have had the same idea. In the shade, there was an unfortunate amount of garbage consolidating in wind-forged clusters. "I probably shouldn't care, but I don't want to add to the mess," I said, tapping my cerveza can.

"You finished?" he said with a hint of disappointment.

"You're right, it did a good job pretending to hydrate." I was somewhere between dehydrated, hungover, and starting a fresh buzz.

Mat reached for his pocket, hesitated, rested his hands on his lap, then reached for his pocket again, where he retrieved a wonky tube of paper and a lighter. It took a moment to light, probably sweaty. "It's basically schwag, but it does the job," he said as he exhaled and passed the joint to me.

It burned unevenly as I took a drag, the ash crumbling and wads of paper and green falling to the ground, "Sorry." I passed the mess back to him.

He licked his finger and performed emergency first aid on the paper. "There we go." I declined another hit when he offered. We looked at garbage piles and stony ruins, and while he kept relighting the lost cause of a joint, I mentally composed and edited a line about the great juxtapositions of human civilization—piles of ruins and piles of garbage—but couldn't find the right words.

* * *

I checked back at the desk to see if any late mail had come. When he reached below to retrieve an envelope, I held my breath until I saw my mom's handwriting. I thanked the desk clerk and tucked it away, regretting having given her the address where I'd be holed up a while. He asked me something I didn't understand, then clarified, "*Dinero,*" blushing for being curt when asking me to pay my bill.

"Oh, of course." While I fumbled for cash, my eyes caught with Mat, and I blurted out, "Hey, do you want to share rooms? I don't know about you, but I'm on a budget."

"Um, I mean—"

"There's an extra bed just sitting there untouched."

"Well, I've already paid for the whole week. So…"

"Oh, nevermind." Either he was quite the gentleman or wanted to look like he was quite the gentleman. "Well, I'm going to take a nap. Meet up later?"

"Sure."

"What room are you in? I'll come find you."

"Let's just meet in the lobby. Around seven?"

* * *

Lily,

I need you to know something. It's been weighing on me, and I could never bring myself to say it in person, but it's been nagging at me for so long. You need to know the truth about your father.

He was an addict. I could never prove it. He'd keep his stash hidden. Sometimes I'd catch him, and he'd say it was only aspirin; he told me he had headaches. But I never once saw a bottle of aspirin in the medicine cabinet. I'd hear him every morning. He thought I was still asleep. I could hear the cap and the rattle, the swallow, and the rattle again as he tucked it away.

I wasn't dumb. I'd heard about the pills people were taking. Pain pills that'd dope you up, like the ones Elvis was hooked on. I could see it in your father's eyes. Like he was there, but not quite, like he'd be drifting away someplace else. I tried not to judge. I'd only known him a little while before I'd gotten pregnant. He had his demons, we could work through it, but only if he were honest. But he made me think I was totally off base. Made me think I was crazy.

While he was out running an errand, I tore apart the house looking for those pills. Nothing. Every drawer and closet and cupboard and shelf. I pulled it all out and sifted through. He came home earlier than expected and found the house in a mess.

He denied it all. You were only a baby. He didn't raise his voice, but you were crying in your crib the whole time. He wanted to comfort you, but I wouldn't let him. I couldn't trust him. I screamed in his face and told him to step back. His face changed. He looked at me in a way I'd never seen before. He told me I'd made a big mistake. He called me an idiot. And he left.

The next day, they pulled his car out of that lake.

I'm sorry to tell you like this. I don't mean to burden you with this knowledge, especially while you're out finding yourself, but I want us to be honest with each other. I'm not looking for forgiveness or using this as an excuse for anything I've done, but you deserve to know the truth.

I'm sure you're having a wonderful time exploring the world.

Love,
Mom

I tossed the letter aside and gave the matter little thought. She didn't talk about my father much, but she still seemed perplexed by my lack of curiosity. This new information didn't change much as far as I was concerned, but I guess my mom needed to get it off her chest.

The oscillating fan spun back and forth, the notes on my desk fluttering underneath their paperweights each time the breeze returned. Since it was a lost writing day, I swore to be productive in other ways. I leafed through the back pages of my magazine, scanning the journals that didn't charge a reading fee to see if I'd missed any. I cross-referenced with the rejection letters that had been piling up. A ten-dollar reading fee wouldn't be too bad, right?

The bed had been made, but the sheets weren't changed; the damp from the night was still present. I pulled up the pin to stop oscillation and aimed the fan at the bed. If I fell asleep, it was dreamless.

Night came eventually. I took a shower and got dressed but there were still thirty minutes to kill. I might as well spend them in the lobby where there were people to watch. It was prime check-in hour, and guests stood at the desk while the clerk marked points of interest on a map. Even in Spanish, I could probably recite the spiel from memory, its rhythm unchanged from guest to guest. Lizards climbed the walls with their frantic spurts and pauses, a delight I'd never get used to. The red protrusion that bounced beneath the males' necks must have worked for some or they wouldn't have kept trying.

Mat still had his cap on when he arrived twenty minutes late. His eyes were red enough to tell me I had some catching up to do.

"Do you want to get some dinner or—" I started, realizing there wasn't really an alternative.

"I should probably eat something," he agreed.

The menu had enough I could identify, or at least identify which meat was in it. He said I could decide between *pollo* and *carne*.

"It's funny that we give animals other names when we eat them. In Spanish they call it *pollo*, but they have a different word for a live chicken. *Gallina*, I think. But for us, chicken is chicken is chicken."

"And we use chicken as an insult, too. Don't get any respect."

"No regard, neither," he said in a goofy voice with his eyes bulging.

Food and drinks arrived, and we told stories, and we continued our banter, and we talked about nothing in that way that talking about nothing felt more important than talking about something. The way we responded to each other's jokes said more about us than knowing where we were from or how many siblings we had or how we earned a living before we came here. It was flirtatious but it didn't feel like he wanted to sleep with me. The drinks were so cheap it made it easier to lose count. I was drunk by the time we left. Drunk enough that I knew I was drunk but not too drunk that another drink seemed like a bad idea.

"Nightcap?" I suggested walking past a place with a dusty dog lying on the stoop. It could've been mistaken for someone's house if not for the neon cerveza sign.

"Um, I know a better place," he said, quickening his pace. A couple people craned their neck around the bar's entrance, intrigued by the English voices. One of the guys jeered something I didn't understand, but I did catch him say the name Mateo.

Our nightcap turned into a bottle left at our table to pour as we pleased. It was a clear liquid or a brown one or maybe it was both. Regardless, it burned something awful when it came back up. I was in the bar bathroom or the hotel bathroom, or maybe it was both. The spins came, and the chills, and then another round ensued. I got it all up before I got tucked in.

Morning somehow managed to feel worse. I tripped my way to the bathroom, not wanting to open my eyes and make the pain real. If I could keep them shut, I could trick my body into staying asleep. But the pain was too strong, and I succumbed to the daylight.

Like a gentleman, Mat had slept on the floor. He was surrounded by his liquor bottles and his books and a TV and VCR he'd set up on top of a dresser full of clothes that weren't going to be packed into a suitcase anytime soon.

Purgatory

I'm continuing my inspection of the basement, noting every room of empty bunk beds. The monotony causes my mind to wander; my movements become muscle memory. The sound of my footsteps echoes in the elongated hallways and becomes a steady cadence.

Step, step, step, step, step, step, step. Door 24. Thumbprint. Beep. Open swoosh. Check, check, check, check. Close and latch. Notes, notes, notes. Step, step, step, step, step, step, step. Door 25. Thumbprint. Beep. Open swoosh. Check, check, check, check. Close and latch. Notes, notes, notes...........

While immersed in this mesmerized search, I unpack a theory:

***

It's not how I pictured it, but this is purgatory.

I wouldn't have expected the cold, or the other guests, but, most of all, I wouldn't have expected technology. When people came here before, centuries ago, it must have looked different. There may have been a series of tests and deceptions, but there wouldn't have been computers. This place relies on gradual deconditioning, a steady erosion of the familiar. But it needs to look professional, futuristic even, to create the guise of trust. The computers look sleek and distinguished to my late-twentieth-century mind. I'll bet they used to rely on cryptic theologians in cloisters for the same effect.

In either case, after establishing the foundation, they strip it away. Rather, *we* discover the flaws and begin to tear it apart. It's better if we work in teams because it helps us keep our sanity to see other people undergo the same deconstruction.

The Medicament does something. Perhaps it triggers a response in our body chemistry, so we react differently to stimuli. If we're occupying a different physical realm, we'll need to be conditioned. Or it might be a placebo, but it's one we need to point to as the source of our transformation. It makes it easier when we can attribute the cause of the drastic change. Either way, the effect is the same. It helps us believe.

Hector figured it out first. Maybe his revelation was expedited by his near-death experience, or whatever you want to call it. That's why he's been acting so strange. He found out what was happening before he was ready.

Anna is lost just like me. She's dealing with conflicting evidence and struggling to believe and disbelieve, and it's not easy. That's why we're here. In a medical facility. They've recreated a safe and clinical environment so we'll have the resources we need to feel comfortable. If we panic, they'll be able to help. They are here to help.

Quinn has disappeared because he must have moved to a stage beyond us. He's younger, so he has less from his life to reconcile. We may have been wrong about his moods. When I saw him being glum, he was being stoic. When he looked ornery, he was calm and serene. Perhaps we were even sensing reality differently by the time he left. He was so odd; I wouldn't doubt that he was in some transcendent plane that was literally imperceptible. All we could do with our feeble senses was see someone in a mood. But he might have been blissed out with, I don't know, super-receptors or some such.

I'm still trying to figure out this place; I'm not worried about what's next yet.

They called it a suicide, but it was something else. It might be similar, though. I hope leaving here won't require anything like that.

Still, I pause. Everything that brought me here was logical. I remember struggling with the decision to leave home. I remember packing my belongings into storage. I remember what I had for breakfast the morning before the flight here. It was all deliberate. So, if this is purgatory, when did I die?

* * *

Step, step, step, step, step, step, step. Door 41. Thumbprint. Beep. Open swoosh. Check, check, check, check. Close and latch. Notes, notes, notes. Step, step, step, step, step, step, step. Door 42. Thumbprint. Beep. Open swoosh. Check, check, check, check. Close and latch. Notes, notes, notes.

When I open Door 45, at first I'm upset that it disturbs my rhythm. There are no bunk beds. Instead, there's a library. Volumes of bound books line the walls. A maroon high-backed leather chair sits in the room's center with a carafe of water and an ashtray sitting on a table beside it. Nearby, an ornate globe rests in a wooden stand. The monotony of the search may have put me in a trance, but I'm not hallucinating; I've seen this place before, but not in person.

I pull a book off the shelf at random and flip through it. Every page is blank. I try another, and there's not one word. The books on the top shelf are cardboard boxes with a page pasted on them to look like the spines of a set. Less detail has been paid here because they're not the focus of the frame.

In front of the leather chair, atop a tripod, a video camera watches the room. Cables protrude from the device, which lead to an arrangement of receivers, a monitor, a VCR, and a machine called *My First Video Editor*. A stack of VHS tapes sits on the VCR. Most are unlabeled, but one tape says *Pretest Screening 1982* and another is called *Orientation 1991.*

I write furiously in my notes, detailing every piece of the showcase.

When I conclude the inventory, I write two words, which I underline:

Arthur Romaine

In some regards, The Medicament is magic. It has enchanted us, but the performers haven't been able to maintain their act. They might even be magicians, too, but they're sub-rate showmen.

* * *

After a few more storage rooms, I'm nearing the end of basement exploration. There are only a couple doors left.

Door (51) Residence. Men's Clothing (White). Clean. Spartan. Books. Non-Fiction—History, Science and Medicine. Poetry. No photographs or other personal items. Most likely Dr. Samesong's Room.

Door (52) Residence. Women's Clothing (Yellow).

I'm feeling invasive in Peggy's room. I scan the room as quickly as possible, taking brief mental notes. There are stacks and stacks of paperbacks scattered about. They're well-worn, and they give the room the scent of a used bookstore. I'm brought back to the memory of perusing shelves, hoping to happen upon a gem, but always feeling too snobbish to try something pulpy. I hover over Peggy's nightstand, reading through the titles, and try to refrain from similar judgment.

I'm lost in the cover of a book that's either a thriller or a romance; regardless, there's lots of sex in it.

I startle when I notice Peggy sleeping less than a foot from me. She's soundlessly bundled up in the blankets; I just didn't see her. I back away and knock a stack of books from the nightstand, which splats onto the floor. She doesn't flinch. If the blanket weren't rising and falling with her breath, I'd wonder if she were alive.

It's a surreal intimacy, and I can't help but admire her peace. If she woke up, I'd feel like she'd apologize for not being able to accommodate my request sooner. I leave the room, feeling sheepish for invading but tickled by her serenity.

Dr. Samesong sees me exit. He's standing outside his room, not menacing, but still. I blush.

"I hope you didn't look under my mattress," he jokes.

"What have I told you about those magazines?"

Not knowing where to go with the dumb joke, he feigns a laugh before asking, "Find anything interesting?"

I realize I'm still holding Peggy's romance novel, having left abruptly after spotting her asleep. I tuck it under my arm. "Interesting. Yes. That's a word for it." I'm not sure if we're still playing or not, so I change tone with some honesty, "Peggy scared me in there. She's out. Like, dead asleep. I didn't even notice her."

"Yeah," he says running his hand over his chin as he finds the words. "Like I've said, we need something to do. Something to keep us busy."

"What? Sleep?"

"Uh huh," he says, yawning.

I get the message. "Enjoy your nap."

He goes into his room, but I don't hear the door latch. I futz with the romance novel, debating if I should return it now and pretend like I hadn't taken it. Flipping through the pages, something falls out.

A Polaroid lays at my feet with two familiar figures looking up. The faces are caught in a candid shot, seated side-by-side on a tweed couch I recognize from the lounge upstairs. The woman is in a blue smock-dress, and the man wears a white button-down shirt. Not looking at the camera, she has a natural and bright smile even though she isn't posing. He looks like he is mid-gesture as if telling an animated story. In black marker, the photo is labeled in Peggy's handwriting, "Peter and Me – 1974".

The Duration

I will be paid for one year. That's what the contract says. I'm poring over the details, trying to parse out the legalese and see if I've missed anything.

… As compensation for participation in the study lasting (one) calendar year, subjects will receive a stipend totaling no less than ($100,000). Thereafter, participation in the study may continue on a voluntary basis. In the event…

When I read this the first time, I didn't pause. Not because I skimmed it—I was sacrificing a year of my life; I took the time to diligently read and reread the contract—but because "voluntary basis" never registered as a possibility. After a year, there'd be no chance I'd volunteer to stick around.

It might not be a choice, though. Not a practical one, anyhow. After everything that's happened here, I'm not sure when I'll be ready to leave. Especially if it means giving up The Medicament. It's only been four months, but the expiration date begins to feel portentous.

With the spring thaw, it's almost pleasant here. There's still a brisk wind, but in the heat of the daytime, I can enjoy the outdoors and the scenery. The isolation has become therapeutic.

I reread the contract again, trying not to let my eyes glaze over. Many of the details involve the breakdown of financials. It doesn't seem like it should matter, but our meals and clothes and supplies are all accounted for with dollar values down to the cent. For tax purposes, they'll qualify as income. Nothing stands out, but it's hard not to become numb to the enormous spreadsheet.

The emphasis on financial details causes me to pause. There is a business here. Perhaps I shouldn't be surprised. In fact, it was the professionalism of the contract that legitimized it in the first place. A facility like this doesn't come from nothing. It takes investors and fundraising and a promise of return on investment down the road. Since being here, however, it's felt less and less connected to the modern world. There's disharmony between what we're experiencing and the cogs of capitalism that make it possible. Whoever is in control, they must be trying to make money off this place and monetize The Medicament.

Then it hits me like an epiphany. I paid enough attention in European history to know selling indulgences was a bad idea. It must be a test. They are doing everything they can to tempt us with riches, but I need to reject the money. Anyone who is driven by the cash won't be able to transcend.

No one can profit from granting time out of purgatory. Or something.

Predictability

We cling to our diversions like a crutch. Hector, Anna, and I continue to work through Anna's film schedule. We are watching a forgettable one with a midrange score of six. The title doesn't matter; it's only background. The acting is hammy, and the production value is poor, but Hector has a different complaint, "I've seen this before."

He hasn't seen this exact film, but we understand and share the sentiment. We are tuned in to the conventions of plot and narrative structure. It happened in an instant— every film, every book and story; it's like we've heard it before. Predictability is an unfortunate side effect of wisdom.

Tired of the movie, I head to the lounge's rear and fire up the pinball. The movie is loud enough to drown out the dull thuds of the flippers and bumpers. Hector joins me and offers me a Redlight which he sparks before lighting his own. Anna has moved to the exercise bike, though she keeps her eyes on the film. I miss the ramp bonus, and my ball bounces straight past the waving flippers and down the center. Hector switches places and begins his turn.

"I keep wanting this machine to play better. Like I keep trying the same thing, while expecting different results. Some call that the definition of insanity."

"Better lock you up." The joke lands with a thud. Hector's ball hits a dead bumper, he tilts the machine, but to no avail; the ball slides through the side gap, ending his turn. He smacks the machine. Watching his frustration gives me an idea.

"I was just thinking," I begin as I step into position for my turn. "What do you think it would take to arouse security? I've only seen someone once. You think they'd show up if we staged a fight or something?"

"Ha. You know security is a joke, right?" Hector ashes out his cigarette. "I recognized the pilot right away when 'security' showed up for Quinn." He gestures the quotations. "He'd shaved his beard, but that dragon tattoo on his arm was pretty obvious. They probably have the guy on call whenever they need him. It's quite the operation, really. All they've done to make this seem like they've got everything under control."

I hold the ball with the flipper. "Yeah, you're right. It's the same with the professors. I'm still not convinced they do anything."

"It feels like a cult. They've fully bought in and don't question anything," he whispers. "Though, I admit, I could hardly blame them. They've got one hell of a product in this drug."

I release the ball and flick it up the ramp. It hugs a rail as it exits the chute and flies right past my flippers. "Dammit," I complain, shaking the machine.

"Here, I've got an idea." Hector says as he lifts up the ceramic ashtray. He looks to me for permission, and I shrug. "Sorry, Anna. This is going to be loud." With that he slams the ashtray into the case, shattering the glass sheet.

"Whoa!" I shout as glass scatters everywhere. Hector still holds the ashtray as he stares to the security camera. The bulbs over the doorway remain unchanged.

"Just as I thought. Nothing. No one's watching," he places down the ashtray and picks a few shards out of his hand. "Sorry. I'll clean this up. And I'll see if I can fix some of the issues while I'm at it."

I poke my head outside the lounge to gauge any reaction. Peggy and Dr. Samesong are talking down the hall. They're deep in conversation, unfazed by the commotion with the pinball. It's one of those conversations that demands the discretion of hushed tones even if I weren't in earshot. They mutter a few more things back and forth as I close the door again.

"Actually, hold up a minute, Lily," Dr. Samesong says, interrupting his own thought and then returning to address Peggy, "that makes sense to me. As long as we're on the same page."

"I think so." Peggy, remembering her manners, now turns to me, "If you wouldn't mind, we'd love to speak with you."

"Am I in trouble?" I weakly jest.

"All of you," Dr. Samesong responds without humor.

* * *

Peggy makes sure we're all comfortable and apologizes for interrupting us. They have us stay in the lounge. Dr. Samesong sees the broken glass and Hector's bloody hand and does nothing more than retrieve a first aid kit affixed to the wall. The emphasis on comfort evokes thoughts of palliative care. Comfort is all they can control. They want to ditch the formality. It's a conversation, they assure us. The image of a paused action sequence sits on the screen with the projector's beam hovering over the room.

"We've reached a turning point in our study," Dr. Samesong begins. "You have surely noticed some aberrant circumstances, and we'd like to do our best to provide some explanations. That's not to say we have all the answers, but we do have experience with what you're going through."

"Give it time. It will start to feel almost normal," Peggy adds.

The three guests—Hector, Anna and I—look twice as confused and half as anxious as Dr. Samesong and Peggy. Whatever they're trying to communicate, it's lost in their nebulous words that sound important but mean nothing.

"Can you please stop speaking in riddles?" Hector demands on behalf of all of us.

They pause, "Well, it's—"

"—we need you—"

"—it's out of our control."

"What do you think The Medicament does?" Peggy says, finding the right words.

"It makes you feel no pain."

"It makes you heal."

"It prevents disease."

They're nodding along in affirmation.

"So, what does that tell you?"

"Say what you're too afraid to say," Peggy urges.

I try to forge the words, to articulate all of my conflicting thoughts, all my misgivings about purgatory and deception and all the other impractical madness. Except it makes perfect sense; I just can't communicate it, just like they're unable to communicate it now, and I'm circling back and forth trying to decide how to say something I can't say because I won't be able to take it back, and when I focus on the words, I don't want to say it because then it becomes real, and I don't have to because Anna says it for me.

"We are all dead," she chokes out.

"And this is purgatory," I add, equally morose.

"This is a test of our faith," says Hector, not quite echoing us, but looking like he needed to say something.

A quiet falls over the room. It's happened. The truth has

emerged, and we can't possibly be prepared for whatever comes next. It's a relief. My eyes wander the room, not wanting to focus on anything, trying to gather every bit of this fleeting moment. The blinds are drawn but fading daylight creeps past the edge of the frosted windows. Plumes of smoke waft past projector lights, and a blurred image of a man rushing through a forest sits on the screen. A pillow beside me has a loose feather protruding from its threads.

I can't make eye contact with Peggy or Dr. Samesong. As they said, they don't have answers either. I don't want them to see me disintegrate like this.

But they're not leering or gawking. They look confused. Peggy whispers under her breath, "Should we tell them?" Dr. Samesong nods his head forward in affirmation. She calmly says, "I want to show you something."

Orientation 2

No one has an appetite; everyone has a drink. A whole bottle of wine for me. I had paused on a bottle of whisky, but I settled on the wine, wanting to be numb but not absent.

Dr. Samesong and Peggy have returned with a stack of papers. The scent of fresh photocopies wafts by as they hand each of us a warm packet. Their copies have well-worn glue bindings.

* * *

The Medicament Project

"Feel free to page through for a moment," says Dr. Samesong, "but when you're ready, I'd like to highlight a few things."

The language is dry and technical. There are no photographs or graphics. It begins with orientation information about schedules and the project's objective summarized as:

A pharmacological examination of a medicament's effect on the infirm.

I note the lack of capitalization and change of article. Anna leans over to me to point out a marking on the front cover. It had been obscured by Xerox blotches, and the faint letters suggest it was originally written in pencil. Of course, Peggy is the sort to write her name on an orientation packet.

"Do you see a year anywhere?" I say in a hushed voice, instinctively.

Not sure if she should honor the whisper, Peggy hesitates, then answers us, "1971."

We give a nod of thanks, and she blush/smiles. Hector isn't reading through his copy. Instead, he's futzing with the wrapping on a fresh pack of Redlights, trying to catch the plastic ribbon with his fingernail. He's over the theatrics. Sensing this, Dr. Samesong says, "We're sharing this because we want to renew our trust and be as transparent as possible."

Hector's eyes wobble. He's not impatient. He's drunk. He must have snuck a few nips during the break. In solidarity, I take a slug of wine straight from the bottle. I flip through a few more pages and spot Dr. Samesong's name listed as a researcher. The others are sitting with closed packets in their laps, evidence they're ready to begin.

Dr. Samesong begins, "We'll do our best to explain what we know. As you've discovered, this isn't the first time the project has been conducted. What you may not know is that it has changed."

Peggy takes over, "You are a healthy group. As you can see, however, I was part of another trial. I was sick. Lung cancer. Stage four." The Redlight smoke hovers, self-aware. "Don't worry. I'm better now."

History

Peggy was already dead, so it was no decision at all. Even the most optimistic prognosis didn't give her more than two years. At the very least, it would be a nice hospice. A medical staff and facilities, and—judging from the brochures—an amazing view.

Her body was so frail they thought transportation might be an issue. But she was a perfect candidate, and she was adamant.

In the early days, she hardly left her room. The cancer kept her still. There were others, she could hear them, but they were the anonymous sounds she'd learned to ignore from years in and out of the hospital.

Withdrawal hurt. She needed to be taken off her prescriptions and painkillers and transitioned into an exclusive dosage. It began with nausea and vomiting, before her muscles grew sore from the heaving and caloric loss left her weak. She couldn't keep down food or water, and a fever coursed through her body: shivers turning to tremors without relief. The pain, unmuted, nearly killed her.

That's how they lost the first one. If Peggy had been more lucid, she might have feared the screams and panic from the neighboring room.

She slept. Each hour drifted into the next, and wakefulness would last for a few moments before she soon found herself asleep again. This cycle turned time irrelevant. Days felt like weeks, but weeks felt like only hours.

For a while, she thought death had already taken her. Her body became foreign as the pain started to leave, and she misattributed the relief. It was springtime when she stepped out into the crisp beauty. She stayed outside for hours, not wanting to retreat into the haunting space of the facility. They had to chase after her. She apologized. She didn't want to be a bother.

Meeting the other guests was surreal. For a while she was convinced that they were angels. When one of the angels cursed, she grew suspicious. When he drank and smoked cigarettes, it was unexpected, but who was she to judge an angel? When he told asinine, overly detailed stories without purpose or narrative flow, the fantasy was broken. Angels who curse and drink she could believe, but she couldn't believe angels could be boring. His name was Robert. Robert the Boring Angel.

They weren't angels; they were only themselves again. After so much illness, being healthy didn't seem real. There was elation and downright giddiness. With a new lease on life, they wanted to rediscover the world, but, as per the contract, they'd have to restrict their exploration to the range of the facility and its immediate surroundings. This didn't temper Peggy's optimism, however. Her joy was reborn.

***

Maria was the likable sort. She attributed her joviality to the southern hospitality with which she'd been raised. Most traces of her accent had been shed after years of itinerancy with her father, a political organizer who traveled to community events nationwide to register voters. The lifestyle taught her to be sociable with strangers, to find shared interest and common ground, and to meet people where they were. She was the type of person you want to be there when you're mixing groups of friends for the first time, someone charming and sociable and having such a way with people you'd almost be jealous, that is, if you weren't grateful for her spirit.

Peggy, by contrast, worried she wasn't sufficiently interesting. There'd been so little room for cancer-unrelated conversations, she'd felt like she'd forgotten how to be a person. This fear was misguided. Maria liked the way she listened. Not only was Peggy an attentive and active listener, but she was intimidatingly smart. Maria tended to ramble, circling around the crux of what she was trying to say but never quite managing to arrive. Peggy could succinctly rephrase it without effort, articulating exactly what Maria meant to say. Maria never failed to be impressed by this, but Peggy reassured her that the hard work had already been done for her because Maria wasn't afraid to express herself.

Maria's extroversion and Peggy's warmheartedness complemented each other, and with scarce other options, they became inseparable friends.

They didn't have anything against Robert. He was just dull. He would hijack conversation and relate the topic back to his own experience with a small network of friends in the Chicago suburbs. Peggy might make a comment about mosquitoes which would cue Robert, "That reminds me… Did I tell you about my friends Amy and Bruce?" he'd ask without waiting for reply before launching into an anecdote everyone had heard before, "They used to sit on their front porch for hours in the summer. Never touched bug spray, and I don't think they got one bite." Behind his back Peggy and Maria would joke about needing Amy and Bruce grade deet.

"I try to see the best in people. I really do," Maria lamented to Peggy. "But every time he begins to talk, I brace myself. He's such a buzzkill. And such a complainer, too."

Without the excuses of normal life available, ducking out from undying chatter required tact. But this became tedious and exhausting in its own way, so the options became: A) Avoid him. B) Tolerate his dull and endless stories. C) Be direct and rude. While Peggy opted for Options A or B, Maria was less delicate and embraced the blunt Option C.

When Peggy confessed the nickname she'd given him, Robert the Boring Angel, it only took Maria a moment to set the name to music to the tune of "Rudolph the Red-Nosed Reindeer." It wasn't mean-spirited at first, but as Robert's entrance and exit were always accompanied by Maria's whistling of the seven-note melody, the rift among the trio became all the more obvious.

He might not have understood the specifics of the inside joke, but Robert knew he was an outcast, being picked on like Rudolph, with the song becoming an anthem to his mockery. One time, he spotted Peggy and Maria heading out for a walk. Peggy offered an invitation, but Robert picked up on Maria's body language and declined, adding, "Enjoy your reindeer games."

Despite their bullying, Robert persisted, at least with Peggy. He needed a social outlet, too. Though it began as pity, Peggy came to respect and appreciate Robert. There was an earnestness to him that softened her. She began seeking out his company (there were so many hours to fill), if only for a change of pace.

Robert misread, though. To Peggy, he was a casual friend, an alternative to Maria and the maddening solitude of her own head. They may have developed a rapport, but it was nothing close to the chemistry Robert thought they had. When Robert kissed her, she was too polite to tell him to stop.

Sensing her lack of passion, he eased off and pretended like nothing had happened.

It might not have occurred to him that Peggy wasn't interested in men. She kept this quiet as she always had.

He began spending more and more time alone. In his self-imposed exile, he ruminated, becoming short-tempered with the others and making sarcastic, cruel comments at every opportunity. The isolation intensified his paranoia. Every sound echoing in the hallway was another secret joke. When near others, he began to whistle the tune himself as a strange taunt. All of the other reindeer.

Robert hadn't been sick in the same way as Peggy. For years he had suffered from chronic pain. An accident left him with a shattered pelvis and pinched spinal column that never healed quite right. Sometimes the pain was minor, and he could almost ignore it. Other times routine motion triggered excruciating pain. Either way, it was always there.

***

Dr. Samesong was too distracted, too eager by the promise of a medical breakthrough to have taken notice of Robert's withdrawal. During their checkups, he was relieved by Robert's soft-spokenness because it meant shorter exams and less paperwork. Robert could wear a convincing guise for one hour each week.

He went months without conversation. Whatever truth he discovered during that period of introspection, there was no one to question him, no one to dissuade him. Being laughed at would have been preferable. Gossip meant people cared. He needed to act, to find a way to be noticed.

***

The guests and staff gathered together on the day of the big announcement. They didn't yet know what they were celebrating, but they couldn't help but notice the bottles of champagne.

Not only were they healthy, but they were no longer aging. It couldn't be possible, but they felt it was true. They shared stories of the miraculous: allergies had disappeared, Maria could see without her glasses, and walking for hours never made anyone sore.

Except Robert didn't share. He listened and drank from his glass and watched the happy women celebrate the marvel without considering how the change affected him.

His glass shattered, and the shards stung into his palm. Maria let out a shriek while Peggy grasped at the base of her chair. Expressionless, Robert watched the blood drip down his hand as the others sat frozen, too horrified to intercede. "Why don't I feel anything?"

"You do. You just don't feel the pain," Dr. Samesong corrected, trying to stay calm and putting a hand over his mouth. Robert watched as the blood continued to stream down his hand.

"You're right. I feel its warmth."

* * *

From there, Robert's behavior became more unsettling. Sensing the reaction he'd received from the glass incident, he'd intentionally act to upset the others. Once, he passed Maria in the hallway and, without preamble, sprinted into the wall and bashed his head. Over dinner he started hacking something up, attracted attention, then reached into his mouth to pry out a tooth. Dr. Samesong came into the exam room to find him with a plastic bag over his head. "Three minutes and counting," he announced.

Something needed to be done, but there were no clear solutions. Dr. Samesong put in an emergency request to Arthur Romaine to remove Robert but was denied for fear a hostile actor might expose their project to the outside world. Keeping him on board risked everyone's safety. Imprisonment was a violation of protocol but might have been the only viable option.

The facility became a hostage state. The guests retreated to their rooms at any sign of disturbance, and most hours were spent in refuge behind locked doors. For weeks they maintained this bleak stasis, not upsetting the balance. If they pushed him, there was no telling what horror would come.

* * *

It was a wet and dreary spring afternoon when Peggy and Maria entered the lounge to find Robert playing chess against himself. Maria turned to leave, but Peggy waved her off and asked if he wanted a partner.

"I don't need your pity," he said, without looking up.

Maria had had enough. "Listen, Robert. Whatever this grudge is, whatever problem it is you have with me and Peggy. Would you please—"

"Not Peggy," he interrupted. "Just you." He moved a white piece, rose, and shifted to the opposite side of the table.

"Okay, fine. You have a problem with me. Let's talk about it. Like decent people," Maria pleaded.

"Decent people," Robert scoffed as he studied the chess board. He whistled the seven-note song and shook his head. "You couldn't have made it clearer what you thought of me. I was having a great time until you two became thick as thieves."

He moved a black piece and returned to the other side. "Can you imagine how I felt, Peggy? Years of pain. Gone. And when I gave you a friendly hug of relief, you recoiled, made me feel like I was some sort of monster."

"Robert, I'm sorry, but that's not what happened. It wasn't just a friendly hug.

You—"

"Enough," Robert interrupted. "All I know is I never saw that side of you until you and Maria started conspiring. She's a bully. Don't you see that? A two-faced bully."

Maria snapped and raised her voice, "Robert, Peggy's not interested in you! She never has been. She's too kind to admit it, but any attention she ever gave you, any sign of interest, it was only pity."

"That's enough," Peggy whimpered, not meeting anyone's eye.

"No, you should know the truth, what she said about you behind your back," Maria raged, "She said you were dull, a total bore. Do everyone a favor and leave us alone!"

Robert looked to Peggy for denial, but she kept her head down. He left the room without another word.

"Fucking loser!" Maria shouted after him.

Rain pattered the windows, and the wind swelled its breath.

***

It was almost twenty-four hours before Robert's absence was noted, and he was declared missing. A half-hearted search party swept the facility and its immediate environs but discovered only that a pair of boots and a parka had disappeared as well. A days-long storm system had settled in, and a torrent of rain and hazardous winds made an aerial search impossible.

His departure was met with both worry and quiet glee. While Dr. Samesong expressed dejection for having failed, even he couldn't hide his sense of relief. With the departure, the menace had lifted.

When the weather cleared and airplane scouting missions revealed no trace, their routine returned to some semblance of normalcy. They continued on with their dosages and pastimes while speculating on the nature of Robert's fate.

Escape into the wilderness seemed the only possibility, though a brutish one. The Medicament's residual effect would have protected him from pain for a period of time, but even so, navigating a trail through the wild and weather would test anyone's tenacity. Any mishap—a misbegotten path, a rolled ankle, a fall from height, even an animal encounter—might have rendered Robert incapacitated. Dr. Samesong wouldn't declare him to be dead; he had enough faith in the drug's potency but conceded any existence out there could hardly be considered life. Robert would most likely succumb to the elements as the drug wore off and his body weakened. It was only a matter of time.

* * *

It surprised Maria and Peggy when he asked them to join him for a meeting. The study had become much more casual, so a sit-down was notable. Once seated in the dining room, Dr. Samesong spared preamble:

"I just received word from a source outside—Robert was found several days ago. Apparently, authorities were alerted when a disheveled man made his way to the post office, where he began rambling about a secret lab and experimental treatment. He was transported to the nearest hospital to be placed on a seventy-two-hour hold while he underwent a psychiatric evaluation and was treated for minor injuries."

"Does that mean—"

"Let me finish. His condition stabilized. They treated small lacerations he'd sustained on his hike out and administered a mood-stabilizer to regulate the psychosis. He was lucid, and even though he'd been sedated, he spoke manically about what he'd endured, that is, until he suddenly lost the ability to speak. When they performed an examination, many irregularities were discovered. His vitals were erratic, and symptoms didn't follow any standard diagnosis. As his energy dropped, tests confirmed perilously low oxygen levels, and he soon lost consciousness. Before they could attach him to a respirator, his bandages resaturated with blood, and he began flatlining shortly thereafter. Attempts to resuscitate him failed, and he was pronounced dead yesterday morning," Dr. Samesong paused. "The autopsy revealed multiple organ failure, but no infections or toxins were detected. While exposure to the elements had weakened him, that alone would not account for such a sweeping decline. They listed his cause of death as Anomalous Rapid Deterioration and Delirium, which, to my knowledge, is a novel diagnosis. Now, there's a lot we don't—"

"When did you find out?" Maria interrupted.

"Yesterday. I was just given authorization to debrief you. The administrators thought it would be best if you understood the ramifications."

A pause before Maria asked, "Ramifications of what? You mean withdrawal, right?"

"Yes. We don't know everything, but we have reason to believe it might be fatal regardless of the trauma he suffered during his escape. We don't have much data. No one has ever gone off The Medicament regimen as far as we know. His last dosage was ten days ago."

* * *

It was weeks before anyone mentioned Robert again. Peggy took hours-long walks, while Dr. Samesong and Maria caught up on their reading. There was little laughter, and meals were perfunctory affairs.

Arthur Romaine made a personal visit to offer to triple their compensation. They attempted to barrage him with questions raised by Robert's disappearance and discovery (about the scope of the operation, details on withdrawal, The Medicament's ready-ability, their proximity to the town Robert had found) but were only offered vague explanations before being redirected to the contract. It was possible they were being deceived, but leaving the project and risking their own Anomalous Rapid Deterioration and Delirium was unthinkable, so the women signed and followed instruction.

* * *

While Peggy seemed content in her solitude, the isolation had worn on Maria. Dr. Samesong offered some social outlet, but his pomposity had always irked Maria and left her wanting to vent to her friend. "He just walks with such an air about him. Like we should be grateful for his presence," Maria ranted to Peggy during an encounter at the coffee pot. "I get the sense everything he says is rehearsed. Like he's reciting some dinner party stories that hit all the right beats. And if you don't laugh or make him feel like he's the most charming person you've ever met, then he's got no need for you. He wants an audience; it doesn't matter who."

Peggy stirred her coffee and remained quiet.

"He's talking at you, that's what it is," Maria went on. "I've never known how some people can be so clueless, you know. Like, hey, you're not as interesting as you think."

Peggy moved to put her spoon in the sink, breathed like she might say something, decided against it, then turned to leave.

"Hey, what's going on? I've had enough of this silent treatment."

Peggy stared into her cup before letting out a deep exhale and looking Maria in the eye. "Robert was right. You're not a nice person. I didn't see it before. I guess I was lonely, or maybe I wanted to indulge in a little gossip myself. But I see it now, you really see the worst in everyone. You seem to relish it."

Maria rolled her eyes and scoffed.

"And I don't think you feel guilty at all about Robert," Peggy continued. "We were mean to him. Cruel even. But it's like you're proud of yourself. I'm sorry, you're not someone I want to be around."

"Really? That's it? Fine!" Maria raised her voice. "Put me down if it makes you feel better. Project all your insecurities onto me. At least I'm honest. I'm not the one who's living a lie."

"What's that supposed to mean?"

"Please. You don't think I've noticed?" Maria jutted her head forward in a scowl. "It's obvious. How you act. How you carry yourself," she paused and looked Peggy up and down. "How you look at me. Pathetic."

Peggy clasped her coffee mug and spoke in a firm tone. "That's enough, Maria. Now, I'm going to pretend you didn't say that, and we can do our best to be civil. But no, I don't want anything from you. I don't want to be your girlfriend. I don't even want to be your friend. You're nothing but a bully."

She turned to leave, but Maria reached for her arm and tugged her back. Gripping Peggy's wrist tight, she looked her in the face and called her a name that need not be repeated.

Peggy winced, took a deep breath and composed herself. "That's so disappointing," she said, shaking her head. Once again, she turned to depart, but Maria's grip wouldn't relent, and they were caught in a struggle. Not wanting a fight, Peggy clenched her body, hugging the mug to her chest. It sloshed and spilled until Maria's hands found it and threw its hot contents into Peggy's face.

No one screamed. The liquid steamed off Peggy's face as Maria released her body. Peggy didn't look back to her once. Not in horror, or disgust or betrayal. She walked to retrieve a napkin, wiped her face and exited the room, the plumes of heat still dissipating off her upper body.

* * *

The two never spoke again. After the conflict, a team was brought in to reassess the project and alter its terms. Maria was reassigned to another facility and Peggy was given an opportunity to restructure a new contract. They gave her an empty notepad and let her take her time to draft her own terms. She didn't blame the SL Company for the trauma with Robert and Maria. She was still grateful for the life they'd rescued for her, but she thought she could be of use. There was a new group of recruits scheduled for the next year, and she wanted to stay—as an assistant, a helper, someone who was there.

It was a voluntary position. She could come and go as she liked, and sometimes she did leave, but she always returned. For almost twenty years, this was her home.

Dr. Samesong's Story

If Peggy is lying, it's fully convincing. The story was plain-spoken, though at times it felt like she didn't want to relive every detail. We prodded her, and her responses weren't rehearsed. They were the conflicted descriptions of a lived experience.

When it's time for Dr. Samesong's story, he pulls out a book of his own. It's a worn leather journal that looks like it might turn to dust. "There's always been protocol," he says, leafing through the delicate pages. Before beginning his story, he adds the caveat, "It's been so long since I was given this. I don't remember everything."

* * *

It started with a business plan. He didn't know anything about mining, but Otto Peters, as he was then known, saw the Fairbanks Gold Rush of 1902 as an economic opportunity beyond the claims. Having previously failed to more established competition elsewhere, Peters raced to the Alaskan boomtown to found the region's first pharmacy. His career as a chemist was still in its infancy, but with high demand for pain remedies to alleviate the ailments associated with mining, the business was an overnight success. While herbs and ointments did provide some clients with relief, the bulk of his sales came from customers demanding a more potent substance—laudanum.

As more miners came to the area to strike it rich, a new batch of clients sought Peters's drug, and his business continued to grow. When winter set in, however, he found ennui got the better of him and he began partaking in a dosage himself. The dark months passed in a haze, and Peters knew little of the competition which had sprung up on the opposite side of the camp. A new salesman had come to town to pitch elixirs from his wagon, a man named Arthur Romaine. With a barking voice, tailored three-piece suit, fine top hat, and a signature waxed mustache, Romaine pitched his product as a cure-all and miracle drug.

Insulted by the obvious charlatan, Peters eventually noticed many of his regulars had stopped frequenting his pharmacy, instead favoring the theatrical newcomer and his wares. With profits dwindling and morale sinking, his reliance on laudanum was exacerbated until he made a grave mistake.

Deep in a haze, he'd forgotten to lock the back entrance to his shop. While he was cashing out his register a masked robber entered and pointed a gun to Peters's chest. A fight ensued, and in the commotion, Peters was shot in the abdomen.

When he came to, he was surprised to find his competitor Arthur Romaine crouched by his side. In a whisper, he explained he had been summoned to help after Peters was found. "You're lucky you're this tall. A few inches higher and—"

Peters didn't feel lucky, he interrupted, "Laudanum. Please."

"With your permission, I'd like to try something different. I hope you're not offended, but my clients find my product even more, how should I say, invigorating."

Peters scoffed and looked away.

"Please, I want to help you. But I need your permission."

Wishing nothing more than for the pain to subside, Peters gave his rival a silent nod.

* * *

Within weeks the two entered into a partnership. Peters swore off the laudanum but maintained a steady dosage of Romaine's elixir, which managed his pain and recovery. Romaine never accepted any form of payment—only his service.

He made this same deal with all his clients. Those who insisted on paying in cash received a placebo instead. He wasn't interested in customers, he wanted believers. Actually, he wanted a believer and non-believer rolled into one. An intrigued skeptic who hadn't made up their mind, one who could hold contradictory thoughts—that this man was both a huckster and a miracle worker, that this drug was real but inexplicable, that there is order and rules and design in our world, but that our perception, our knowledge, will always be limited. He wanted people who showed humility, who knew they didn't know everything: those who allowed for the possibility of the transcendent no matter the packaging.

* * *

Romaine educated Peters on his craft. The elixir defied explanation, but his tactics did not. They were recruiters and relied on a system to find the optimal candidates.

Boomtowns were ideal ground, he'd explained, citing a protocol handbook. They shrank the world to a microcosm, with societal roles appearing and being filled overnight. People were solitary, desperate, and willing to take risks. They were also malleable. "Press upon them," he'd say. "And they'll change shape."

His task was to identify candidates for a unique society, so while witnessing the creation of one, he could scout the peacekeepers and dynamos, the kindhearted and the industrious—those who kept the strings of civility taut and knew the benefit of communal good. The others—those who descended into the cutthroat world where their greed and vice were unhidden—forfeited their eligibility.

* * *

Romaine's theatrics were designed to garner a response. The wagon, the snake oil, even the mustache—it was all a way to make himself seen. What the clients didn't know, however, was that while his quackery attracted a crowd, he had eyes on the crowd, too. One of his protégés had insinuated himself into the camp as a scout. This accomplice never broke cover, even Peters never learned their identity, only that they existed.

The scene culminated with a magic trick. Romaine would invite a volunteer to his stage, where he'd lay out a hammer, a few nails, and a plank of wood. He'd ask the volunteer to hammer a few nails to prove the tools were what they seemed before laying his hand across the plank and instructing the volunteer to strike it. After resisting, the crowd would goad the volunteer, who'd eventually drop a blow onto the hand. Sometimes the crunch of bone could be heard, sometimes a spurt of blood, but what never came was a hint of pain from the host. He'd step into the crowd to showcase his damaged hand up close before wrapping it in a bandage and returning to the stage. His pitch would continue for another minute or two, articulating the miraculousness of his potion and such and such, and as grand finale, he'd remove the bandage for the crowd to see. When the hand was exposed without so much as a bruise, the crowd would erupt into applause.

***

In watching those who watched the charade, many could be weeded out. Those who lined up immediately could be discounted as uninquisitive, and those who refused to engage were close-minded and non-persuadable. The scout was looking for another faction, the curious doubters, those who didn't buy in at first, but who lingered and would return another day.

The scout would track these individuals, taking note of their everyday behavior. They'd stage happenings—a fall into the mud, a forgotten wallet, or even an overeager dog—to generate a reaction, which helped evaluate their character. If, unbeknownst to them, a candidate passed the screening criteria, Romaine found an opportune moment to approach and present them with a proposition.

He'd offer a free sample. If they accepted, he'd offer another the following day. And again, the next. By the end of one week, he'd present the contract.

Protocol stipulated this one-week deadline. It was enough time to let them feel its effects without building dependence. This fact had been surmised by previous, and unfortunate, trials and errors.

In order for the scheme to work, the recruits needed to buy-in with limited knowledge. Only bits of information could be revealed before inking the deal to ensure their society remained a secret. The recruits were asked to *feel* the truth and accept it without further evidence. Only then could they take a leap of faith and sign the contract.

* * *

Within a year, the team had met their quota. Ten new recruits. Romaine distributed envelopes to each detailing their next assignments, and they made preparations to depart. They'd meet again, he assured them, but he wouldn't estimate when. "I honestly don't know," he told them. "I'm only following protocol."

* * *

When Dr. Samesong finishes, he reads our faces and can tell we are expecting him to continue. He clears his throat and offers, "Death becomes an even worse threat when you know you could have lived."

The Truth

While Peggy and Dr. Samesong tell their stories, none of us look surprised. It's a supernatural account, but it falls on us like a sunshower, weird but explicable. The group is calmer than we've been in weeks, and I see Hector and Anna nodding along as though responding to a sermon or stump speech. They're agreeing to the ideas they haven't been able to articulate for themselves. When Dr. Samesong opens for questions, Anna doesn't delay:

"When were you born?"

"My birth certificate says 1857, but my regimen on The Medicament began in 1903." Dr. Samesong says. "I haven't celebrated a birthday in some time."

Anna nods and turns to Peggy who also answers, "1932. And my trial—"

"Class of 1950, too?" Hector interrupts with a laugh.

"Yes, it's funny, isn't it?" Peggy smiles and continues, "And, as you know, my clinical trial began in 1971."

They let the information hang in the air, but no one is surprised.

"And these studies, you've been trying to perfect this miracle drug somehow, to make—"

"Hold on, hold on. Sorry to interrupt you, Anna," Hector says. "They're really spelling it out for us, but I feel like we're still tiptoeing around the big question. Do you mind?" Anna waves for him to proceed, "The Medicament, it keeps us from aging, it heals disease, it ends pain. Now, I think we need to know the truth. Is it a cure for death?"

"Well, that's a nice way of putting it," Peggy says to Dr. Samesong, like it's an inside joke.

* * *

What follows is an existential debate about the nature of our state. We have not died; we are still on earth, and it is still 1991. However, we cannot die as long as we continue to take The Medicament. They shy away from using the term immortal, because it's contingent on a steady dosage, they think, but for all intents and purposes, we are not going to die. It becomes philosophical when we are sidetracked by a Möbius Strip of an argument of whether we're alive or dead; if, relative to the state of non-existence, we are alive, but relative to the concept of mortality, we are not really alive. It's dull. I am blessed with eternity and boredom is my first reaction. Might as well start chain-smoking.

Anna begins a barrage of questions, trying to understand every permutation of this reality, "What if, say, we shoot ourselves?"

"Don't."

"It's messy."

"But what will happen?"

"You'll heal."

"And what if…"

The way they talk about it, I have the impression they've tried a few of these methods. They're detached when they describe it. Like undoing massive trauma isn't miraculous, though they concede decapitation or dismemberment should probably be avoided. I'm less concerned with these possibilities.

* * *

The revelation is a calming and welcome alternative from the frantic unknown we'd been stumbling through. In a way, mistaking the change as purgatory is understandable. We've been conditioned to expect the possibility of an afterlife.

Continuing to live, unaging, makes sense. Well, at least it's a concept I can wrap my head around. There aren't metaphysical quandaries, coupled with moralism and routes to salvation blah blah. I'm relieved.

Death has always been the abstract phenomenon. Even though I've always known I was going to die, it was in a more academic sense. It's never felt like non-existence was a reality. Perhaps because it's a crippling notion. Whenever the thought enters my mind that there is nothing after you die—an empty blackness, a void of consciousness, a cruel absolute—it hurts too much. I push it from my head, because what other choice is there?

So, continuing to live doesn't seem like a big deal. It feels natural. All I've known is being alive, so the alternative doesn't make sense. Religion tells us of an afterlife, heaven, paradise, Valhalla, whatever. Even reincarnation involves the continuation of life. But nothing prepares us for the inverse. On a philosophical level maybe, carpe diem, etc., but these are only ways to trick our psyche. A state without consciousness can't be perceived with a conscious mind. It takes too much thinking to perceive the absence of thought.

* * *

"Listen. Not everything can be explained," Peggy interrupts Dr. Samesong during a digression about cellular chemistry. "But I found this helpful." Peggy opens her packet, turns to an introductory letter signed by Arthur Romaine and begins to read.

"At the end of the 18th century, the world was introduced to a new concept: the vaccine. This preventative treatment was developed to prevent smallpox, revolutionizing medical science and redefining what was possible. By letting a tiny bit of a disease in, it could teach a body to combat it.

"Only a few decades ago, the first medical cure was discovered—penicillin. Prior to its use, illnesses and ailments could be treated but not cured. Penicillin, however, not only eliminated the symptoms of bacterial infection, it also undid the illness itself.

"Further these principles and introduce small amounts of cellular death into the body (a natural process as human cells are constantly dying and rebuilding) and combine it with a prescriptive theory of treating deterioration with a medication, and it's hypothetically possible a person could be immunized from death itself.

"A surprising amount of agreed-upon science defies explanation. While the why is understood, the how is often puzzling, or vice-versa. Chlorophyll converts sunlight into energy because the plants need it to. The nuclear reactions of stars create more energy than they consume. If it helps, think of The Medicament as supernatural. To someone in the seventeenth century, penicillin would have felt like magic, too..."

My mind wanders. Just as irrational as the nothingness of death is the sprawl of eternity. It's inconceivable. I blurt out my thought process, "So, we could live forever, in theory. What happens when the sun burns out?"

"That's millions of years from now."

"But still."

The room's volume swells, then dissipates with asynchronous rhythm. Back and forth we shout chaos before settling into contemplation. The orientation packet rests in my lap. It's filled with hope and ambition, its optimism spilling out, begging to be celebrated as a historic achievement. It was to become the focus of history, an event that will rewrite the calendar with a before and after.

People will pity those on the unfortunate side of that timeline, those who came before—the forgotten age when people lived and then died. No, disappeared, ceased to exist in an act of cosmic cruelty. We'd envy their unwanted courage, inherent to all those who knew of their fate but had no choice but to carry on.

Yet, they were from long ago. We do not pity the dinosaur, or wooly mammoth, or Neanderthal. They had the misfortune of coming before. Except it hasn't happened like that. There have been mistakes.

The cigarette ashing itself onto my lap snaps me from my stupor. Anna is continuing her barrage of questions. Her preoccupation with impossible methods of death is disconcerting. Impalement? Bloodletting? Oxygen deprivation? I begin to understand her curiosity. She's not asking for herself.

I interrupt on her behalf, because now I'm wondering, too, "What happened to Quinn?"

They look around, unsure how to answer. I think about the hysteria as we began to process what was happening to us. Maybe he figured it out first, but then he freaked out. I bet he's being hidden from us, in a cold sweat, fighting paranoia, unable to cope. They're keeping him safe from us and from himself, so he doesn't cause worry.

"Where is he?" I demand.

"He's dead. Please believe us on that count."

"But how? I mean, if we were all—"

Dr. Samesong waives off the protestation, "He was switched to a placebo about a month ago," he pauses to let that register. "He violated the contract. We followed protocol. As expected, it only took about a week for withdrawal symptoms to surface, so we moved him near the end."

"So he didn't kill himself?" I ask, "You let him die."

"It's a matter of semantics. He made his choices." Dr. Samesong says, glancing toward Anna who keeps her head down as she can't help but fiddle with her hair. "But we should take a break. Have something to eat, if you're hungry. We'll be here a while."

Everyone else shifts their weight out of their chair, ready to take a moment, but I'm not, "Something doesn't add up." I'm suddenly using the exasperated tone my mom employed when giving me a lecture. "This study. All this history and protocol. Clearly, you already know The Medicament works. It cures cancer and heals wounds instantly. So, you aren't testing the drug. You're testing us."

They let me have the final word.

6/2/1991

Mom,

I was probably about three or four when I first called you a liar. It was at the earliest stage of my conscious memory. I remember sitting with you in the kitchen when you told me everyone had to die. I couldn't handle it, I knew you must be lying.

I knew death was a possibility, from disease or accident, but not a certainty. I cried for hours. One of your friends was visiting and wondered what was wrong. You explained and she said something along the lines of, "Yup. It's a bummer." I'm sure she didn't use those words, but she might as well have.

As harsh as the truth was the calmness with which you seemed to accept it. I wanted to push back, to convince you you were wrong. Someone must have figured this out. There must have been people working to fix this. Through my tears I asked, "What about the scientists?"

I don't remember what you said.

Love,
Lily

Note From the Editor

When I returned to Fairbanks, I called home to check on Germany. My brother assured me he was content, but he missed me. I was still secretive about my research and didn't say much. At the end of the call I asked to borrow money to continue paying for a dumpy motel.

I visited a thrift shop to buy a VCR, which I set up in the motel to view the orientation tape. When the tracking resolution settled, I watched as the pseudo-corporatized production laid out the project's aims. Only moments into the film, I paused to focus on the image. His face was caked with makeup, but his eyes matched those of the man I'd met in the facility. Either Arthur Romaine had been played by the actor I'd met, the actor had, in fact, been Arthur Romaine, or Arthur Romaine did not exist.

***

At the Fairbanks Historical Society, I did what I could to research Fairbanks's first pharmacy. There was not much information, but, based off a photo of Downtown Fairbanks in 1909, I could at least pin down where the pharmacy had been.

The building was still standing on the main strip, and though it was no longer a pharmacy but instead a regional bank, I found a form of confirmation in its cornerstone. Inscribed beside its establishment year of 1902 were a set of letters—*SL Corp.*

Chapter 7

The exhaust started getting to me, so I stepped into the station. Rows of plastic molded chairs were mostly unoccupied, as all the other passengers had already retrieved their luggage, found their people or taxis, and departed. It was an early March afternoon, and a wintry mix of slush and sleet had forced hangabouts inside who didn't look like they had any bus to catch. A woman with a baby swaddled into herself tried to sell me chocolate, and I declined. It wasn't uncommon for my mom to be late, I reminded myself, though I made sure I had a quarter for the payphone.

A half-hour passed, which felt like an eternity after the bus ride, and the flight, and the layover in Panama City, and another flight, and the bus before that. I'd woken up on another continent only eighteen hours earlier, and I could feel each step of the journey in my body, which wished I weren't sitting in a plastic groove. I ambled to the window again, hoping to catch a glimpse of my mom's car turning into the depot, but again was left disappointed. Maybe I had given wrong instructions or been confused about time zones, but I knew better. I just wished she weren't so predictable.

The answering machine was prompted after four rings, and I hung up, hoping to have my quarter refunded, but enough of the call had completed, and I was out of change. I was too anxious to read, so I stayed put and waited. Every time the door opened, and it was someone besides my mom, I became more frustrated, both with her and with myself for having expected anything different.

***

"You wouldn't believe what happened," she ranted as she drove home through the sleet, having picked me up almost ninety minutes late. "The neighbor's dog, you know Luca, the beagle mix... No... I'm sure you know Luca; they've had him for at least a year, sweet puppy... Well, in any event, I was all set to go, when I saw him walking through our yard. He was covered in slush, looked like he must've been out for hours. And, of course, the neighbors—

"Mom!" I interrupted as she cruised through a stoplight that had already gone from yellow to red.

"Lily, would you please... Anyhow, the neighbors, of course, are nowhere to be found, and I don't even have a leash or anything. I just have these visions of Luca out on the road, all helpless... Anyhow, so I found some rope in the garage..." I stopped listening, focused on the road, and mentally seethed. "... and then I was so filthy I couldn't even get into the car without showering first. But I couldn't believe it, the neighbors hardly thanked me. Can you imagine?"

I was twenty-six but felt thirteen again as I responded with an emotionless "That's crazy." She asked if I'd seen some new TV show, which obviously I hadn't. My eyes wandered over her face as she drove. It had been less than a year since I'd left, but I could see the time in the wrinkles next to her eyes, the tone of her skin, and the gray in her hair.

"Peru was incredible. It was probably my favorite," I offered. "Such history and scenery and—"

She spotted the red light this time, and as she broke, the

car skidded across the wintry road. "Yeesh. Something's wrong with this car. I've been meaning to have it checked, but they'll probably tell me I need to just buy a new one. Oh, that reminds me, I saw Mrs. Lerner the other day. You remember her? Her son had that muscle car. In any event…"

* * *

"Are there any clean towels?" I shouted downstairs, half-undressed in the bathroom. The dog bath hadn't been a lie. There was mud and dog hair all over the tub, and it looked like every towel had been used.

"Check my closet." She shouted back. "I moved some things around. Sorry, it's a bit of a mess right now. I tried to tidy everything before you got home but kept getting interrupted."

I put my dirty clothes back on and moved to her bedroom. Indeed, she had been rearranging. Clothes clumped all over her bed and chair, some of which still had tags. It looked like she'd bought a new stereo system, but the cables were unattached. Her bedside was the usual mess of books, knickknacks, and stray items of questionable utility, like a threadless sewing kit and a singular earring. Pill bottles lined her dresser more than usual. I picked one up and noted the date from months earlier, though the container was mostly full. A stack of musty towels rested on the closet shelf, which would suffice.

"Hey, look what I found!" She startled me on my way back to the shower. In her hands was a mix of loose-leaf and typewriter paper. "I'd forgotten I'd saved these until I cleaned out the closet. I thought you might like to read through some of your old work."

I glanced down and saw the heading for Mrs. Payton's second period English assignments. "Thanks, Mom. I'll take a look later." I could smell my own stench and pushed past her.

"I always liked this one. About the kid at the new school. I think that's when I knew you were a better writer than me. It was so believable, the way you inhabit those characters."

"Thanks, Mom." I held the towel up as a gesture and half-smiled as I went into the bathroom and shut the door behind me.

"I'll just leave these on your bed," she said through the door as I heard the papers shuffle. "I thought you'd get a kick out of it." I noted the time on the frog-faced clock beside the sink. I'd only been home twenty minutes.

* * *

"Sorry for giving you the brush-off before. I just really needed a shower," I said, coming downstairs with a towel wrapped around my head while I carried the stack of papers. "But thanks for saving these. I'm sure some are pretty embarrassing but worth a laugh."

She was sitting in the living room watching the news on TV. "Looks like it'll warm up later this week. About time. Everyone's sick of this winter."

"Yeah, it's a bit of a shock coming back from the heat. Colombia was roasting."

"—but it looks like it'll still be pretty gross tomorrow. Maybe if it's nice in the afternoon we could go for a hike or something." A commercial came on for a luxury sedan, and my mom turned the volume down.

"So, how are you?"

"Um. Fine. Tired. I think I could sleep for two days straight. But it was a really good—"

"Oh, I can't wait to see this." She turned the volume way

back up for a movie trailer. "Everyone's been raving about it. And Sean Connery is in this one, too." The trailer ended with a crack of Indiana Jones's whip.

"I never saw the second one."

"It was weird."

We continued watching TV together, making light talk during lulls. I removed the towel from my head and shook the remaining droplets out of my hair.

"I think there's dye upstairs, if you need it," my mom offered, looking at my roots. "I haven't been using it as much."

After the news, *Wheel of Fortune* came on, and we guessed along and both agreed the winning contestant's outfit was dreadful. As the episode ended, my mom retrieved and uncorked a bottle of wine offering me a glass in a tumbler. "This is the last proper wine glass I have," she said, gesturing to her own stemware. "The others kept breaking when I'd wash them." A cop show came on, and she resettled on the couch. I didn't know any of the characters, but that didn't seem to matter.

During a commercial I asked if she'd been reading anything.

"Not really, to be honest. I can't seem to keep focus. And nothing has grabbed me of late."

She topped up her wine and my own. "What do you want to do for dinner?" I asked.

"I'm not sure. There's plenty in the fridge. Have a look and see if anything looks good to you."

* * *

The fridge was overstuffed with food and drinks. Multiple bricks of cheese were stored in Ziploc bags, though two were covered in mold. A couple of half-full bottles of soda sat beside a jug of expired milk. Leftovers upon leftovers had been stacked and piled in their Tupperware, and wilted lettuce spilled out of the crisper. There was enough salvageable for several meals, but a thorough cleaning would be needed when I had the energy.

"The pasta salad is fresh," she called to me, reading my mind. "Red container."

I spotted it, and as I rearranged the stacks an unlidded bowl tumbled out and splattered onto the floor. It was some sort of oily dip or sauce, and the mess immediately seeped into the cracks in the tile.

"What was that?" she shouted.

"This damn yellow sauce. Why didn't you put a lid on it?" I got on my knees with paper towels.

"Because I'm tired, okay!" she screamed from the other room in a sudden change of tone. "Some of us have been busy while you've been off doing… whatever."

I could feel the heat beneath my skin as I stared blankly at the mess. I took a deep breath and refrained from responding. After I cleaned up, I plated some pasta salad and asked if she wanted any. "That'd be great," she replied, turning down the tenor.

We ate and focused on the TV as a million thoughts raced through my mind, none of them related to the cop show. My mom seemed unfazed by her eruption. She ate and drank and chuckled at the banter in the police station. It looked like they got the bad guy, and the detective made a pithy comment to sum up before it cut to commercial.

I'd finished eating and put down my plate. "Listen, Mom, are you alright? You seem a little off. Have you been taking your meds? I saw all the bottles upstairs and—"

"Please, Lily. I can take care of myself."

"But you didn't answer the question."

"I've been taking them off and on. No, don't say it. I don't need the third degree from you, too." She let out a sigh and sunk back into the couch. "You know I don't like the idea of needing a pill to feel like myself. Sure, when I've had a stretch of bad days, I'll take one. But I don't think there's anything wrong with taking a break here and there. You know, ground myself a bit."

"What did Dr. Forester say?"

"Same thing as always. I need to be consistent. But I disagree, I'm managing just fine, don't you think?"

It wasn't what I wanted to hear. Long breaks from her meds inevitably led to a stint in the hospital. I didn't answer. My eyes wandered the room finding the familiar decor that had been displayed since childhood—the clay elephant I'd made in second grade, the framed quilt work from Amish country or wherever, the photo of us at the beach when I was a toddler. There were still no pictures of my father, of course, but I now understood a little better.

"I shouldn't have left," I muttered.

"Fine. Feel sorry for yourself if you want, but you don't need to feel sorry for me," she rose and took our plates to the kitchen. I heard the creak of the stairs as she stomped upward. If she was going to act like this, I'd happily move out. I didn't have a ton of money left, but there was probably enough to get started. The stairs creaked again as she descended. When she came back into the living room there was a hint of red in her eyes. She remained standing and, like I'd always done when she launched into a lecture, I couldn't meet her eye.

"I know you think I'm a mess. And maybe you're right. Sometimes. Sometimes I lose track of time or get sidetracked or let chores pile up. But I'm not clueless. I just don't care! I don't care what other people think of me. I haven't for a long time. I like tinkering around and bouncing from one thing to the next and living in this house even if it is a little messy. You act like you're holding this family together, but you're always so annoyed with me. I'm sick of it. Give me a little credit, okay?"

"Okay," I said in a tone she knew too well.

"And here, will this make you happy?" She shook a prescription bottle in my face. "Take once daily to stabilize mood! Here's to stability!" she said as she popped a pill and swallowed with a drink of wine. The cop show went to the end credits with a slideshow of stills elapsing over the theme music.

"Mom, I'm sorry. I just—"

"It's okay, Lily." She split the wine bottle's remains into our glasses.

I took a sip and rubbed my temple while I let my breathing return to normal. "What's on next?" I asked with a half-smile.

Onboarding

"We apologize for having been cryptic. You needed to figure it out for yourselves. We couldn't tell you. There's protocol." Dr. Samesong lifts a large packet of paper and gives it a tap. Peggy moves around the room, distributing a copy of the A4 glue-bound booklet to each of us. "If we told you outright, you'd have trouble believing it. Imagine being taught about fire without ever witnessing it. How much easier would it be to light a match, to let you feel the warmth of a flame?" He pauses before lifting his protocol packet again. "You need to feel it, to know it's true, that The Medicament works, that you are not going to die. In this book, this epiphany is identified as 'Enlightenment.'"

"But what is it? The Medicament?" Anna asks.

"It's a medicine. Derived from grape skin and coupled with compounds found in lobster and jellyfish. Animals whose chemistry doesn't degrade. We weren't lying about that. It was discovered unintentionally by an alchemist in the seventeenth century who was attempting—"

"Who?"

"That we do not know. My guess is even executives aren't totally sure at this point."

Anticipating questions, he clarifies, "Now, we have been a part of this for some time but have only dealt with a limited number of participants."

"So, a secret society of immortals?" Anna asks with a sarcastic laugh.

"Essentially," he answers without humor.

"How many are there?" I add.

"I'd only be guessing, but I'd say hundreds. Maybe thousands," Dr. Samesong says as he looks at Peggy, who gives a concurring shrug.

* * *

Next, we watch another orientation film. It's the same format as the others. Arthur Romaine gives a corporatized spiel about what the hell is going on. It's a learner's guide to immortality; they lay out a plan with a series of graphics and charts accompanied by fuzzy audio. One segment uses rudimentary animation, zooming in on a stick figure's head while the voiceover asks, "What does this all mean for me?"

Well, a rotational schedule of 'The Program' is illustrated with a diagram of a wheel, dubbed 'The Color Wheel,' divided into segments of blue, white, yellow and purple.

At present, Hector, Anna, and I are part of the rim, not the tire, but the blue rim. We're essential because we give shape to the enterprise and support the component parts—a structure to hold it all together. We don't have an active role, but by simply existing we are important.

Next comes the white tire. These are the ambassadors who maintain contact with the world and provide a comforting cushion in each direction. Dr. Samesong pauses the video to let us know that in addition to conduits like himself, these are the people who first contacted us regarding the study. It sounds like they were keeping tabs on us for some time beforehand.

Then there are the yellow spokes. These are the administrators. People like Peggy. They oversee operations and implement policy. These folks know the rules, but they do not challenge them. This is important. Security also falls under this purview.

The hub, they assure us, is not the top of any structure (especially not a pyramid!), but rather another part no more or less important than another. These are the executives, responsible for decision-making and adjustments to The Program. This portion of the color wheel is purple.

The voiceover uses the word "essential" at least a dozen times while explaining each component of their human wheel.

Given that these roles could be filled ad infinitum, they adhere to a rotation. Each individual spends a five-year tenure in a position before following their rotation schedule to the next part. There is a series of tests which must be passed before transitioning between roles. Dr. Samesong pauses the video to explain some highlights:

1. The rim is essentially a training period. Service in this phase need only be accomplished once, though in certain circumstances a participant returns to this phase for retraining. Our service in this five-year phase includes the one-year trial period which began the day we first signed up to come here. Contact with the outside world is limited and supervised during this period.
2. A half-century of service is required before one can assume an executive role.
3. Anonymity during all stages is imperative. No families. No children. An individual obtaining notoriety will be relocated and protected by the administrators.
4. Violence (including self-harm) is strictly prohibited, with breaches leading to contract termination.
5. Twenty percent of pre-existing personal funds and

assets are to be contributed to 'The Collective,' a term for the organization and its participants, upon enrollment.

6. Compensation is non-monetary, though everyone is ensured basic needs of food, clothing and shelter in perpetuity. Many have inconspicuous jobs to provide supplemental income. Also, previously offered cash payments will still be furnished.
7. The Medicament may not be exchanged for currency under any circumstances.
8. A six-month sabbatical period is observed after every two rotations of service.
9. On the yearly anniversary of the contract signing, special requests for material or services will be proffered by administrators within reason.

It turns out we have been allowed unlimited special requests during our trial period, which has apparently ended now. I guess I should have asked Peggy for more every time she offered.

I raise my hand since it feels like a classroom. "Where do you get the money for all this?" I ask, gesturing around the room. "This doesn't seem like a real business since you aren't selling anything."

"Well, there's no shortage of rich people who want to live forever," Dr. Samesong answers flatly. "They're screened and approached in the same way as everyone else, though many are not made offers due to a perceived unwillingness to shed their high profiles. Or they're too stubborn to believe there's something they don't possess which they can't get for themselves. There are also people like Arthur Romaine who amass a fortune after enrollment and voluntarily contribute to The Collective."

"So, to be clear, a secret society of immortals funded by a shadow economy?"

"Yup."

We're paging through our protocol booklets while Dr. Samesong and Peggy field questions. Everyone is reading with rapt expressions: Hector massaging his temple, Anna mouthing the words as she reads, and my fingers finding every itch on my head. There are a number of flowcharts and decision trees that detail common eventualities like handling overcurious consorts, misplacing one's dosage, and rectifying security breaches. Side bubbles highlight new terms for our lexicon, like an "in-network buddy," who is a fellow participant one is encouraged to contact with any concerns or queries. A "case manager" shall adjudicate said concerns when necessary.

"—if in the event a one-year trial—" Anna begins reading aloud, first to herself, then extending it to the group. "—doesn't elicit 'enlightenment,' an independent subcommittee determines the course of action." She holds her finger in the booklet and turns to Dr. Samesong. "Okay, so what happens if someone doesn't figure this out within the one-year trial?"

"They do."

"Every single time?" I ask.

"Yes. There are tactics we use. Like the evidence we've left around. Or the incident in the ice field. There's an escalating series of methods to create awareness. We didn't need to implement most of the options this time." Dr. Samesong taps the packet again. "But there's protocol."

Hector starts laughing, which turns into a coughing fit, which returns to laughter. "Excuse me," he coughs. "Sorry, none of you find this funny?" He sits still. There's a placidity to him that has been there for weeks. He hasn't shown emotion since his fall, which was my fault. I led us across that perilous ice field. Lured away by nothing. Except it wasn't nothing. A beacon drew us in. The purple. Perfectly placed to provoke curiosity.

"You wanted him to fall," I gasp.

"We wanted you to know your limits. Or lack thereof."

Hector shrugs, unfazed by their trick language. It's hard for me to be more upset than him, the victim, so I let it drop. Still, I'm brought back to that moment when his body was numb, frozen in a hidden depth.

"You talked about dissolution of the contract in cases of violence," I begin, remembering the consequences of Quinn's action. "It seems like a subjective term to me. Who decides when it crosses the line. I mean—" I look towards Hector, who shakes his head, imploring me not to mention smashing the pinball machine. "It seems like we have to trust anonymous people to make decisions affecting our lives."

"That's hardly a new concept. I think you just described government," Dr. Samesong says before chuckling. No one else laughs.

* * *

For the next few days, I do little else but read the protocol packet in the library. It's labeled as the 5th Edition, 1990, indicating several adjustments over the years. Hector's right. It's absurd, but, at the same time, I'm struck by how normal it feels. Eternity contained within a measured protocol. When you learn you're going to live forever, you'll have lots of questions. And I have the answers to page through.

Still, there's an inevitability to all this. There might as well be a flowchart where all paths lead to me reading this packet. My spot in the library has become littered with Redlight butts, unfinished cups of water, and wine glasses dry with residue. Peggy has to remind me multiple times to eat something.

Choice

This place consumes you. I don't think Peggy told us her story so we would side with Robert, but that's where I am. I don't want to leave, but I can hardly stay either. This place is wearing on me. I am repulsed by its beauty.

There are even darker stories buried here, I know, but I can't resist the pull of wonder. If I am contained, it is by the walls of comfort, like a pet who remains in their cage when the door is open.

It's not possible to know how you'd react if someone led you into the woods at gunpoint, handed you a shovel, and told you to begin digging your own grave. Those who have dug the graves are dead; those who refused are dead. We can't ask them what they were thinking. Most choose to dig. Perhaps they cling to a scrap of hope they might escape, that lightning would strike their captor or they'd dislodge a sinkhole and the earth would be their savior. Or perhaps they don't believe—even though a gun is being pointed at them, and each shovelful brings them closer to the inevitable—death was meant for them. Or maybe they know they're going to die, but these last moments, as terrible as they are, are their last to experience life and need to be savored. Whatever the reason, they'll dig and dig and try to keep digging like if they don't stop digging, maybe it will save them.

* * *

It's easy to be caught up in the details as we navigate the contract. There's plenty to pore over and each element is a factor in whatever may happen next. However, it really boils down to a simple decision. Join them and live, or shun them and, you know, perish. Not much of a choice, really. The contract creates the illusion of choice, but it was the initial 'choice,' the one to come here and ingest a mystery drug that brought us to this point.

I've never liked the term, but I've always known I have a soul. I'm not sure about the rest of all that spirituality, but there's more to me than involuntary chemical reactions in my body responding to a physical world. There's something that makes me me, and I'm happy to call that a soul.

But this drug has me muddled. I'm feeling better than ever, better than I could've thought possible, and I owe that feeling to a compound of atoms and molecules. And so it goes, The Medicament has become a part of me, and I too have become a variable in an equation. A person, yes, but one beholden to a much more powerful apparatus. There used to be innumerable paths ahead of me, but now there are only variations on a single route that will always lead me back to them—the people in charge. If they ask me to jump, they'll already know how high I can go.

I don't feel tricked, though. In fact, I'm grateful. I never would have agreed to be a guinea pig in the testing of an immortality drug. It would've felt preposterous, and my skepticism would have kept me home, along with my debt and lack of prospects.

I wrestle with these contradicting thoughts, but they don't keep me awake at night. I sleep as though I can take my time. I don't have to worry. Worry is the instrument of those who can't afford to make mistakes.

* * *

I'm hoping Hector or Anna will make a decision. I might not follow, but at least their action might compel my own. If I choose to stay, I want it to be a choice and not just the result of indecision. Peggy and Dr. Samesong still haven't made a choice.

I shouldn't be afraid. We are taken care of. It's foolish to seek something better and risk sacrificing contentment. I worry about withdrawal—if that is indeed true. I'm hoping that it isn't, that I can reject everything and return to myself. They may have been telling the truth about Robert's deterioration, though.

I need to rest. Time is my greatest luxury. Decisions can be made tomorrow or maybe the day after that.

Chapter 8

I was never the sort of person who could do work in a coffee shop. 1) There was the unknown etiquette of how long one could stay after ordering a single coffee. 2) It was impossible not to eavesdrop, and, though it could give me good observational material, I more often turned into a misanthrope who noticed the banality of people who weren't me. 3) It didn't feel like the type of place to talk to strangers, but maybe I was wrong, so shame on me for becoming irritated when someone tried to strike up a conversation, or, no, they should be able to read my body language and stop violating the goddamn social contract.

The library was a better place. It had rules. Sometimes they were even posted on the wall. And the heavenly shush of the librarian. Yes.

Our library was ordinary—a boxy one-story building that felt like it should have had a higher ceiling. There were stacks of periodicals and a general mustiness and lighting not dissimilar from a hospital and folks who came in every day to read free newspapers, but it offered the potential for anonymity. I knew all of the librarians and regulars by sight but none of them by name, which would seem rude in most other settings. Presumably, they had families and lives outside the library, but I knew nothing of them, nor was I expected to, but the passive smile we'd all exchange communicated as much as desired.

There was a series of posters depicting genres of fiction—romance, science fiction, horror, etc. One poster, under the heading "Adventure," showed a bear snarling at a helpless hiker, but I wasn't sure if it was a scene from a real book or not. If it were, there's no way the story should have ended well for the hiker, but since it was called "Adventure," it probably did.

I'd find a book to bring to my table and hold it as a prop while hardly turning the pages. Its weight made me daydream. Half-formed thoughts and little notes that wouldn't amount to anything were scribbled down on a pad next to me that I'd never look at again, but I would have the muscle memory of writing.

Sometimes voices from the children's annex would drift in. My mom used to take me to pull a cushion from a stack and listen to a reading where they'd do funny voices, and kids would giggle and say 'ewwwwww' during the gross parts. During summer, they had a reading program where you'd get a sticker for each book you read, and the more stickers you got to put on your yellow brick road, the closer you'd get to Oz. My road found a place on our fridge and stayed there longer than it should have.

* * *

I was sitting and pretending to read and pretending to write and thinking half-ideas for stories that sounded good in my head, but when they came out, they weren't really more than a sentence or two, and not even a particularly good sentence or two. There were some computers now, but there was always a line to use them. People who had never been to the library started coming in to see what all the fuss was about. I'd heard they were good for writing because you could delete parts and move paragraphs around without having to write a whole new page. I would have tried, but even if I did wait in the line, I didn't want people getting antsy behind me when they wanted to play Frogger or whatever.

Someone was upset because they had booked an appointment for the computer for four o'clock, but it was 4:15 already, and some kid wasn't giving up his turn. The librarian wanted to help, but she also wanted him to lower his voice. Their voices became unignorable, drowning out the voices in my head that were trying to create mediocre sentences.

* * *

It wasn't a terribly large place, and the shelves were easy to navigate. They'd once been a labyrinth to me, though. One time, I had read through my books and was ready to leave, and I'd stacked up my cushion, and my mom was taking forever to find her book in the adult section. The librarians didn't like it if you went in there without an adult, but since I didn't look up at them when I pushed the door open, I couldn't see the disapproving look they must have given me. It wasn't like I was going to make a lot of noise or anything; I knew that much. I was systematic and went up one row and down the next and double-checked to make sure I hadn't missed her, and then there was a woman with similar hair who I called mom, but I ran away when the stranger turned. A librarian was going to shush me, but I was already rushing out of the adult section, so they didn't have the chance.

In the foyer, an older man waiting to check out caught sight of the frantic little girl and came over to console her. He crouched down and spoke gently and asked, "What is the matter? Let's see if we can find your mom together, okay?" And he held up his hand to give me a high-five. His hand looked too hard, and I didn't want to touch it, so I squirmed away to dart back into the kids' section. He followed me. My mom looked as frantic as I did when she saw me. She thought she lost me, she said, and we must've zig-zagged right past each other. Then she saw the man who was sort of out of breath from chasing after me. He looked relieved, but she had a look on her face like I'd never seen before, or maybe it was like when I chased after a ball that started rolling into the street. I got brushed aside. Whatever she said to him, he let her say it. When we left, I heard the librarian ask the man if he still wanted to check out his books. Maybe next time, but I don't think there ever was a next time. He probably started having the newspaper delivered to his house.

* * *

They mowed the grass often in the summertime. The days were longer, and the grass grew quicker, but that didn't mean my concentration cooperated with the din. When he neared the window, I began to brace, and the whir reached its climax, and then the motor turned and the sound faded until it met the Doppler effect. My pages remained scribbled upon, but maybe this one thought would come to something if only I could... Whirrrrrrrrr... I returned to the book as prop as crutch.

The writer described the scent of orchards. They might have been apples, but my mind wanders to orange orchards, or maybe they're called groves and orchards are for apples. On my paper I wrote, orchard vs. grove? The grocery store was a little out of the way going home, but I needed orange juice and maybe a few other things, but I should call my mom to check what she might need. Whirrrrrrrr... I checked and I had a quarter. Just one.

Leaving my table claimed with book and notes, I went to make the phone call in the foyer. They had added a stepladder for the book drop. Now kids could step up and watch as their books flipped/folded down the chute to thud at the base of the metal contraption. While on tiptoes, I used to glimpse the books' disappearance. That's where they keep the imagination, my mom used to say, that's why it's so secure. If a thief could just check out a book for themselves, why would they bother with trying to crack the book vault? Because thieves are the sort who want to skip ahead to the end.

There would be three rings, and my mom would answer. She didn't like to seem overeager to answer the phone. I needed to be direct, I only had the one quarter, so I prepared what I would say, already getting irritated for when she would inevitably drag out whatever she was going to add to the shopping list, and it would go over the minute, and I'd have to break a dollar and call back, but, like, seriously be quick this time. Somehow, the lawnmower found me here, too, and the kids in the next room erupted in laughter, and I heard the step-step thud of the book drop and the clickity-clack of the new computers, but no voice answered on the other end of the phone. My quarter clinked down into the coin return slot.

A poster depicted a tree growing out of the pages of an open book.

Null and Void

Hector's wheezing has gotten worse. It's been a month since he's been off The Medicament. I've begun to forget what pain feels like, but I know what it sounds like. They keep giving it to him, but he refuses to ingest it.

Anna and I have been holding steady, keeping our options open. It didn't take him long to decide. He said he didn't want to continue carrying two lives inside him. I carry others inside me, too, but it's not the same. I've never given half of myself away. Hector speaks of it little, but I know he's lost someone. He wasn't sure how long he could go on, but this way it won't be forever.

Cagey

Ghosts are said to pass through walls because they walk the same pathways that existed in their lifetime. Even ghosts are creatures of habit. Everything has become so ingrained, it's not hard to imagine Peggy or Hector or anyone passing through a newly constructed wall to maintain the routine. Maybe ghosts aren't actually dead, maybe they're people who have been around so long we don't notice them.

Even with eternity, we choose our routine, its sameness and comfort. They may be alive, and I might be the silent one, but I have become a ghost chronicler.

Anna is the most optimistic; not that she's excited, but relative to the others, she's least passive. Her routine fits into that space of things she wants to do, not things she feels like she has to do. It may be small, but when she says she can't wait to see a movie, it's a display of something we all lack now—anticipation. She still exercises constantly, and even though we all look effortlessly beautiful, she's the most stunning. It's almost as if she pushes herself so that we have an ideal of what to strive for.

Peggy and Dr. Samesong are hard to differentiate from each other. They're resigned to it, to their existence. It's neither bleak nor rosy; it's just matter of fact. They sleep for long stretches. They're not immune to pockets of joy like an odd chuckle or the satisfaction of a good meal, but they mostly just exist. It's like infinity has made them procrastinators, and it's hard to blame them.

Hector exists apart from the others. His routine has become one of quiet. I know Dr. Samesong is impossibly older, but Hector evokes a greater sense of aged wisdom. Accepting his fate has lent him a mysterious credibility.

His health is failing. Or maybe it's just the stark contrast to the rest of us. It doesn't keep him away from the Redlights, a fact I find perversely respectable. He's going to stay true to himself even if it kills him.

He has appointments with Dr. Samesong more and more often. Bandages have begun to appear where his skin has thinned. He sleeps for long stretches, too.

He's taken to watching the sun cresting over the mountain ridge each morning. Not for any spiritual reason, he says, but because he's awake and it's there. Sometimes he watches the shadows disappear; sometimes he faces away and watches the dew evaporate off the grass. A routine, but with distinct variety.

Puzzles are his only exercise, he jokes repeatedly. They give him a tangible goal. He's not convinced anyone gets better at jigsaw puzzles the more they practice. He can't think of any other activity where that's true.

Solstice

The days are long, and the nights are short. No matter how many times we see the sun at midnight, it's still remarkable. I suggest a solstice bonfire, and the idea is met with enthusiasm. No one checks the calendar to confirm it's the correct date. It's clear at twilight (the sun dips enough to give the earth a hazy glow without fully setting) so we've agreed to call it the solstice.

We gather on a small hill where the dome of the conservatory is the only man-made object in sight. It glimmers in the light as Hector slowly walks up to join us. I had offered to walk with him, but he wanted to take his time. If we burn all the wood we have, we'll have the tallest and longest lasting fire I've ever seen.

Some of us stand, others don't. Some of us drink, others don't. The hues turn dusky, and the dimming light of the sun competes with the fire for control of the shadows. The wind breathes its constant exhale over the peaks, echoing into the valley and silencing into the wet earth.

We start with our voices muted in reverence, but as the evening proceeds, and we begin to shout over each other in that way people speak when they are too excited to control their volume, the surrounding nature quiets to hear us.

Each time another log is placed on the fire it is met with appreciation. We watch in awe as it is consumed by the flames.

The hypnotic fire dictates our voices. It's as though our words don't come from us but originate elsewhere. Despite the atmosphere, the chatter is trivial, silly even. We make jokes:

"What has two wheels and is holy?"

"Swiss cheese. Like, two cheese wheels. In a shopping basket."

"The pope on a bicycle."

"Is that really a joke? I prefer my answer. It's just as accurate."

"How many popes have never ridden a bike?"

"Is that a joke?"

"It's an honest question."

"How could we possibly know the answer to that?"

"I guess it was more of a musing."

"I thought my answer was more amusing."

Hector begins laughing more than is warranted by the joke. There are tears in his eyes he thinks it's so funny. We do not talk about the circumstances. When Hector's laugh turns to a cough, an awful and frightening sound, it does little more than change the conversation's tempo. There's a pause, but no one brings drama to it by offering concern. No one wants to be the person to kill the vibe, so the chatter turns into a competition of who can maintain the silliness.

Hector stays seated on a rock and does a lot of listening. The few things he does say are hard to follow, and I try not to think of the delirium setting in. He's underdressed but seems unbothered. The breeze kicks up, and he doesn't shudder. I offer him a drink from the whisky, and he takes a small sip. When he returns the bottle, he holds onto it, giving it a joking tug like I can't have it back before he catches my eye. "Cheers," he says before releasing.

FUNERAL

The ground is harder than I thought it would be. Most of the snow has melted, and most days are warm enough to go outside without a coat, but the soil is compacted and cold. I volunteer without telling anyone since I don't want help. When I take a break, the sweat sticks to my skin, cooled by the breeze. Letting a cigarette sit on my lip like a cowboy, the ash dangles as I resist using my hands to flick it off. I lean against the upright shovel and take stock of the day's work. A long way to go. Starting again, the sweat regroups and drips down my face. My tarry breath clashes with the fresh air, but it feels right, nonetheless. I didn't do any measurements, I have a pretty good sense of the height, but it's hard to estimate height when laid on the ground.

–Don't underestimate your capacity to underestimate yourself.

I'm remembering them wrong. They're too well-edited, too pithy and sage. He was repetitive, but not tautological. And he certainly wouldn't have said capacity. I sit down, exhausted. The shovel drops and clangs further down the hill than I want it to.

The plumes of smoke puffing from the facility's generator are the only evidence that it's nearby. There were few options flat enough but still out of sight. He was clear on that point.

—Something tucked away. A destination. A place you'll have to go out of your way to get to. And with a view.

Whether he meant to obscure the view from here to there or there to here doesn't really matter. He wanted to be close enough we couldn't pretend it didn't happen, just not that close. He tried hard to act like he didn't care about much, but there was dignity in acknowledging he cared about this.

—Everyone I've known is dead. Death is a part of me. Funny that I'll be the last person you know who dies. Should we do a puzzle? Yosemite falls?

There's always so much planning to do when someone dies; you don't have time to be sad—finding the right minister and the right venue and the flowers and the catering and contacting relatives and making an announcement in the newspaper and deciding about the casket and trying not to care about price but not wanting to spend too much on someone who is dead and definitely won't care about price, so you find a budget that shows respect and frugality and doesn't reflect poorly on you because you might not be the one in the casket, but you're the one that paid for it. When the funeral is over and they're in the ground and you have a fridge stocked with strangers' bowls of casserole and potato salad that you promise to return if you can keep straight which bowl belongs to who, and everyone says to call if you need anything, but they've already given you so much of them and their time that you know you can't call soon, that's when they're gone. That's when you can be sad.

—Just in case. (The box holds a mix of puzzle pieces and over a month's worth of green pills.) I'm sorry there's not more.

Before I began digging, I scrounged for a bag I could use to transport his body. Bag feels too crude a word, but when the only option has Samsonite written on it, it's either a carry-on or luggage or a bag. His body doesn't look like a person; it looks like a body. He's been dead for over a day, enough time for the life to seep out of him and transform him into something I have to deal with.

–Do you know how to whistle? I never learned.

Last words never mean as much as the listener thinks they do. The words themselves don't matter as much as the fact that they were the last expression of life. A smile or a squeeze of the hand could mean many things, involuntary reflex even, but words are something we don't come to by instinct, they're evidence of a life lived. It may have been another episode of delirium, but I'd like to think it was a good joke.

I wrap him in a blanket before I pack him inside the bag. The zipper is stretched in the middle, and I have to pull the sides together with one hand and inch up the zipper with the other. Once past the resisting section, it completes the seal with the satisfying sound.

(Coughing continues. The lights from the projector flicker over the room.)

I'm chilled from the breeze, so it's time to start digging again. Each shovelful is going to go back the other way in a few hours, so I leave it loosely packed by the grave's side so I can scrape it back in after a few ceremonial scoops.

(The fluorescent lights brighten, and the theater turns back into a room. He is resting on the couch. The coughing has been infrequent. Or maybe stopped altogether.)

Near exhaustion settles in as I make a push to finish. My heart pounds as the thin air fails my quickened pace. Some parts are deeper than others, and I've had to give up on removing some of the bigger rocks. There's enough space now, but a little bit deeper would be better. My hands blister on the wooden shovel. It doesn't hurt, but I know if I stop, I won't want to start again.

(Out of instinct, I find Dr. Samesong since you're supposed to call a doctor.)

My head is light with runner's high as I amble back to the facility. I splash through puddles without trying to avoid them. I'm already filthy. It's fine if I'm muddy at the funeral, too.

They ask about the mud, and I point to the bag. They're happy to help me carry. It's heavy. Sometimes we have to drag it. The blanket should keep his bones intact. It's a tedious haul. He's heavy, and we need to take a break every hundred steps. We count them. Our progress is slow, but the increments give us something to focus on.

(There's less color in his skin by the time we return. He checks for a pulse or, at least, puts his fingers on his neck even though he knows there's nothing there.)

No one wants to open the bag, so that's how he'll stay. A bag in an irregularly flat hole. I'm not sure if I'm joking or not when I suggest unzipping the top for an open-casket ceremony. The comment is met with an odd silence; no one else knew if I was joking or not, either. We've caught our breath now.

(I reach for a tissue and take one. Dr. Samesong takes one, too. Neither of us cry. The tissue crumples into a dry wad in my hand.)

Since no one else takes the lead, I begin, "I guess we should start." They shift their weight and stare downwards. "To be honest, I didn't know much about Hector. I didn't even know his last name. He was a private person. We know that." A wheezy exhale to my left. From Anna, I think. "But that doesn't mean he wasn't a friend. Someone who will be missed." Another wheezy sound I can't attribute. "Someone who is already missed." My voice begins to crackle. "I feel fortunate for the time we—" The wheezy sound distracts and causes me to look up. I don't find tears and red, wobbly faces. Anna's brow is furrowed, and the others are blank.

Anna, whose scoffs I mistook for sobs, is waiting for me to make eye contact, "What are you doing?"

"I'm sorry?"

"This. This eulogy. This funeral."

Peggy steps forward, not saying anything, but making her presence noted.

"I'm, I'm not sure. I thought we should—"

"Exactly. *You* thought that *we* should. What? Bury a man? Perform a hasty funeral and move along."

"By no means. I thought—"

"Stop!" she screams. The sound reverberates through the landscape and bounces back. Hearing her voice a second time, Anna recedes. Peggy steps back and Dr. Samesong continues to stare at his feet. "I know you were up to something. The two of you. I bet you put him up to this. I saw him stashing his pills."

I'm caught in the place of not wanting to say anything but having lots I need to say. My sinuses begin to twitch and I fight it; I swallow the tears back and breathe. I focus it into anger; I don't want to look on the brink of crying. I catch Anna's face; her tears are contagious. I can't help but release just a few, and I wipe them aside. The bag lies motionless in the hole.

My breathing stutters. Not wanting to speak, and for lack of anything else, I pick up the shovel and drop a dirt pile on top of the bag. I extend it to Anna, who follows with the same motion, as do Dr. Samesong and Peggy.

"I don't know what to say," I offer, finally.

"None of us do," answers Dr. Samesong, speaking for the first time this ceremony.

(A sheet rests over his body. "I wish I understood it, but I don't. I suppose it doesn't matter if you believe me. It's fair if you want to hold me responsible. People only want to play God, but they don't want to be him. I'm speaking in metaphor, of course.")

The dirt is pressed into a soft mound, and we begin to head back. I walk with Peggy, who has drifted to the back of the group. We step slowly, and the others pull further ahead. "How do you do it?" I ask. "How do you keep this up?"

She doesn't respond at first. She looks around, at the scenery, at the rest of the quiet group, then turns her gaze downward, "One step after another."

It sounds like a company line. "Okay. But what's next?"

"Something. There's always something. Sometimes it'll be better. Sometimes it'll be worse. All I can do is try to make it something better."

"But don't you ever feel guilty?" I ask. "Like you shouldn't be here? That you don't deserve it?"

"Of course, I do. Every day." The trail dips, and she leans into a rock for balance as she steps downward. When it's my turn, she reaches a hand up, and I let her guide me. "Haven't we always felt sorry for the dead? Be honest. When you hear about scores killed in an earthquake or read an obituary of a cancer patient, isn't there a part of you that thinks, 'Glad it wasn't me?'"

"I suppose. But these aren't strangers I'm talking about. They are people we have known. Like Quinn. And Hector. Why are we here while he's in the ground?" I pause before adding. "And how about Maria." I look at Peggy, thinking I might catch her off guard. But there's a stoicism to her expression, like she's already reconciled these losses.

"We learn from our mistakes. Each of us. I never said I don't get sad. But they made their choices. And I've made mine. I choose to continue; to try to do good. And look..." She gestures to the scenery. "It's a beautiful day."

The conversation lulls, and we walk in silence. Wind rushes overhead as birds soar across the valley. A pair of streams converge into a creek before us, and we choose which stones to step on. It's bright daylight, and it will be for several more hours.

Chapter 9

They always let you in. Even if you showed up a minute before closing time, they wouldn't lock the doors beforehand. If you were returning something, they'd prefer if you handed it to them so they didn't have to key open the vault, but then you'd miss out on the magic of book evaporation.

At least they weren't peering out on the street, standing with their hand on the lock. Instead, they were fussing with the checkout cards and emptying the vault when I rushed in. I still needed to b-line it for my book to avoid aggravating them further, but they could handle it.

The stacks looked different at night. Lonelier, like the other books begged me to take them with me, too. But I snagged the one I came for and ignored the rest. The librarian had his stamp ready for me. I thanked him, hugging the book to my chest as I left.

Reading seemed to help. Well, the sound of my voice helped, but reading gave me a way to focus it. If I tried to ad-lib a story, I started repeating myself and, honestly, became a little bored, so I stuck with library books. The doctors said there was no way to know how much she could hear, but her face made small, almost imperceptible movements that weren't quite smiles but were close enough.

Usually, when I read aloud, I wouldn't really hear the words. I could speak deliberately and do voices and everything, but I'd still lose the meaning as the page turned to sound. Had it always been this way for her, too? She read story after story that made no sense because she was the one reading them, but nevertheless, she continued because of the movements in my sleepy face that weren't quite smiles but were close enough.

It might have been an accident. Medicines are unpredictable, they said. There's a lot of trial and error.

They didn't say any of this in the aftermath, but they'd said it enough before.

Dr. Forester wasn't himself when he stopped by. He couldn't meet my eye when he said there was nothing we could do but hope.

* * *

I knew we were out of eggs, of that I was sure. I was even proud that I'd remembered. There's a part of me that would like to blame the happenstance. The cosmic injustice of my delayed arrival home. But it wasn't like that. When I got home, delay or not, I wasn't prompt. I futzed with the mail, I unpacked groceries, and I flicked on the TV and channel surfed.

The water was so cold. It must have been sitting for hours. She felt like ice when I pulled her out of the tub. I was sure she was dead. Her body was lifeless, and her eyes were open and dull. Still, somehow, she continued to breathe. Splinters lay everywhere. The door had been easier to kick down than expected. I lay her in the puddle of tile and splinters and rushed for help while her body continued to rise and fall with impossible breath.

* * *

It took a while to adjust to her eyes: the right perpetually bloodshot and the left faded and unfocused. They closed when she slept, and when awake, they gave emphatic, elongated blinks. If she could see, her eyes did not belie it. They were vacant, as if they'd forgotten how to see. Her hair was different, too. I'd never seen it so gray.

Still, she was there. When I spoke, I sensed she could hear me, and that was something, at least for a time.

Evidence created a muddy picture. The toxicology report indicated she had no trace of drugs in her system but did have a 0.12 blood alcohol content. There were plenty of pills available and more wine in the bottle—an abnormal truth, if she'd wished self-harm. She was unclothed, which could have supported either theory, depending. Either she didn't care about being indecent when she was found, or she wasn't planning anything, and it was pure accident.

The water was shallow enough that she didn't drown entirely but deep enough that she lost oxygen for several minutes. Most likely, she passed out and slid beneath the surface, causing the water to rise to the level of the emergency drain, where it slowly seeped out and let her breathe again. If it was intentional, it was unlucky; if it was unintentional, it was unlucky.

It may have been bad luck, but that didn't mean I couldn't be mad at her. I was grateful that she was responsive to my voice, that she was somewhere behind those eyes, that she wasn't gone. Her presence, her still, living body, gave me somewhere to direct my emotion. She held physical space in a non-abstract way, and that mattered. I didn't have to talk to a ghost.

* * *

During my next trip to the library, I held my book as a prop and underlined ghost vs. body on my notepad. Routines were important, they told me, even if they were talking about her. Home was too quiet and too full of space that collected dust not long after you cleaned it. Dust is a fitting auto-antonym, one of those words that means the same as its opposite. "To dust" means to remove dust, just the same as it means to add dust. No matter where you are in the process, you're always dusting.

Daydreaming spurts were hijacked by thoughts of the envelopes. More came each day and became easier to neglect. Insurance and the hospital and the ambulance and the clinicians and the pharmacy. With her absent, the person I turned to with adult problems was also absent. I didn't have anyone to talk with about the financial woes. The letters became an insurmountable mass, a different physical space to direct my emotion toward.

The poster of the bear and the hiker watched me. His plight seemed a manageable adventure. A kid sat on a computer clacking keys to make a pixel frog cross the street. He must have been squashed by a car or missed a log because the kid let his anger out on the machine. The librarian shushed.

I reread the page of my book as prop, the same one I read the night before and would continue to read that night, still not finding the story, even if I read the words again and again.

When home at night, I still walked the same path to avoid creaking floorboards.

Summer

The mornings are cold, but they're the best time to move. If a storm comes in, I have enough time to retreat in the daylight. Also, when I get up and go in the morning, I won't put it off and make excuses, I'll actually do it. By the time the sun crests over the mountain range and the valley begins to warm, I've already worked up a sweat, and I'll forget I had wished it warmer only an hour earlier.

Cartography isn't my best skill. I'm a shoddy drawer, but I've managed a decipherable representation of the area. Perched atop the crater's southern *arête*, the wind howls as I focus on the descending range and the geography beyond. I shade the mid-foreground with diagonal lines on my map to denote forest. I'll measure more efficiently soon, but for now I write the estimation: Seven miles.

I turn the page and review the chart. Southern Arête—2395 steps, three hours, twenty-three minutes. It's the highest of the peaks I can summit without gear. Directly opposite: the Saddle—3100 steps, four hours, seven minutes—recesses below the northern peak. Its view was largely obstructed by the craggy rock face of the peak and the jagged slabs protruding in the approach beneath. Extending to the north lies a valley covered in a glacial field that looks unnavigable. The Eastern Rim—4800 steps, five hours, eighteen minutes—required a long and winding approach. It proved to be a false summit, and, having exhausted myself on that day, I still haven't pushed myself to return to scout the panorama of the true summit, which extends at least another mile past the rim. The entire western edge is unapproachable. Within the crater, wind has swept ice and snow to make the walls sheer. Scouting from the southern base, it was obvious the thick forest and incline make ascent impossible. I could chart the west through the forest, but without an aerial view to give me an idea of its geography, I stick to documenting the other areas. The southern route is most promising, and since we're in the northern hemisphere, a southern route will lead to something eventually.

Visibility has only been good every third day on average. That likely gives me two days to prepare for an overnight.

Glaciers roar as the ice shifts with summer melt and the echoes bounce upward. It's too early in the season, but the blueberries will ripen soon, their white flower buds broadcast their nearing appeal. I need to quit smoking. I'm surrounded by space that becomes greener every hour, and I'm possessed by cravings.

* * *

I want one year. One last hurrah away from all of this. The last few weeks, I've only been taking one pill a week and stashing the rest. It hasn't been hard; they've long since stopped inspecting our mouths at dosages. Adding to what Hector gave me, I have enough to live out a year. I could always stay with them for a time, then disappear once I feel like I've lived enough, but I don't want to be a part of this anymore.

My decision was made during Peggy's story. Ever since hearing it, I've felt an underlying dread. There wasn't any specific detail in her story, but horror movies don't need to show the gore to be terrifying. The camera turns and the audience fills in the space. I don't want to continue to live in the first act of a horror movie.

The others are uninterested in my work. Dr. Samesong even caught me testing a few codes on the medicine safe, and he played dumb. I haven't had to make excuses; if anyone asked me what I'm up to, I'd tell them, but they've retreated into themselves. I hardly see anybody anymore. I spend the days outside or in the library. The resources are a bit dated, but there's still enough to give myself a crash course in wilderness survival. Following water will eventually lead to human settlement in most cases. Packing food will get me pretty far if I ration, but there's no knowing how long I will need it to last.

Anna is determined to restore normalcy. Her movie regimen has resumed, and she invites Dr. Samesong and Peggy to viewing parties. When we talk, there's a strain to her voice that sounds like an actor stumbling their way through a new accent. The words don't come out quite right. She talks about the good old days as though there's a mutually agreed upon past in which things were perfect. It's not clear if she's talking about the start of the project or before our arrival. Either way, she says it enough that it has become true for herself.

I try not to look in the mirror. If I pause for too long, the image will persuade my decision. I have never looked as perfect as I do now.

My writing is finished, at least that's what I'm telling myself. It could always be better, but that attitude becomes dangerous when it compels me to stay. It's finished and imperfect.

During the gloomy days I work on my tent. If my paintings were better, I might feel bad about re-purposing them. The waterproof canvas is flexible and lightweight. It tears easily, but if I'm careful it shouldn't matter. I save the scraps for patching. I can't help but coordinate the color arrangement for aesthetics. It's still going to be a hodgepodge, but a conscious one. The patterning is inefficient; I'm having to resew lines because I didn't plan it out well. Still, it's coming together.

The frame is a more difficult task. One of the library books suggests gathering tree branches at each camp, but with the unknown landscape ahead, I'll need something more reliable.

I save my good weather days for scouting, so it's pouring rain when I set out for the mine to pilfer. The path is thick with mud as the rain and melting snow flood down the mountainside. I trudge through, and even though the cold rain doesn't cause me pain, I'm not immune to misery. Each step is bleak—my boot disappears into the boggy murk, and the suction doesn't want to let it go. But I need something to do.

The mine is even less inviting when I'm alone. Voices pour from the falling rain outside and tell me not to disturb the past. I focus on the metal. The IV stands will need to be sawed at the base, but they're about the right length. The forceps and dental equipment could pass as stakes. I might not use the wheelchair again, but for now it'll work as a shopping cart to haul the load.

When I return, I shower the mud off the equipment and myself simultaneously. My feet begin to prune as the drain clogs. The sludge gurgles and slops with my efforts to unclog it, and a foul, earthy odor is unleashed. I recoil and bump into the arrangement of metal I've cleaned and set aside. It destabilizes, and the equipment clangs its way back into the sludge. I hate it for being loud. I watch the mass submerge itself and resolve to pace myself.

There should be no urgency. My panicked response is not rational. Firefighters don't actually rush out of the firehouse. They are methodical. They tie their boots and double-check their equipment. Mistakes could be catastrophic, so it's more important to be correct than it is to be fast.

7/1/1991

Mom,

You used to tell me if I had a hard choice to make, I should flip a coin, not because I should make big decisions based on fifty-fifty chance, but because my relief or disappointment from the result will show me the decision I've already made.

When I went back to gather supplies at the mine, I'd already made a choice. I'd convinced myself I was preparing myself for all possibilities, but now I realize I was already leaving.

The others made a choice, too, even if they don't realize it. Inaction as choice.

Our minds find all sorts of ways to rationalize; we don't like cognitive dissonance, so we shield ourselves with an internal logic no one else understands. Because it doesn't make sense. Thoughts make sense to us because we're the ones who thought them, and we're using the same brain to examine them.

You taught me that reading would challenge myself and my ideas. It might be uncomfortable, but I might see something in a new way. More often, though, I read to find ways to validate my opinion. See, I'm not crazy, someone else thinks what I think.

I'm sorry for leaving. I can hear you fighting for me, wishing I would reconsider, take in the other perspectives. I'm not sure I'm right to leave. If I watch the others, it may challenge my belief. I may find that I'm wrong, but I don't think they are right.

Love,
Lily

Cold

The cold doesn't hurt, but I feel it. When the night began, it was a mere discomfort, but as the hours passed, it's become all I can think about. It creeps into my feet and sticks inside my chest. I cuddle into a ball and contort to find a position that will let me doze off. But the cold and sleep are incompatible. The chill feeds upon itself until I lie awake wishing to feel nothing.

My insomnia began with the cold and midnight sun, but it's my head that keeps me awake. It's easier to blame the physical—the icy ground below, a flicker of shadow on the canvas, an unignorable tickle, a pang of hunger—than to slow the spin of mental discord.

My trial night is a disaster. I had set out at morning and made camp after a five-hour walk on the southern route. Finding a suitable site proved more difficult than expected. The ground was often too sloped or too rocky or too swampy. When I eventually settled on a spot, it still rested on a double-fall incline. Whatever sleep I might find, it'll be hindered by the urge to seek equilibrium. Flat rest is an impossibility, I know, but my subconscious feels differently and tries to compensate.

The walls slump, but not for lack of trying to make it otherwise. My tent would've been sorry in the best circumstance, but on unlevel ground without trees nearby from which to suspend support, I was stuck propping the rods with cairns. Fist-sized rocks slipped if they weren't supported by the hefty slabs I dubbed cinder blocks. My fingernails filled with dirt as I dug up the cinder blocks and schlepped them over to the tent whose walls had fallen in the absence of erect rods. If I roll over, or if gravity pulls me too far, I'll dislodge the Jenga cairn and be wrapped in painted canvas.

A body in motion stays in motion, and a body at rest stays at rest. And a body in the ground stays in the ground, but it still moves. The motion of gravity and centripetal force of the orbit around the sun: the motion of rocks. The conversations are jumbled, and some are imaginary and some are remembered wrong but that doesn't make them any less present. What I did say and what I should have said and what I'm going to say and the gaps I fill in with whoever I'm talking with because it isn't me; the people in my head are real, they just aren't here. A body at rest is not a mind at rest.

Alcohol could have helped. It was weight, and I didn't want to carry nonessentials. I have to think hard to remember the last day I went without booze, and I stop counting. Redlights wouldn't have weighed much, but I wanted to think I didn't need them.

Building a fire can still be hard even when you have a lighter or matches and know how to make a teepee of kindling inside a log cabin. None of that makes firewood any less wet.

Books were definitely weight, not that I could've held one for long without my fingers freezing.

Stargazing is underwhelming when it's overcast, and the sky is never pitch black. It's darkest before the dawn, but it's also coldest and miserablist. This is a practice day. It could be raining next time.

I'm focusing on the negatives so I can convince myself to

stay. There are a lot of negatives, though. It's not irrational pessimism. They don't want me, or maybe they do, or maybe they don't know what they want either, and emotions overwhelm, and we just buried a man, and none of this is normal, so there's no one to blame, and we're scrambled because we don't communicate, and we rely on each other to help when we can't help.

A list of needs! Like counting sheep, I itemize and watch them jump over the fence one after the other: more warm clothes, a paperback I can read and reread, whiskey, fuel, even more clothes than I think I'll need because I'm going to need them, pen and paper and backup pens and backup paper for when the paper gets wet, and a few pieces of chocolate or candy or something that I can have as a reward when I deserve it.

It will be heavy, but I'll take weight.

I break down camp because whatever sleep I get is going to be conscious sleep or waking dreams. The sun is up. By the time I start moving back, it'll be heating up, and my pack will be heavier because of the zero sleep, and I'll start sweating and wonder what it feels like to be cold.

Procedure

Canned goods won't spoil anytime soon, but they're heavy. Microwavable meals are bulky, and I doubt the possibility of cooking them over a fire. I've already snagged a small pot from the kitchen for boiling water. Dried foods—pasta and rice—pack more easily and maximize the weight-to-calorie ratio. I loathe the thought of weeks of tasteless meals, so I'll supplement with some sauces. I can't justify too much extra weight, so I'll have to ration. Once per day, I'll spoil myself with the luxury of a tomato or sweet-and-sour sauce. Some mountain climbers cut their toothbrushes in half to reduce weight. I'll reassess once I'm packed. I might have to compromise and carry nothing more than rice and protein powder.

I try to be discreet as I raid the pantries, but I think they know something is up. When Dr. Samesong sticks his head in, I start babbling a fake explanation, but he cuts me off. "You have a birthday coming up, right?"

Surprised, I put down the pasta box and look him in the eye. "In a few weeks," I say. "I haven't thought much about it."

He shuts the door behind him and steps into the room. He finds a box of cake mix. "Good. We still have plenty." His eyes drift up to the part in my hair. I know some gray has returned, but he doesn't mention it.

Emphatically, he slumps into a sack of potatoes in the corner. He's making an effort to establish sub-ordinance. "I know it's not perfect here," he laments. "But believe me, we're trying our best."

"Is this some tactic from the admin protocol book? Admit flaws in an effort to appear trustworthy?"

"Okay. Fair enough," he shifts his weight on the irregular seat of potatoes, "I understand why you might not want to trust me. And I apologize for any deception, but, as we mentioned, you needed to be skeptical at first. Otherwise, you wouldn't believe any of this."

It occurs to me I can reduce packaging weight if I consolidate the pasta into one container. "Yes. I was skeptical. I still am, just not about the drug."

"Believe me. I understand." He seems to think I should know what this means. "I wish I had your strength."

I lean against a shelf of dried apricots and raisins. The unbranded products are labeled with black letters on white packaging as though they are trying to convince me of their blandness.

"Look, it's not easy. This life. Being alone. Being anonymous," he says as he stands again to look me in the eye. "But before I came to Fairbanks all those years ago, I had some dark times." He pauses and looks down. "You can't choose your family, right?"

I give a reassuring smile to let him know I'm listening.

"And when Arthur found me, I was an even bigger mess. A failing business. A drug addiction. He took advantage of me. He knew I was lost. I'm not so sure he didn't send that robber in himself, to be honest. I know there were scouts, and it wasn't hard to see I was an addict. There were times I thought I might stop breathing, and I was fine with that. Everything I had done. It was a way to escape the pain."

"But what is life without pain?" I ask.

"Is that the title of your book?" he responds, smiling like he's proud of me. "I'll answer you, though—it's boring and it's easy to get lost."

I look back to the shelves and remove a can of tomatoes to feel its weight. "Or, maybe," I turn to face him again. "Like you say, it's something to do." I shrug to add a hint of sarcasm.

He doesn't look as hurt as I expect him to. He pauses and says simply, "We are here to help."

I hesitate before telling him what I've been wanting to say for weeks, thinking it'll land like a knockout punch, "You aren't gods, you know."

"Ha. No, definitely not," he laughs, deflating my intent. "We're only people who are too scared to die."

I turn to go. Part of me expects the pantry door to be locked, but it opens without resistance. He's standing still, not making any motion to follow as I'm holding the door, "Do you want this open or—"

"Either way. Happy early birthday," he says as I leave.

Anna

Anna apologizes. She doesn't do it in front of the others. She waits and doesn't force it out. We're sitting beside each other on the lounge couch, and as she speaks, her face goes through a range of emotion—as if an actor posing for headshots—at moments on the verge of tears, then smiling with sincerity, and then with just a hint of worry. As she performs, I can't help but marvel at her. Her hair and skin are perfect and radiant, with the contours of her face symmetrical and alluring. Her voice sits at a register that almost puts me into a trance.

I know I have changed, too, but I don't see myself like her. When I watch her, she's present and natural; the words are almost incidental. Her veneer confuses and obscures. It makes it difficult, but not impossible, to see the undercurrent of her speech—fear.

"When we lost Quinn, no one was to blame. He had his problems, and it was easy to move on. We were sad, sure, but it was hard not to feel good, too, you know? I know you feel it," her eyes sway me to agree. "Are we that selfish? Two people have died, and I pity them. I'm mad at them for being so stupid. Why is it so easy?"

"I don't know," I say before pausing, thinking through what I want to say, even if it isn't really a response to what she's saying. It's what she needs to hear, what I need to hear myself say, "I'm afraid."

"Me too," she pauses for a long while. Her eyes aren't focused on anything, and her breath stutters. "I know I belong to them now. Whatever they need from me, I'll be there. I can't stop. All I can do is hope they're the good guys." Her fear is quiet. It's in her voice and my own and in the silence. "They know you're leaving," Anna adds. "They told me. I guess Peggy really was keeping track of everything with her clipboard. Sorry. I might have tipped them off at Hector's funeral."

And now I understand her mix of emotions. She knows I'm abandoning her. She's the last one of our group. "It's okay. What did they say?"

"They mentioned it almost as an afterthought," Anna tells me. "I didn't want to believe them. Even after I saw Hector's stash of pills, I thought I might have misunderstood."

"You could come, too. I have a plan. And we won't even have to give up The Medicament. It sounds crazy, but I think they want me to have it. It could be a trick, but—"

"No," she cuts me off. "I don't want to."

"Why not?"

"I still have movies to watch," she smiles at me, and I watch as it fades.

"So, what should we do?" I ask. "A hug?"

"Sure." We share a seated embrace, and our breath settles.

"It would be easy to stay," I say.

"Easy."

"And good. We'd feel good," I add.

"Yes."

"But the fear wouldn't go away, would it?"

"I don't know. It might."

We separate, and sit in silence except for the ticking clock and the whir of the air and hum of the lights and the echo of breath and the pounding of my chest and the creak of the walls and the groan of the distant wind and the chattering in my head, the endless chattering.

The Medicament

I enter the four digits of the month and date of my birthday and unlock the cabinet. There are 500 capsules in each bottle. With a weekly dosage to sustain me, I've decided eight bottles is enough. Four thousand weeks. Almost seventy-seven years. I think that's enough. I don't know why I'm sneaking around, Dr. Samesong basically invited me to steal with his clue about my birthday. He might've changed the code for me, if it hadn't always been so.

I've already taken four bottles, and when I reach to remove another, I notice a post-it stuck to the outside. "Don't forget to write." Peggy's handwriting.

They're playing with me. Some twisted psychology to convince me to stay. Or maybe they know I'll leave. Whatever it is, it's working, they're in my head.

Chapter 10

I make a point not to hate anyone. I hate situations, and I hate circumstances, and I hate a number of decisions people make—but the people themselves—I try not to hate them. With one exception. When the forensic analyst testified he could not rule, with certainty, the accident had been just that, an accident, I hated him. Sure, he was just doing his job with his talk about health history and water depth, but I hated him. His stupid suit and stupid haircut and his stupid testimony—they all meant she wanted to do it—to leave me with a vegetable mom to care for, to leave me with guilt when I stopped showing up, and to leave me with the mountain of bills that turned into threatening phone calls.

I only read her letter once. She'd left it where only I'd find it. I felt like a spy burning it afterward, but I didn't want it used against us. It wasn't a suicide note. Quite the opposite. She wrote of wanting to feel alive, to be rid of the ups and downs. She must have known it was a risk to dispose of all her meds, or she wouldn't have written the note. Everyone wanted her to trust her doctors, but she didn't. She didn't want to be like my father. She didn't need drugs to make her feel okay.

* * *

The first knock on the door wasn't a debt collector, but a doctor. I didn't recognize him at first without his white coat, so I wondered why a stranger in plaid was telling me my mom was dead.

The second knock on the door was from a lawyer who had a great deal of knowledge about the case. He thought we could win a settlement large enough for the hospital bills, obviously, but for any additional damages as well. He didn't really wink when he said the last part, but he might as well have. I was implored by the mountain of envelopes to let this lawyer take the case.

The lawyer may have hated the forensic expert even more than I did. But the lawyer also seemed like the sort who would hate a lot of people. After the verdict, he commiserated with me and gave me his business card in case I'd lost the others he'd given me and told me to contact him if I needed anything, but there was no wink this time.

* * *

The third knock on the door (and the fourth and fifth and sixth, and I stopped counting) were from the debt collectors.

Then it wasn't a knock on the door, but a wave from a neighbor who said my name in a confused way, like they recognized me but they weren't sure if it could be me. I don't know what would have happened if I didn't say anything, but I answered, "Yes?" He gave me papers saying I needed to go to court.

The last knock on the door came from a witch doctor. When your empty house is going to auction to pay for the doctors who couldn't do anything but shrug and say anomalous deterioration, and the funeral that put the only person you ever knew in the ground leaves you further in debt, you don't ask too many questions about what makes the beans magic.

July 1991[1]

I don't think anyone is following me. I've had a frantic pace, but, from higher vantages, I haven't seen anyone on the trail behind me. Trail isn't the right word. I haven't trod any clear path. Following the river was more difficult than anticipated. The river carved out a rocky gorge, and sheer drops caused me to backtrack, sometimes for miles.

Instead, while always keeping the river in sight, I hiked along the highest ridgeline. This technique may have added unnecessary exertion, but it kept me from getting lost or having to make many decisions. Parts of the mountains were equally impassable with steep inclines or dense snowbanks, but the obstacles were more predictable from the aerial vantage. I have been charting a map, just in case.

For six days I've been pushing onward, up and down, up and down. I had intended to walk at night, to keep warm when it's coldest, but that notion proved foolish.

The nights never become completely black, only a hazy dark blue. It was the hint of light that made me overly ambitious. In this diffused light, my depth perception was lost. I was tracking up a rocky face, the stone glowing a muted pale, when I misjudged a step. Like taking a step onto an extra and imaginary stair, the rock disappeared beneath my feet, and I lost balance; after a second of looking comically wobbly, I fell.

---

1 Handwritten, included in the cache.

My hands lunged out to brace me, but my face still smashed into stone. Without the pain, it took the taste of blood to alert me to the missing tooth. My upper right canine knocked clean from my mouth and hid in the earth. The blood seemed like it would never stop.

I can't keep my tongue from finding the gap as it tries to familiarize itself with the smooth and foreign space.

The tent is a disaster. I've resolved to turn it into more of a bivouac casing, an extra layer I wrap around myself while I try to sleep. I don't sleep. I sit upright and occasionally nod off before the startle of a myoclonic jerk. Still, my mind wanders enough that there's little distinction between my waking thoughts and subconscious dreaming. Even while walking, I enter a near-hypnotic state, the pack weighing on me and the steps automatic.

When I stop to draw my map, I make a rough calculation of the distance. It's an inaccurate system that depends on time estimates and a difficulty gradient. On flat ground (Gradient – ten) I know I average about three miles per hour. If it's a moderate incline (Gradient – six), I'll factor it in, and I'll only go sixty percent of the distance relative to flat ground pace. Since it's pretty rough terrain with an average gradient of seven, I don't make it more than thirty miles in a sixteen-hour walk day. I don't have a watch, so all the times are wild guesses. I probably overestimate how long I've been walking so I feel better about my progress. Four days, thirty miles per day, equals 120 miles. Still no signs of people. I'll give it five hundred miles before I worry.

* * *

There's a part of me that doesn't want to find anyone. I'm trying to prepare what I'll say when I do. It's a loose story about hiking in the wilderness and getting lost. I'll have to work on the details. If they start to ask questions about the area, names of towns and such, I'll have to play along. That's assuming they speak English. I have been speaking out loud periodically, so I won't be startled by the sound of a voice.

Destroying the generator wasn't difficult. Once the fuel tank was ruptured, the job was pretty much done. I'm sure they heard the banging. It was thunderous, each swing reverberating with an echo of the action's importance.

The blankets were a harder task. They filled two storage rooms, and then there were the extra clothing layers, too. Each trip outside, I was sure I'd be caught, but no one ever came. I wasn't trying to be ceremonial or insulting by starting the fire close by, I just didn't want to haul them any further. The bedding in their rooms was spared, at least.

I would have stayed to watch, but I needed to start moving. Someone may have seen it; I won't know. The flames were still roaring when I dipped past the horizon.

The frost is settling, so I need to keep going. The air is cold, but it's not impossible. It's a clear day, and those always feel warmer even if they aren't.

I'll bury this at the first sign of people. It's too risky to keep. If no one reads this, that's fine, but I couldn't not write it.

Note From the Editor

After returning from Alaska, I needed a break. Seeing the facility firsthand left me shaken. What began as a pause in my research eventually led me to determine I wouldn't continue. I didn't want to keep digging and digging and hope it would save me. It's been several years since I found any leads, and I'm now convinced this is where the story ends. If any of the participants are still out there, they've gone underground and may never resurface. As disheartening a conclusion as that is, it's one I've come to accept. The project may have been a failure, but I don't view my work uncovering it to have been in vain. Like Lily says, some stories need to be told.

* * *

Germany has been gone for a little while. It happened suddenly, and it still hurts. He's looking at me from a picture frame on my desk. I'm used to having a reason to go outside.

* * *

There were two sealed envelopes in the cache I left unopened for years. For a time, I thought my research would lead me to a point where I could deliver the letters myself. I've hit enough dead ends to know that isn't the case. The letters were private, but they might reach their recipients this way.

July 13, 1991

Peggy,

I've addressed this to you. If it finds its way to someone else, that's fine, but know that it is for you. I've sent this to you because you are kind. I don't know you well enough to know if you're good (you may well be), but I'm sure that you are kind. Since I may never see you again, I wanted to thank you for this.

I apologize for the damage. I hope you can forgive me, but if you don't, I'll understand.

Whether or not you'll accept my explanation, I won't know, but I feel that I owe you one.

You may not hear it downstairs, but at nighttime the wind howls over our rooms. For a while it was pleasant, like rain on the rooftop, a gentle song to doze off to and make me grateful for the warmth of my bed. But as the months wore on, the howl turned to menace, a reminder of the cold outside. Without realizing it, I grew to depend on the warmth. Even as pain disappeared, I needed the security.

When spring came, the days turned warm, but the nights stayed cold, and the wind continued. A constant screech that made the nights inaccessible. I dug a hole in the ground for Hector and felt the cold earth that would consume him. It's not a fate I would wish on anyone, especially myself. Yes, I am selfish. Death no longer frightens me. It can't. I had the cold to fear instead.

There was no real threat of losing warmth inside the facility, but knowing it was lurking outside stoked an irrational fear. Cryophobia. Fear of cold. Once I learned its name, I couldn't escape it. The window could break, or the shower could stutter an icy output, or maybe even an avalanche could come crashing through the walls.

I forced myself to acclimatize, to adjust and tame the fear, but no matter how far I got away, I'd always be drawn back. I knew I'd be able to walk for days before the urge overwhelmed me, and I couldn't help but retreat. The only way to stop was to destroy the heat.

I am selfish. I apologize. You are resilient. I know you'll be able to fix it, if you desire. I didn't do it to hurt you; I did it to save myself.

If you want to chase me, if that does anything for you, it won't be hard. I'll be heading south along the river until it reaches its endpoint. It's the only reference I have.

From there, I don't know. I'm sure there are others out there, too. People who are part of this. People with secrets they don't know what to do with, but who can't help but continue on regardless. Every time I see someone smoking a Redlight, I'll think they're one of us.

Goodbye Peggy,
Lily

July 13, 1991

Dad,

WHAT?

Protocol Section 4.48. No individual shall forge romantic relationships beyond the membered group. Bringing a child to bear is strictly forbidden in all circumstances.

They say you can't choose your family. I'm not so sure about that. All you have to do is break a few rules.

WHY?

Zeus had an arsenal of lightning bolts and the love of a goddess wife, but he would still turn into a bull or a satyr or an ant so he could mess around with mortal women. Sure, some of the bastards turned into kings or gorgon slayers, but they didn't become heroes because of their dad. They were anointed, and they were special, but he watched from afar while their mothers raised them. He probably threw down a lightning bolt or two to let them know he hadn't forgotten.

I don't think you were trying to be cruel. You may have even loved my mom—or convinced yourself you did. I just know you didn't descend from Mount Olympus only to die in a lake-submerged car with faulty brakes.

I know why you broke the rules. The same reason as me. It's lonely up there.

HOW?

It wasn't chance that brought me here. Someone took a special interest in me. I was found. I know it was you.

Whoever you are, you've been around long enough to know people who will help you. Maybe you're Dr. Samesong, or Arthur Romaine, or they're only following your instructions like Dr. Forester did. All those prescriptions, the conflicting diagnoses—that was your hand at work.

She tried so hard to convince me she wasn't crazy. I used to be so frustrated with her because she couldn't be a normal mom. She'd be okay, until she wasn't. And how could she be? I'm not saying all her issues were your fault, but you certainly didn't help. She was lost and you gave her a broken compass. Maybe you thought you were saving her, or maybe you wanted to return and sweep her off her feet; in either case, she was an unwitting element in your experiment. I'll never know which version of her was real.

You know enough to know your way around protocol. It seemed so official. *5th Edition*. I wanted to believe in the glossy finish, that you'd sorted it all out.

But it's all so sloppy. The guise of control. The blinking lights. The 'Security.' The wax in Arthur's mustache. All of it is a facade. It only took me until page 3 to spot a typo in the protocol.

The Medicament might be genuine, but the fraud comes with everything you've orchestrated to contain it. It could never have been kept secret. There's no beauty in a life unshared.

Rules would never have worked. You needed competence and a secret kept, and you thought bureaucracy was the answer? It's comical—trying to restrain the infinite. There'd be no myths if all the gods behaved.

You may have had noble intentions, but there were always going to be unfortunates: Robert, and Quinn, and Maria, and my mom.

You gave me special treatment—you signed me up, you let me break the rules, you allowed me to steal. You wanted me to be safe. And you wanted to keep me tethered, one way or another.

You probably felt trapped. Like we do. You wanted to feel normal, to feel connection, and you may have, but you couldn't stay. You wanted to undo the damage. The damage that was us. By keeping us safe you could feel something like love. That was all you had. It was something to do.

You may well find me. You certainly have the resources. I didn't want to hurt you, but I couldn't stay either. Staying is too easy. Too much certainty.

I need to make my own mistakes.

—Lily

Acknowledgments

I'd like to thank all the people in my life who made this book possible. Without your support and guidance, this project would never have found its way:

The team at Blackwater Press for helping shape, edit, and put this novel into the world—Elizabeth Ford, Luca Guariento, Vivien Williams. Thanks also to John Reid and Maxwell Donaldson.

My Mom and Dad for being my biggest fans since the beginning. My partner, Trina, for her loving support throughout. My readers, Frank Shannon and Andrea Stout, for their helpful notes. My pup, Germany, who made every one of the days better. And, finally, a genuine thanks to you, the reader, for giving my story a place to go.